BAD NEIGHBORS

BAD
NEIGHBORS

Isidore
Haiblum

ST. MARTIN'S PRESS
NEW YORK

Library of Congress Cataloging-in-Publication Data

Haiblum, Isidore.
    Bad neighbors / Isidore Haiblum.
        p.   cm.
    "A Thomas Dunne book."
    ISBN 0-312-04263-9
    I. Title.
PS3558.A324B3   1990
813'.54—dc20   89-78095
                                          CIP

First Edition

10 9 8 7 6 5 4 3 2 1

BAD NEIGHBORS

PROLOGUE

THE OLD MAN CLIMBED THE STAIRS. HE CARRIED A HEAVY SHOPPING bag in one hand, a newspaper in the other. He rested for an instant on the first landing, then continued up; he was limping slightly. His gaze fixed on the stairs, he failed to notice the two men on the third floor until he was almost even with them.

One grabbed his arm. The other sliced a metal pipe down on his neck with terrific force.

The shopping bag fell from the old man's fingers. His mouth opened in a silent scream. He toppled headlong down the stairs.

The two men plunged after him, leaped over his body, and kept going. Out on the street they turned east, in the direction of Broadway, and raced up the block.

The young man in the second-story window nine houses up the block saw them. He had been snapping pictures of people entering a corner red-brick building for the past six days. He had no special interest in the pair sprinting toward him—that was not his job—but their frantic gait made him curious.

He snapped their picture as they ran by.

CHAPTER 1

I HAD JUST FINISHED GOING THROUGH THE SPORTS AND ENTERTAIN-
ment sections of the *New York Times* and was giving serious
thought to whether I ought to tackle the hard news or quit
while I was ahead, when I heard the door to our reception
room open. My partner, Harry, and I took turns greeting our
callers. It was his turn. I slipped the *Times* into a desk drawer,
tossed my empty styrofoam cup into the wastebasket, and sat
up in my swivel chair. More, no man could do.

"Pliz," a woman's voice said, "Mr. Shaw, he here?"

It shook me. I thought I recognized that voice, but that was
plainly impossible. I considered crawling under the desk
anyway just to be on the safe side. I didn't quite make it.

She came chugging through the doorway like a pint-size
locomotive, a short, squat oldster in her late seventies. A
green-and-yellow polka-dot dress flapped rakishly under a
moth-eaten black coat. White hair was braided around her
head. Wrinkles crisscrossed her face like lines on a road map.
She was carrying a faded, oversize purple handbag. It looked
heavy.

She churned to a stop before my desk, glaring at me
accusingly. "You change name," she said.

"Occupational necessity," I told her. By then I had a smile
on my face. I waved her to a chair. She sat, still clutching her
bag as though convinced I might try to grab it away from her

3

first chance I had. The real me, the latent purse snatcher, must have been showing through.

"How'd you find me, Mrs. Kazmir?"

"Police."

"You went to the police?"

She nodded. "They say ask Captain Rogers."

"And of course, you did."

"Sure."

"Good old Captain Rogers." I had run afoul of Rogers on my last case, but I'd never figured him for a squealer. On the other hand, I hadn't sworn him to secrecy either.

"You are detective?"

"On my good days."

"I think you detective all along. So many questions you ask. I see plenty on TV."

"Good old TV," I said.

"Pliz, I want hire you."

I sighed. My gaze, as if hunting for better, more encouraging sights, drifted to my window. Down below, on the west side of Madison Avenue, between Sixtieth and Sixty-first streets, a bank and a number of high-powered retail shops were pulling in the customers as if by magnets. With all that money floating around, you'd think some of it would drift up here. Guess again. My guest, I knew, might very well have been the Belle of the Balkans circa 1910 and awash in spanduliks or whatever they used for currency in those regions. But now, unfortunately, she was merely a grade-A candidate for the welfare rolls, someone who could do me or the agency no good at all.

"You work, Mrs. Kazmir?"

"Not no more. I cleaning woman long time. Now I retired."

"On social security?"

She wagged her head.

"Mrs. Kazmir," I said, "I don't know what your problem is—"

"Is big trouble in building."

4

"Ninety-fourth Street?"

"Sure."

"You're in trouble?"

"Everyone. Is very bad."

"The *whole* building?"

"All of block. Second Avenue and Ninety-third Street, too."

"Sounds big, all right."

"You be rich."

"Yeah, rich." Those tenements, I knew, were only a couple of notches above skid row and sinking fast. I hunted through my usually adequate vocabulary trying to find words that would embarrass neither of us.

"Mrs. Kazmir," I said, "I've got to be perfectly frank with you. I don't think you can afford me."

"We all chip in."

"Who's we?"

"From buildings."

"All of them?"

"Lots."

Welfare mothers. Factory workers. The aged, unemployed, and infirm. Need a lap to cry on? Come to Shaw. Bring your nickels and dimes. Hurry. Before he becomes one of you.

I shook my head. "Even so, Mrs. Kazmir, I *honestly* don't think—"

"Look." She had stood up, clutching her bag. I wondered if she was going to swat me with it.

Three steps brought her to the edge of my desk. She raised the bag, upending it. Money flowed out. Green dollar bills. Wads of them. A veritable torrent.

"Is for you, Mr. Shaw. All for you."

CHAPTER 2

"IT'S ALL FOR ME," I TOLD HARRY, "YOU CAN'T HAVE ANY. THE LADY said so."

"Who wants it? Probably fake anyway."

"Probably."

"How much is it?"

"Close to three grand. Two thousand eight hundred and seventy-three to be exact."

"In the Moojooe Islands we'd be millionaires."

"Gods probably."

Harry sighed. "Can't do better than that."

"Right. Here, of course, we're still paupers. But another five thousand gets us out of hock. For a while, at least."

"Another five million we can retire."

The money was piled on my desk in neat hundred-dollar stacks. Harry was seated in the client's chair, his curly blond hair in its usual state of advanced disarray. A round, boyish face, white nonsmoker's teeth, and even features made him appear ten years younger than his thirty-three years, and totally innocent. A great boon for a detective or pickpocket. Harry was wearing a gray tweed sports jacket, white shirt, blue-and-yellow paisley tie, and dark gray slacks. The gentleman's gumshoe. Quality bred.

"What'd she do," Harry asked, "give you her life savings?"

"She didn't have any. This represents the wages and welfare checks of hordes of tenants in that lousy slum complex I was staking out. They want me back."

"Can't be your personality."

"Landlord trouble. They've got a new one who may be planning to kick everyone out. They want me to protect them."

"Can you?"

"Lord knows. The old girl's hard to follow. Lawyers and state agencies usually handle stuff like that. Anyway, they're holding a tenants' meeting tonight, so if I trot over, I should get the full picture. Trouble is, I may be busy hanging myself or taking poison just then."

"Well," Harry said, "it's a good thing you told me all of this. I have the solution."

"Thank God. I was beginning to lose hope."

"I'll go in your stead, kid, what are partners for?"

"Would that you could, old buddy, but they insist on the genuine and true article. I've still got an apartment there, paid up till the end of the month. I'm known as Stuart Gordon. The idea is, I'm supposed to work undercover."

"Why, in heaven's name?"

"As far as I can make out, they don't want to offend the new landlord yet."

"How can you offend a *landlord?*"

"Precisely."

"Who's they?"

"Tenants' committee. I seem to have been Kazmir's brain-storm, Mr. Fix-it on the spot. Somehow, she convinced them to shell out for my services. They may be poor, but there are lots of them. Forty-five houses' worth."

"What happens if it's all a false alarm? If the new owners turn out to be sweethearts?"

"Depends how long I'm on the job and how generous we feel. If nothing comes of it, I guess most of the money goes back to the needy."

"That's us, no?"

"Them, unfortunately. We rob from the poor, how could we look ourselves in the eye?"

"Trick mirrors?" Harry asked hopefully.

.

CHAPTER 3

I HAD NO TROUBLE ATTENDING THE MEETING. I WAS GREETED AS AN old friend. So were a couple of unshaven gents who looked as if they'd wandered in off the street to grab forty winks. I didn't take it personally.

We were in the cellar of one of the Second Avenue tenements. Someone had thoughtfully swept away most of the cobwebs and gotten the dust and grime off the floor. But the odor of mold hung around like an honored guest. Trucks, cars, and buses out on the avenue kept up a steady din. No heat came from the boiler or heating pipes that ran across the walls. The blue-and-green flannel plaid shirt, jeans, and lined denim jacket I wore—a usually dependable combination— didn't quite ward off the chill. Neither did the lukewarm cup of coffee I'd taken from the table when entering.

My vantage point near the rear gave me a pretty good view of the crowd. Close to a hundred people were assembled. They came in all colors, shapes, and sizes, a poor man's miniature UN. Some of the mothers had brought their toddlers along; the tots looked none too pleased. Oldsters predominated. They weren't beaming either.

Mrs. Kazmir sat up front in a solid-black dress that reached to her ankles, facing the rest of us. Six other members of the tenants' committee were to the right or left of her. Their faces had a yellowish tint in the dim light as if their new public roles had already undermined their health.

I nodded to Carlos the super, a short, wiry Hispanic with jet-black hair, who was leaning against the wall near the doorway, and got a grin in return. I recognized some of my other neighbors from the building, a couple from down the block. The rest were just strangers.

A tall, cadaverous, sixtyish man who had been sitting next to Kazmir slowly rose to his feet. He had sunken cheeks, a lined face, and thinning, close-cropped, graying hair. He wore an ill-fitting black suit and tie and wrinkled white shirt. Here was a guy right out of Norman Rockwell's *Town Meeting* forty years and a couple of dozen layoffs later; it gave a body pause. He said his name was Ned Hawks and he was chairman of the tenants' committee. He spoke slowly, carefully, in a voice as dry as withered leaves. He said a lot of rumors had been circulating and this meeting had been called to set the record straight. He wet his lips, looking around as if expecting someone to object. No one did and Hawks continued. The buildings, he said, as everyone knew by now, had been sold. Primrose Real Estate was the new landlord. He had called Primrose and been given a Mr. Berk, the new building manager, who had not been wildly informative. Plans for the property were still in the air. Berk said he would know more in a few days and promised to be in touch. That was a week ago.

Hawks paused again; he looked grim, as if debating whether it was too soon to go to the men's room or maybe head home. I figured the bad news was about to put in an appearance. The crowd did, too, apparently. They had been fidgeting up till now. There had been murmurs and whispers. All that stopped. The traffic outside seemed to grow louder in the silence.

Hawks said, "I guess we've all heard some pretty bad things about what to expect from this outfit. A lot of us are worried, and maybe with good cause. Mr. Nesbit here thinks he knows these people, and I'm going to ask him to tell us what he can, right now."

Hawks sat. Nesbit rose, taking a few tentative steps toward the crowd. He was an old duffer, maybe pushing eighty. His lined face was long, yellowish, and freckled with brown liver spots. His few strands of hair were white and disheveled. He wore an ancient cream-colored, wide-lapeled suit that had been the rage of the fifties, old hat in the sixties, camp in the seventies, and high fashion again in the eighties. At this rate it figured to outlive its owner. Nesbit's wide tie was pale green and orange over a yellow shirt. His collar was starched and too loose around his scrawny neck. He peered out quizzically from behind thick glasses, looking a bit like a rabbit poised for a quick getaway.

He identified himself as a retired clerk whose main wish was to live out his golden years in peace and quite. Here, no less, among his friends and neighbors where he'd spent so many happy low-rent years. The crowd murmured its approval. It was a desire they could share. For most of them, the alternative was probably a park bench or a welfare hotel.

"Where would I go," Nesbit asked in his quivery voice, "if they put me out? Where?"

The floor remained silent. No one had an answer.

"When you're on social security," Nesbit said, "there is *no* place to go; none at all. That is why we simply *must* do something."

Five days ago, Nesbit said, he had been chatting with Mr. Glickman in front of his tailor shop on Second Avenue when a car pulled up. Two men climbed out, then went around the corner to Ninety-fourth Street. Presently they returned with Carlos, the super, who let them into the empty storefront, three doors down. Nesbit was sure he recognized one of the men and asked Carlos who they were. The super said that the shorter of the pair was Tom Berk, the new building manager, the other, a Mr. Rensler from Primrose. Berk was planning to use the storefront as his headquarters.

Nesbit went up to the plate-glass window for a better look.

There was no doubt in his mind that he had seen the building manager before. The memory of it made him shudder.

After this Berk took charge of three brownstones on West Twenty-ninth Street, Nesbit said, the houses were vacated within three months; luxury apartments stand there now. This was two years ago. Nesbit was only a sometime visitor at one of the houses, where his friend, Mr. Shultz, had resided. But he would never forget Berk as long as he lived. All services stopped. Strangers prowled the building. Shultz's place was broken into twice. They took his TV, a radio, and phonograph. They even ran off with his record collection. There was no heat or hot water. And this was midwinter. An old woman died. People were coming down with pneumonia. Shultz gave up, packed whatever he had left, and went to live with his sister in Nebraska. At least he had somewhere to go. Others weren't so lucky.

Berk was the building manager, Nesbit said, but his name wasn't Berk then, it was Lacy.

Nesbit was done. He stood there, his mouth slightly open, breathing hard, lost behind his thick glasses.

Hawks rose, put a hand on the old man's shoulder. "Thank you," he said.

Nesbit woke up, shook himself, and shuffled back to his seat.

"I guess," Hawks said, "most of you have been hearing stories like that for the better part of a week."

"Damn worse," a thick-voiced man said from the third row.

"Mr. Nesbit here," Hawks said, "far's I can tell, is the only one among us who has any firsthand knowledge."

"I heard," a stout woman spoke up, "that the owners is *Mafia*."

Heads began wagging. The lady had lots of company. Nothing like the Mafia to make people thoughtful. Some brains have been known to short-circuit at the mere mention of the word, mine included.

"No," Hawks said, "it isn't."

14

"How do you *know?*" the woman asked.

"'Cause I spoke to just about *everyone* who said they knew something. Turned out to be just variations of what Mr. Nesbit here had been saying. Only kind of improved along the way."

That got a couple of laughs. But not from everyone.

"Mr. Hawks," an elderly woman asked, "how can you be *sure?*"

"Nothing checked out," he said.

"Don't mean they ain't Mafia," a black woman said.

A burly, potbellied man stood up in the second row. He had on a checkered-gray-and-black red flannel shirt. The sleeves were rolled up to the elbows, revealing thick, hairy forearms. He was smoking a cigar. The only thing missing was a mug in his hand, and he would be ready to pose for a hard-hat beer commercial. He pointed a stubby finger at the chairman. "Hawks," he growled, "let's cut the bullshit. What're you doin' with our dough? You really spend it on some damn private eye?"

That shook me awake. I sat up taller.

"Part of it, yes."

"Jesus, that's what I heard. This guy got a name? He here?"

"Mr. Caloney," Hawks said, "the private detective we hired will be working undercover."

"Doin' *what* for chrissake? You gone simple, Hawks? What we need is a good lawyer."

"Please, Mr. Caloney. If you give me a chance, I'll be glad to explain it to you."

"Yeah, you do that; you *explain* it to me."

Caloney sat.

Hawks said, "No one has even made us an offer yet. When it comes time to negotiate, we'll get ourselves a lawyer, don't you worry. Meanwhile, we ought to know what we're up against. If our new owners are crooked, we need someone who can make them think twice before they try something."

"Hey," Caloney said, "you been seein' too many movies.

Who'd you get, Clint Eastwood, Charles Bronson? You think this guy you hired is gonna stick his neck out for us? He's gonna take one look at some of Nesbit's prowlers an' shit in his pants. You won't see him or our dough again."

Mrs. Kazmir was on her feet. "He good man," she shouted. "What you know?"

"I don't believe it," Caloney said. "Who'd you get, her son?"

That almost brought the house down. I wondered if I should put in my two cents in defense of the poor, maligned private eye, or ask Caloney who wrote his material.

"Please, Mrs. Kazmir," Hawks said, motioning her back to her seat. To Caloney he said, "The committee's been over this already."

"So what?"

"We believe we've made the right decision."

"Yeah, *you* would," Caloney said. "I think you gone simple, I think we all oughta vote on this. It's our dough, Hawks."

"Mine, too, Mr. Caloney. The tenants *did* vote, they elected this committee. And the committee voted to hire a detective."

"Well, it's crazy."

"That," Hawks said stiffly, "is your opinion, and you are entitled to it."

"Thanks a lot. I think we should vote right now, all of us here, on what we wanna do."

Hawks didn't like that. "The committee," he said, "was set up less then a week ago. We can't canvass all the houses every time we have to reach a decision."

"Then let's get a new committee," Caloney said, raising his voice.

That did it, everyone got into the act. Heads bobbed. Voices shouted. A toddler began to wail, joined by a second, louder one. People were on their feet. Hawks, during all this, stood frozen, giving a fine imitation of a marble column. The rest of the committee sat in their chairs, white-faced and bug-eyed. They all looked ready to bolt.

After a while, the combatants began to run out of steam. Short of taking a swing at each other, there wasn't much left for them to do. They took to their chairs and presently the babble eased off.

Hawks seemed a bit dazed. At least he'd stood his ground. He called for a vote of confidence, and when all the hands were counted, it was clear that he'd got it.

Caloney waved his cigar at the chairman, who nodded. There was no enthusiasm in the nod, only resignation. Caloney stood up.

"Okay," he said. "You an' your buddies won this one. You got what here tonight? A fraction of the people who live in these buildings. That ain't a majority, friend."

Hawks said, "Signs were posted in every hallway."

"Sure. But if people knew what you were pullin', they'd be here in droves."

"I am not pulling *anything*, Mr. Caloney."

"Yeah, so who's this detective, your brother?"

This time no one laughed. The crowd had spent their mirth in the shouting match.

Hawks shook his head as if to say, Have you no shame? What he did say was, "There's been a vote, Mr. Caloney. The issue's settled."

"For you, maybe," Caloney said. "Till the next meetin'." He sat down heavily.

Hawks asked if there were any more questions. There were none. The proceedings were adjourned.

More than half the crowd made a beeline for the door as if any place were better than the cellar; they may even have been right. The rest milled around. Someone had put a plate of homemade cookies next to a refilled coffeepot. I helped myself to one, went over to Hawks.

"Tough audience," I said.

Hawks looked grim. "Frankly, I didn't expect anything like this. You're . . . ?"

"Stuart Gordon, two forty-two on Ninety-fourth. Three-C."

"Seen you around," Hawks said, extending a lean hand. We shook. "Kind of new here, aren't you?"

"Little short of two months. Thought you handled yourself pretty well up there."

"Thanks. Sure didn't feel like it."

"More like the hot seat, eh?"

He grinned. "A little."

"Who's this Caloney?"

Hawks shrugged. "Man's entitled to his opinion. Thing is, last time we passed the hat, we collected from maybe half the folks."

"How much you raise?"

"About five thousand."

"Not bad."

Hawks signed. "This detective could end up costing plenty. And that's on top of the lawyer we're going to need. Caloney gets everyone riled up, there'll be hell to pay."

Mrs. Kazmir came over. "They crazy, Mr. Gordon."

"Free country," I said. Thomas Jefferson couldn't have put it any better, only he'd probably have found a swankier place in which to say it.

"Why they argue? Detective good idea, no, Mr. Gordon?"

"Fine by me," I said, trying not to blush.

We were joined by a couple of senior citizens and I used the occasion to extract myself. Business before pleasure. I found Nesbit alone in a corner. He was just standing there. "Mr. Nesbit," I said.

He peered at me through his thick glasses. I wasn't sure he could actually see me. I introduced myself. "Must have been an awful experience," I said.

"Oh, dear, yes," Nesbit said in his frail, piping voice, "frightful. Much worse for the poor souls who were the victims, much worse."

18

"And you're positive Berk and Lacy were the same man?"

"Oh, yes, quite."

"Forgive me, Mr. Nesbit. Those glasses you wear are pretty formidable. . . ."

"I can see perfectly," Nesbit assured me. "Perfectly."

We stood in silence for a while. Nesbit seemed to be staring at my right ear. Although, for all I knew, he figured he was looking me right in the eye.

I gave him a so long and left.

CHAPTER 4

"Trouble is," I said, "this Caloney is almost right."

Daphne cut herself another slice of steak. "You're not going to tell them, I hope."

"And pass up three grand almost, give or take a hundred? With that much dough I could retire to Mexico, live a life of ease and comfort, maybe even learn an honest trade."

"Become a wetback even."

"Good thinking. It's gotta pay more than this racket, right?" I took a bite of chicken, chewed thoughtfully. "Anyway, no one's asked me yet."

"They are *not* likely to ask Stuart Gordon," Daphne pointed out with piercing logic, "now are they?"

I forked a baby potato. "Goes to show how much *you* know. Gordon has *already* been asked. Along with half the renters. Leaving another half who don't know, don't care, aren't saying, or weren't home. I can report that Gordon was as confused as everyone else, although in the end he *did* come down on the side of the detective. Lord knows why."

"Now, if they asked James Shaw, that would be another matter. Smart. Experienced. Insightful. Tender yet tough."

"That's the steak I'm eating," Daphne said. "Would Shaw at least tell them the truth?"

"He might if they caught him in a good mood; he's a right-on guy. But since Kazmir is his only contact, chances are she wouldn't understand a word he said. Lucky him."

We were in Dobson's—which is on Columbus Avenue and Seventy-sixth Street—seated in the glassed-in section. Aside from the soft rock muttering through the speakers, Dobson's was a nice place to be. The customers looked like the clients Harry and I hoped to attract rather than the suspects we were supposed to collar. The food was tasty. And the prices didn't make you faint with anxiety.

Daphne asked, "How did that happen, Jim?"

"How did *what* happen?"

"This woman . . ."

"Kazmir?"

"Yes. How in the world did she do it, persuade them to hire you?"

"'Them' is only the committee, sweetie, that's seven people counting her."

"Still, you make her sound positively moronic."

"Not me," I protested. "For all I know she's the Demosthenes of cleaning women. Maybe when surrounded by her committee she develops a silver tongue. Or she slipped something into their water glass to make them docile."

I scooped up some fried zucchini, followed it with a slice of steak. While Daphne had ordered only steak, I had opted for the combination plate. The best of both worlds, if a bit less of each.

Daphne shook her blond curls at me. "Seriously."

"It's a puzzle," I admitted, "probably too tough to crack. On the other hand, we don't exactly know the mental capacity of the other committee members, do we? Hawks seems all right, but he might have been overruled."

Daphne smiled sweetly, reached for her goblet of white wine. "I don't believe a word of it."

Daphne Field wore aviator glasses over her large green eyes. Sandy-blond hair, all curls, reached down to her shoulder blades. High cheekbones in a cream-colored face. Full lips with a hint of rose. A long, graceful neck. Her pale yellow dress was emblazoned with tiny green, blue, and red flowers. During business hours when she wasn't cavorting with me, Daphne was a real estate agent and building manager. In fact, she managed my building. Me, too, sometimes.

"Well," I said, "Nesbit might have scared them witless with his tales. Then all Kazmir had to do was sell 'em on me as the boy wonder who could set things right. That's one explanation."

"Think you can do it, Shaw?"

"Bring 'Em Back Alive Shaw can do anything, especially if they pay him enough. Fortunately, in this case, there may actually be nothing to do."

"You believe Mr. Nesbit is wrong?"

"There is a vague possibility, cookie."

"Then Berk and Lacy are *not* the same person."

"Anything's possible. I may be the spirit of Calvin Coolidge returned and much improved. Who knows? However, if Nesbit's glasses were much thicker, he'd need a Seeing Eye dog to read his morning funnies to him."

"Which means you don't get to keep all the money."

"All *what* money? Probably just as well for the old hard-pressed tenants who'll need every penny they can raise to hire the real McCoy, namely a good old-fashioned lawyer to save their hides."

The busboy cleared away our dishes and the waiter brought coffee and pastry, peach pie for her, carrot cake for me. I was being virtuous. Next time—if I survived the coming ordeal, which was doubtful—I'd have a double-chocolate fudge cake with whipped cream and marshmallow topping.

"There's just one thing I don't understand," Daphne said.

"Just one? What's that?"

"Why you're doing this at all."

I sipped coffee from a white mug. "On the off chance, I suppose, that there's really something to it."

"So why does it seem you're being dragged raving and screaming every inch of the way?"

"Because I am. I've put in my time in that flat; another few weeks is liable to cook my goose."

"You expect all your cases to take you to Scarsdale?"

"I wouldn't mind. But every now and then I have my realistic moments just like everyone else."

"Kind of creeps up on you unawares."

"Right. When I'm not even looking. I knew what the job entailed when Uncle Max gave me the agency. And when Harry and I had our office on Eighth Avenue, we handled plenty of crap. Still do, actually. What I hadn't counted on was an extended stay in the pastures of yesteryear. I spent my childhood in dumps like those. The whole idea was to make a daring escape, not keep sliding back."

"It's not permanent," Daphne said. "It's just a case."

"I know and you know, but does my unconscious? Show my unconscious a slum and right away it figures we're camped for the duration."

"Too much nostalgia, sweetie?"

"Too much reality," I said. "And that's even worse."

CHAPTER 5

I ASKED KAZMIR TO PHONE ME WHEN BERK SHOWED UP AND THEN DID my best to forget the whole thing. Up to that point, Harry and I had more or less been sitting on our hands. I was spending lots of time reading Bertrand Russell's "In Praise of Idleness" to get the hang of doing nothing. All of a sudden, during the next ten days, business began perking up. A half dozen medium-sized jobs came our way, and a bunch of smaller ones, too. Wrapping them all up wasn't apt to improve the world any, or lead to our early retirement. But it could put us in the black and then some, a truly laudable objective. We didn't do all the agency's legwork ourselves but used stringers such as Bob Perry, Carl Springer, Dick Hanks, or Lucy Samler. They worked on straight salary and sometimes ended up making more then we did, a situation that did not leave us rolling on the floor with laughter. As the month wore on, Kazmir's fee became less of a lifesaver and more of a potential nuisance. The lady herself called three times as our caseload increased. Berk, she told me the first time, had opened his storefront and was visiting all the apartments.

"What's he say, Mrs. Kazmir?"

"He want everyone move out."

"That's nice."

"He help find new place."

"Any mention of money?"

"He no have."

"Poor guy. Any takers?"

"Mrs. Byankow."

"Why?"

"She no like being here."

"Sounds reasonable. Any others?"

"No."

"You still getting steam, hot water?"

"Yes."

"Anything *bad* happen?"

"No. You come soon?"

"I'll drop by, but first we've got to give Berk a chance to do his stuff."

"How long that take?"

"Depends on him."

"People ask where is detective."

"Off detecting somewhere," I said. "Call me if there's a change."

The next call came a week later. Berk was now offering three hundred for a speedy relocation. A couple of tenants seemed tempted.

"Give it another week," I said.

When Kazmir's third call came, another week had indeed rolled by, and Berk had gone up to five hundred.

"He say no more. You come now?"

"Soon."

"Mr. Berk, he leave note on your door. He ask neighbors where you are."

"Nice to be wanted," I said.

Harry was going through the mail when I strolled into his office. "That was Kazmir," I told him.

"Congratulations."

"Right. What this situation needs is more irony."

He shrugged. "Look, you hate the job, drop it. Money's coming in, what's the big deal?"

I seated myself. "It's a thought," I said. "Thing is, it's not very professional."

"Either are we."

"All the more reason. Also, it's too soon. And it may actually be a mistake."

"I can hardly wait to hear the tortured logic on that one."

"Well, if the landlord turns out to be a bastard, we can always earn our pay and do something about it, right?"

"Like what?"

"Lead everyone in prayer."

"Anything else?"

"Help them find a good lawyer."

"You're really cooking this morning."

"There's another angle," I said. "Do you realize I'm a bona fide tenant over there, a guy with a two-year lease?"

"Don't brag about it, people will be jealous."

"Harry, here it is three weeks and already they're shelling out five Cs. All I have to do is sit tight, keep paying the rent, and by and by cash in on the settlement. I see it as a sort of bonus for having lived a clean, decent life. Mostly."

Harry grinned at me. "Aren't you forgetting one small detail, kid? This thing may drag on for months. Sooner or later someone's bound to notice you're not living there."

"Sooner. Berk's been snooping around."

"So what are you planning to do, hire an impersonator?"

"Show up, it's probably time."

"Brave lad."

"Don't worry, it won't be for long."

"Here today, gone tomorrow."

"That's the idea."

"Figure this Berk got to be building manager by being blind?"

"Look, it's not a prison. Days I can be anywhere. Nights are the problem. He'll expect me to be home sometimes."

"Just like mother."

"Yeah, but suppose I tell him I'm a traveling salesman—out on the road most of the time."

"H-mmmm," Harry said sagely.

"Has possibilities, eh? Set up a phony job through one of our contacts. Let 'em check."

"You really thinking of doing this?"

"Sure. Gives me an excuse for sticking around, not walking out on the downtrodden."

"Didn't know you cared."

"I probably don't."

"But the chance of earning a crooked buck has made you gung ho."

"Let's just say I'm testing the water, shall we?"

CHAPTER 6

IT WAS RAINING THE FOLLOWING MONDAY WHEN I ARRIVED. NO ONE greeted me as I closed my umbrella and entered the dank hallway, climbed two flights of narrow stairs, used my keys, and stepped into my three-room railroad flat. I had vaguely hoped that in the intervening month the place had somehow magically transformed itself. Like a lot of hopes, this one still had a ways to go. The antique bathtub with crow's-feet still hung out in the living room/kitchen opposite the turn-of-the-century stove, which was right next to the lopsided kitchen table. An 1890s efficiency unit dreamed up by some dimwit in a lunatic asylum, and now all mine again. The rust-stained sink adjacent to the bathtub still dripped. No one had bothered to replace the peeling walls during my absence, an oversight I would have to take up with the management.

I tossed my umbrella into the bathtub, put my shopping bag of groceries on the table, and headed toward the bedroom. With each step, the floorboards under the yellow, faded oilcloth seemed to creak in misery as if my weight were a burden they should not have been asked to bear. I reached the window and after the usual struggle managed to raise it. Fresh air rushed into the bedroom displacing the odors of mildew, dust, and decay. I took a deep breath of moist air. Slanting rain beat against bricks and fire escape. The gray sky seemed almost to be touching the rooftops. Across the backyard I could see innumerable windows. They stared back at me like blind eyes.

I unpacked my valise, hung some clothes in the closet, positioned my portable stereo on the nightstand by the bed, and thumbed on Dvorak's bagatelles.

I went over to the fridge, which was one step removed from being an icebox, emptied part of my shopping bag into it. I put the nonperishables up in the cupboard. The only thing left to do was my job. I waited until Mr. Firkusny and the Julliard Quartet were done with Dvorak and went to do it.

"How you say, Mr. Gordon," Carlos asked, "'the bum's rush'? They want I should go last month, but new super, he is sick, so I stay extra." He shrugged a bony shoulder, ran a thumb across his jet-black mustache, and smiled broadly; but there was no mirth in it.

"The union won't go to bat for you?"

"I did not join. The landlord, he say no."

"You got a contract, at least, severance pay?"

"There is nothing."

"Carlos," I said, "what made you take a deal like that?"

"I need money, place to stay. It is best I can do."

I was seated on a beat-up sofa in the super's living room. Carlos held down a kitchen chair. I nodded, looked around. This was the first time I'd been inside his apartment. No surprises. A kitchen/living room in any of these houses would have a bathtub up on crow's-feet in full view. Carlos had rigged a shower in his and bought a flowery shower curtain that looked vaguely risqué hanging there next to the small, blackened kitchen stove. This stove was on legs, too, and it didn't take much to imagine the bathtub and stove waltzing around the floor together. The walls, which had once been a cheerful peach, now looked more as if the fruit had withered on the vine. The windows, being on the ground floor, were fixed up with nice burglarproof bars. The only thing missing was the turnkey with a billy club who whacked you every time you stepped out of line. Whoever tore down these firetraps would be doing humanity a service. I had to remind myself that I wasn't defending the tenements, just the tenants. It seemed a trivial distinction.

"What now?" I asked.

"I go live with sister, she is only six blocks away."

"And then?"

"Look for work."

I wished him well, rose; Carlos and I shook hands. I asked for and received his new address. I left.

"You want tea?"

"Thanks, no."

"Where you been?" Mrs. Kazmir asked. "I think you come last week."

"Had to finish up some business," I told her.

This morning my client was decked out in a long, faded pink skirt and long-sleeved black blouse. Her white hair was braided, tied gaily with ribbons, and hung down her back. She wore fuzzy pink slippers that were large enough to be house pets. The floor-model black-and-white Philco, over in a corner, was tuned to a soap opera. Two might have been company, but the muttering TV made it a crowd.

"I not know what to think," she told me.

"I'm here now," I said.

"Is money all right?"

"Sure."

"I give too much."

"How's that?"

"Committee say is too much."

"They having second thoughts?"

"Not everyone there when I take money, Mr. Shaw."

"Gordon, Mrs. Kazmir, that's what you should always call me around here, so it becomes a habit. That way you won't slip up and blow my cover. Whaddya mean not everyone was there?"

"Only three. Mrs. Patrisky, Mr. Nesbit, and I other one."

"Hawks wasn't consulted?"

"No."

"You three just did this on your own?"

"Committee decide to hire detective. Mrs. Patrisky, she treasurer. We want hire you quick, so she give me money."

"She had it lying around the house?" I felt as though I'd stepped into the middle of *Alice in Wonderland*.

"Mrs. Patrisky, she go to bank. But line is too long. She not have time."

"So she brought the dough home again."

"She have safe place. In chest near bed. It have false bottom, Mr. Shaw."

"Gordon. Any money still there?"

"Is in bank now."

"That's where it belongs," I said. "Don't ask for trouble, Mrs. Kazmir; next time there's a collection, have Mrs. Patrisky rush it to the bank. Make sure someone goes with her. Okay?"

"Okay."

I'd done my bit for reason and sanity. All Kazmir had to do was remember my words of wisdom. That was probably the catch, all right.

"What happened," I asked, "when the rest of the committee found out?"

"Is big fight."

"You won, I hope."

She grinned at me, bobbed her head.

I said, "Anyone besides you know who I am?"

"No."

"They weren't interested?"

"I not tell them."

"And how," I asked, "did *that* go over?"

"Is big fight again."

"I can imagine. You did fine, Mrs. Kazmir. We don't want

to spread the word at all. Chances are someone on the committee will tell their neighbor."

"They not tell."

"Sure. But just in case."

"I understand, Mr. Shaw."

"Gordon. What's Berk been up to? He still at five hundred?"

"Yes. Mrs. Mooney, she crazy. She say she take and go. Ach, she eighty-three, maybe. Not know what she do."

"Have any relatives?"

Kazmir shrugged.

I said, "Hawks should speak to her and find out. If there're social workers involved, they should be brought into this, too."

"I tell him."

"What's my name, Mrs. Kazmir?"

"Gordon."

"That's the ticket."

Thunder went off over my head. When old Beethoven, stone-deaf, lay on his deathbed, a clap of thunder somehow roused him. The great man raised his fist to the heavens and died. I raised my umbrella and started down the block. The wind blew rain in my face. Lightning cut a jagged streak over the rooftops beyond First Avenue. More thunder. The Lord was obviously sending me a message. Maybe to come in out of the rain. I ducked into a building.

Shaking the water off my umbrella, I climbed the stairs to the second floor, knocked on 2B. It took a while for Nesbit to ask who it was through his door. I identified myself and the door opened. Nesbit had on a faded paisley robe over chalk-yellow slacks and white shirt. His feet were encased in black leather slippers. He stared at me blankly through his thick glasses.

"You remember me," I said, "Gordon, from up the block?"

Nesbit nodded uncertainly as if I were some historical

figure whose dates had momentarily slipped his mind. He ushered me in anyway. I followed him into the next room. Nesbit eased himself down onto the sofa. I tried the rocker. I hadn't been in one of those things since my childhood. Swings, a slide, and a sand pile and I'd be the real me again.

I rocked a bit and said, "Berk still Lacy in your book, Mr. Nesbit?"

He wagged his head so hard his glasses almost slipped off. "Oh, yes," he said in his high, flutelike voice. "I'm certain of that. Absolutely."

"You speak to the guy?"

"I see him through the glass. I go by that store every day, you know."

"He didn't come here to give you his spiel?"

"Oh, yes."

"So you got a close-up look?"

Nesbit hesitated. "No, I really didn't."

"Didn't?" I said.

"I wouldn't let him in, that awful man."

"Spoke through the door?"

"No."

"No?"

"I didn't answer him."

"Berk stood in the hall and spoke to you?"

"Yes."

"You knew it was him?"

"I said, 'Who is it?' and he said, 'Mr. Berk.' I walked right away then and came in here. I didn't want to hear what he had say. You understand?"

"Yes," I sighed, "only too well."

"To have that man here, after what I know about him. . . ."

We sat in silence. The off-white walls, I noticed, were yellowing just like their tenant. They had small bumps on them, were cracked and peeling as though suffering from some obscure skin disease. The furniture was neat enough, but rather fragile, as if handled once too often over the long decades. The green quilt over Nesbit's bed had gray stuffing poking through. A kind of phlegmy odor pervaded the place that made me want to be somewhere else.

I said, "Know anyone besides your friend Shultz at Twenty-ninth Street?"

"Only by sight."

"Any idea where they went?"

"Dear me, they must have scattered to the four corners of the earth by now, wouldn't you think?"

"Uh-huh. What about Shultz, you still in touch?"

"Not really."

"Have his address?"

"I'm sure I did."

"That's past tense," I pointed out.

"It was on a slip of paper. We never did correspond, you know; not even a postcard. The address went astray somewhere, I would imagine. Why?"

"Thought I might snap a picture of our Mr. Berk, send it along to Shultz."

"I don't understand, why would you want to?"

"For verification."

"That's certainly not necessary. I told you, I'm positive."

"Can't hurt to get another opinion, Mr. Nesbit. Make sure we know what we're up against."

"Shouldn't we leave that to the detective?"

"See him around?"

"Can't say I have."

"Me neither. Maybe we should give the guy a hand."

"He's being paid."

"Sure. But we live here and he doesn't. Kind of makes a difference, wouldn't you think?"

CHAPTER 7

I COULD FEEL THE RAIN SLOSHING AROUND IN MY SHOES. A SMALL stream flowed downhill in the gutter, bringing nuggets of trash. Soon the blocked sewer on Second Avenue would be overflowing and I'd need a lifeguard to carry me across the street.

Buses, cars, trucks, and delivery vans splashed along the avenue. Pedestrians hurried along under a variety of umbrellas. Lots of activity, but none of it touching the houses. It would take a lot more than rain to wash them clean.

The middle-aged, graying man who ran the laundry was busy with his washers and dryers. But the lady who owned the candy store was just sitting behind her counter staring off into space. The bar was still closed. Sam the tailor, stooped and elderly, was working away as though slave labor were back in vogue. Two of his kids were reputed to have made it big. But Sam was his own boss and the boss showed no mercy. I moved on.

The sign in the window said PRIMROSE RELOCATION CENTER. It was printed in big black letters on white cardboard. I pushed open the door and stepped in. The place was bare of furnishings, except for a desk, three folding chairs, and a lamp. The lamp had no shade and the desk had so many nicks and scratches that it looked like a refugee from some scrap heap. No one could accuse the center of conspicuous consumption. The short, pudgy man behind the desk appeared equally unimposing. He was in his midsixties, round shouldered, with receding gray hair and a slight double chin. He wore glasses and a gray business suit. A white shirt slightly frayed at the collar, and a brown-and-gray-striped tie, rounded out his attire. I couldn't see his shoes but they had to be scuffed. For a guy who was supposed to be an ogre, he still had a ways to go. He and his office looked so down-at-the-heels, I couldn't help wondering if he was going to hit me for a handout. I knew I was in trouble. The guy hadn't said a word yet and already I was feeling sorry for him.

He put down his *Daily News* and I got a smile; it was pleasant enough. "I didn't really think anyone would show up today," he said.

"Thought I'd swim over and see what you were up to," I told him. "You're Mr. Berk."

He said he was.

I gave him my name, address, and apartment number.

Berk held out a soft, slightly damp hand for me to shake. "Have a seat, Mr. Gordon."

I pulled up a chair, watched as Berk carefully removed a green ledger from a desk drawer, began turning pages. He peered at them nearsightedly, his nose almost touching the volume as though trying to sniff out its contents. I listened to the rain drum against the window. Schubert it wasn't. I looked at the bare floorboards, lumpy, discolored walls, and tried to imagine what kind of place this had been in its heyday. Or if it had ever had a heyday.

"Stuart Gordon," Berk said, "three-C."

I nodded.

Berk glanced from the ledger to me and back again as an MD might who had just noticed a suspicious symptom. A frown drew vertical lines down his jaw. "I've been trying to reach you for two whole weeks, Mr. Gordon."

"I was away."

"Away?" He made it sound somehow disreputable, as if he

suspected I'd been doing time, or undergoing treatment somewhere for a socially unacceptable disease.

"That's right," I said. "Out of town."

He sighed. I'd come up with the wrong answer. No prizes for James Shaw this morning. "You have another apartment somewhere, Mr. Gordon?"

I assured him I didn't.

"You're sure?"

"Yeah. My memory isn't what it used to be, but I'd probably remember a little thing like that."

"We'll find out, you know."

"Be my guest."

"We've had our problems with people who live elsewhere, Mr. Gordon. We always catch them."

I had this awful image of Berk turning up in my office, asking Harry to shadow me while I hid under the desk. I said, "You really think someone living in these houses can afford two homes?"

"It's been known to happen."

"I bet they drive here in their Rolls-Royce, straight from the welfare agency."

Berk sat back in his chair. "I'll tell you, Mr. Gordon, my boss would like to clear these buildings. That's no secret. We offer a small inducement for people to move out. Provided this is their legal residence. We find they have more than one address, we can evict them."

"And you do."

Berk shrugged. "It's the law."

"I get the picture," I said. "How much you offering?"

"Five hundred."

"Not exactly a fortune," I pointed out.

"If it were up to me," Berk said, "it would be a lot more."

"That's swell of you."

"I do what the boss tells me."

"The boss?"

"Mr. Rensler. But if you're thinking of going to see him

directly, Mr. Gordon, forget it. He won't see you. My job is to keep tenants from bothering him. He has enough on his mind without taking on my duties, too."

"Wouldn't dream of it."

"We may not offer a king's ransom," he said, "but we do help you relocate. That's worth something."

"What if I like it here?"

"Mr. Gordon, what's to like?"

"The ambiance?"

"These buildings are unsafe, unsanitary, and an eyesore. Do yourself a favor, Mr. Gordon, take the money and move out. We'll help you find a new home."

"Thanks. You paying my new rent, too?"

"I wish I could."

"Me, too. Know what I pay here?"

Berk peered down at the ledger. "Sixty-eight eighty-one a month."

"Uh-huh. You've got enough code violations in these houses to keep a squad of repairmen busy for the next couple of years. You're not going to pour thousands into houses that are eventually coming down. So the rent stays frozen. That's the law, too. If you haven't noticed, Mr. Berk, what you've got here is a renter's paradise."

Berk shook his head. "Some paradise. You know it can't last."

"Maybe not. But handing us five Cs for our homes is the same as putting us out in the street."

"You're a member of the tenants' committee, Mr. Gordon?"

I said I wasn't.

"You sound like them."

"Why not? The law's on our side. We don't have to move an inch unless we want to."

"Now you sound like a lawyer."

"Mr. Berk, what I'm saying is, you'll have to sweeten the pot, if you want some action."

"That's not for me to say."

"Speak to Rensler."

Berk shrugged. "You think he listens to me?"

"He'll listen. If we all stay put, sooner or later he'll get the message."

"You're making a mistake. Why not sleep on it for a while, think it over?"

I half turned, took a squint at the street. It was dark out there as if dusk had suddenly fallen hours ahead of schedule. Rain came down in huge windblown sheets. Passing vehicles were a blur of colors. Pedestrians hurried along as if trying to outrun the elements. Long streams of water trailed down the plate-glass window.

"The answer's no," I said.

"If you change your mind, Mr. Gordon, you know where to find me."

"Right here for the duration."

He nodded.

"And if that proves too long, I bet you have a shortcut or two up your sleeve, eh?"

"I might."

I gave him a grin. "Not something bad I hope?"

"Bad?"

"Rumor has it," I said, "that your company isn't above harassing people every now and then."

Berk scowled. "That's ridiculous."

"Glad to hear it. You ever manage a row of brownstones on West Twenty-ninth Street, Mr. Berk?"

"No."

"Then you wouldn't be Lacy?"

"Lacy? Of course not."

"Just checking."

"Who is this Lacy?"

"A nasty customer. Guy took over those brownstones I mentioned. Got the tenants to jump ship inside of three months. A real expert."

"And what does that have to do with me?"

"Nothing. Only some of my neighbors seem to think *you're* Lacy."

"Preposterous. Primrose is a business, not a . . . a . . ."

"Racket?"

"Yes. Not a racket. We have a license to protect. How long do you think we'd keep it if we harassed our tenants? I'm a grandfather. I have two married daughters and three grandchildren. A few more years and I retire. Let me tell you something. My health could be better. The doctor said, 'Take it easy, Mr. Berk, learn to relax. Get out of the rat race.' Got myself transferred to the field. Pay's a little less, but it's worth it. If I did what you said, badgered tenants, evaded the law, why, sooner or later I'd end up in court, wouldn't I? And why? So the company could make a few dollars more. Does that sound right to you?"

"Can't say it does," I admitted.

"Thank you. Try and give me the benefit of the doubt. And at least think about our offer."

"I'll think about the next one," I said, "the new, improved version."

"That may be a long wait, Mr. Gordon."

"I've got plenty of time, Mr. Berk."

CHAPTER 8

I WENT HOME, DRIED MY SOGGY SHOES IN FRONT OF THE STOVE, AND fixed myself a bite to eat: a tuna salad on onion rye, sprinkled with dill. I cut up some kirby cucumbers and egg tomatoes to keep the tuna company. For dessert, I toasted myself and my levelheadedness with a glass of grapefruit juice. Danny, my health-conscious brother, would have given his blessings to this meal, except maybe for the bread, which being bakery bought was standard Jewish rye, made up mostly of white flour rather than whole grain and therefore a sure death trap. But what Danny didn't know wouldn't hurt him. Just me. And my body had been hardened by years of intermittent junk food. I was tough. But probably not tough enough to brave the downpour without rubbers; mother wouldn't have liked it.

I sneaked a look out the window. The rain showed no sign of letting up. I fiddled with the radio, landed an early Mozart piano concerto to counteract the weather, sank down in the old, battered easy chair, and mulled over my session with Berk. It was nothing to celebrate. I had pushed the guy to his limit, which unfortunately was still five hundred. I had squeezed moving expenses out of him and the committee would consider that a plus. But we were still talking nickels and dimes. The Lacy missile had gone off like a dud. So what did I have besides a dumpy railroad flat and wet shoes? I wasn't sure. Being a private eye hadn't quite prepared me for the intricacies of the real estate racket.

I picked up the phone, dialed a number. The switchboard responded on the fifth ring. From it I went to the secretary and from her to the boss lady herself. I couldn't complain. I had only been put on hold twice and not disconnected even once.

"Honey," I said to the boss lady.

"So," Daphne asked, "how did it go?"

"That's what I'm trying to figure out. I was hoping you might take a stab at it, cookie, based on your long years of experience."

"Let's not overdo it, Shaw, four years."

"And what lucky years they were to have *you*."

"How sweet. He resorts to flattery. You must really be *desperate*."

"I'm at your mercy."

"That's how I like them."

"Berk just offered me a hefty five hundred, the going rate, plus moving expenses. He'll also help me find a new home but not for what I pay here."

"No one will find you a new home for what you pay there."

"I know. My question is: Is this guy cheap, or is he cheap?"

"You may not believe this, Jimmy, but their offer, at this stage, is really quite generous."

I laughed. "Your four years in this business have addled your brains, sweetie. They stand to make a fortune, put up a tower that'll equal the pyramids. They're handing out five hundred smackers. *That's* generous?"

"Yes, it's a start. My firm might not be much different."

I sighed. "That's what I was afraid of. What happens next?"

"Anything they want. They can raise their offer a bit at a time. There will always be *some* takers. Ultimately, when only a few occupants remain, they can raise the ante into the thousands. It's called a buyout. That will usually do it. By then the buildings are half empty, perhaps with only one or two families to a floor. The landlord won't have to employ scare tactics. Any sensible person would be scared on his own. And *very* motivated to find a new apartment. A well-placed word to the less imaginative will often start them on the right road, too. That and the money. What I'm saying, Jimmy, is that there is a gray area between legitimate and illegitimate pressure."

"And you can tell the illegit by the blood on the floor."

"Something like that."

"And I thought *I* was in a tough racket."

CHAPTER 9

I GOT OFF THE LEXINGTON AVENUE SUBWAY DOWNTOWN AT THE Bowling Green station and climbed topside. The rain had stopped during the train ride, leaving the streets and office buildings clean and shimmering.

Thirty-nine Broadway was between a Godfathers Pizzeria, Express Food, Lamston's, Roy Rogers, and a restaurant that merely identified itself as "Breakfast." I fought back a wave of heartburn and entered the lobby. An elevator presently arrived and I shot up to the ninth floor. A sign said DIVISION OF CODE ENFORCEMENT. HOUSING COMPLAINTS. LOFTS. MAINTE-NANCE. PRESERVATION. An arrow pointed to a door. I entered a large-portioned hall.

A few dozen people, half black or Hispanic, sat facing me on long wooden benches. Those who didn't look downright sullen appeared dazed.

A young black kid on the bench said, "You gotta take a number, mister."

"That for complaints?"

"Yeah."

"Which way for Multiple Dwellings?"

Some heads turned my way. Multiple Dwellings was where landlords registered. I had suddenly become *the enemy.*

"There," the kid said.

I took a second look and saw the sign right by my elbow.

Something about government bureaucracies that instantly turned my otherwise keen intellect to mush. I stepped around a shoulder-high partition. The desks to my right screened complaints. The three interviewers behind them struck a dishearteningly familiar note. They were all guys around my age, and any one of them could have been me if my craving for insecurity hadn't won out over common sense. They seemed a tad shopworn but game; justice might yet prevail. The tenants they were talking to looked glum—they knew better.

The registration section was over on the left. Middle-aged black ladies held down three of the five desks; two were empty. Some ancient green filing cabinets leaned tiredly against a smudged white wall. Tenants weren't the only demoralized bunch around here. The cleanup crew could have used a pep talk, too. The ceiling was low, porous, giving off an odor of stale cigarette smoke as though it harbored a secret vice.

The complaint section was bottlenecked, moving at a crawl. But no customers were in sight at registration. One of the lady clerks was sipping coffee. Another was going over some documents, presumably something to do with her job. The third was reading a paperback.

Daphne had given me instructions. I asked the nearest clerk, the reader, for Agnes Lathem and was directed to the drinker. I took a seat and introduced myself.

"You a landlord?" she asked.

"Uh-uh."

"A law clerk?"

"I look like a law clerk?"

Lathem was maybe forty. A large-boned black woman with shiny, dark, medium-length hair, a round face set on a long neck. She wore a wide-collared gray dress with a purple sash around her waist. "You in the right section?" she asked.

"Yeah."

"So what *are* you?"

48

"I'm still working on it." I slipped her a card. "Here's my latest incarnation."

"Private investigator?"

"Yep."

"My, my, never met one of those before. That as exciting as it sounds?"

"Nothing could be that exciting. On good days I manage to stay awake."

"More than we do here," she said.

"Lots of activity, though."

"That's complaints. Here's kind of peaceful. Pay's steady. Get to see a good number of law clerks. That's from the big firms. The rest are small landlords, just peewees."

"But suck the blood of the poor anyway, I bet."

"Not to hear them tell it. Some can hardly make ends meet. Just praying for a change in the rent laws. Don't get rid of the controls, they go on welfare."

"That true?"

"You the detective."

"Right," I said. "You know a Robert Reise?"

"Goodness. This isn't about him, is it?"

"Perish the thought, he's my reference."

"You know him?"

"His boss, Daphne Field. What I'd like you to do, Ms. Lathem, is pull the file on a firm I'm checking out."

"No law against that. If I were real busy, I might ask why."

"But you're not real busy."

"Don't seem that way. Which firm?"

"Primrose. Know them?"

"No. But I will soon enough, I imagine."

She rose, tossed her empty cup in the wastebasket, and went over to one of the battered filing cabinets. I sat and looked at the complainers. The current crop consisted of two women. One was young, black, and calm. The other—white, middle-aged, and dumpy—seemed a fraction away from genuine hysteria. The third was an elderly gentleman who looked as though he'd been put through the ringer once too often. Neon-light panels up above had drained these folks of color as though Dracula had been busy sucking their blood. Just being here made me feel like a victim.

Lathem returned after a while with a handful of eight-by-seven form cards and put them in front of me. "Look through these."

There were nine in all, one for each Primrose property. Only two principals were listed on each card: the owner and management agent. Edward Jenkins, a name new to me, was down as owner on all the forms. The agent, however, varied from property to property. Some worked out of the Primrose office. Others were independent. I dutifully copied every-one's name, business, home address, and phone number. If nothing else, I could always pester this Jenkins by calling him after midnight and breathing into the phone. Berk had said a Mr. Rensler was the boss. No Renslers on the cards. Which meant nothing, of course, since the owner could hire anyone he wished to run his business. Just one of the perks of success.

I returned the cards to Lathem with a thanks.

"Satisfied?" she asked.

I nodded. "Can I trouble you for one more thing?"

"No trouble."

"Okay." I gave her the address of Nesbit's Twenty-ninth Street brownstone. Lathem went to her filing cabinet, re-turned with another card.

"Investigator's paradise," I told her.

"Wait till they computerize this office."

"When's that?"

"In a hundred years."

A large residential tower stood on the block that had once housed the brownstones, a monument to change if not progress. King Enterprises was the proud daddy and one Gerald Munsy was listed as the firm's owner. Lipsky Man-agement ran the building. I glanced at my Primrose jottings.

Leo Lipsky managed a couple of their properties, too. Small world.

"How about the old brownstones that used to be on that site; they registered?"

"Were. That would take a little digging."

"Can you manage it?"

"No rule says I can't. Got to do it on my own time, though. Old files are stored in back."

I gave her my card along with a five and a twenty folded double.

"Goodness. This for me?"

"Yeah, just a token."

"It come out of your pocket?"

"I have a generous expense account, Ms. Lathem."

"Then it's all right. My, I think you woke me up."

"That's what I came for," I told her cheerfully.

CHAPTER 10

DUSK SETTLED OVER THE CITY. I IMPROVISED DINNER: SARDINES ON rye, chopped onions, egg tomatoes, and kirby cucumber. I tossed in a couple of leaves of Boston lettuce, but the whole thing was suspiciously like lunch. If I was going to put in any time here at all, I'd have to stock up. I toasted that notion with a glass of orange juice, which reminded me of breakfast. I was in a culinary rut. I went downstairs to the corner mom-and-pop grocery and bought a pint of double chocolate-chip ice cream and devoured it in one sitting in my easy chair, the morning's *New York Times* spread on my lap, a kind of overgrown napkin. Finally, I'd found a use for the *Times*. A sugar rush from the ice cream hit me, giving me a momentary high. The calories I could feel instantly turning to fat inside me. The cholesterol was, no doubt, forming roadblocks in my arteries that would presently prove fatal, probably within the hour. The sardines were starting to complain that they didn't like chocolate chip.

I got out of there fast before something *really* bad happened and went to work.

Mrs. Nash looked to be in her late eighties. Her hair was white and thinning. Her hands shook and she used a cane. At least she was alive, which was a lot more than could be said of most people her age.

"Five hundred dollars, Mr. Gordon, that's what Mr. Berk said he'd give me."

"It'll go up, Mrs. Nash," I told her.

"Oh, no. Mr. Berk assured me it wouldn't; he was very precise on that point."

"That's what he tells *everyone*. Take it with a grain of salt and wait for a good offer; it'll come along, believe me."

We were seated in her living room on the fourth floor of one of the houses overlooking Second Avenue. The place was spotless, but the furniture wouldn't have pulled in ten bucks at a flea market. I didn't even want to think about how the old girl managed four flights of stairs. Outside, street noises kept up a constant racket, all but climbed through the windows and sat in our laps. Mrs. Nash didn't seem to notice. She was probably deaf, too.

She smiled at me out of a white-powdered face. "He told me a secret."

"Berk?"

"Yes, but I see no reason to keep it from you, young man. If we wait too long, he said, we won't even have the five hundred. His employer will be very, *very* angry and take it away. And then they'll *make* us move."

"Mrs. Nash, they *can't* make you move."

"Oh, they can. But I'm not concerned in the least. The Lord has always provided for me, young man. When Mr. Nash passed away, I had some terrible days, I don't mind telling you. But as you can see, I'm perfectly all right now. And if you ask me, none of us will have to move, not a soul."

"Why not?"

"Oh, Mr. Berk will just go away and things will be as they were before. This is my home, I wouldn't want to leave it. And the good Lord wouldn't want me to."

I looked at the old girl. "I'm sure He wouldn't want to inconvenience you," I said, "but sometimes the higher powers need a little help from us down below." I gave her a long lecture on her rights.

Mrs. Nash nodded and smiled vaguely as though some unseen presence had just passed her a celestial valentine card. I was making as much headway as an ant swimming upstream in the Hudson.

"Mrs. Nash," I said, "when Berk sees you again, I'd be grateful if you'd let him know I was here. And repeat what I've been telling you."

"Of course, young man," she said. Her eyes were fixed somewhere on the wall behind me, as if she expected Mr. Nash to step through it any second and offer me *his* slant on relocation. I left.

Carl Benjamin told me he drove a cab. He was a short, compact man in his midfifties with broad features and a firm, gray-stubble-coated jaw. We spoke in the hallway, mainly because he wouldn't invite me into his flat. As good a reason as any.

"You with the committee?"

I said no, explaining I was just trying to size up the new situation. "Berk dangle his five hundred at you?" I asked.

"Sure. I told him to go shove it."

"He say anything about relocation?"

"I wasn't interested."

"Holding out for more bucks?"

"Not me. I like it here. Rent's dirt cheap. A and P's up the block. Shopping center on Eighty-sixth Street. IRT three blocks over. Why should I leave? Say they get bighearted, hand us six, seven grand. What damn good is it? Nothing doing in this city under eight grand a year, and that's usually shit. Where am I gonna live, in an SRO?"

"Mr. Benjamin," I said, "what happens if everyone moves out?"

"Tough."

"You just camp here all by yourself?"

"Yeah, if it comes to that."

"Sounds terrific."

"What's it to you?"

"Just curious," I said. "What about trespassers?"

"What about them?"

"They'll be all over the place."

"So?"

"You figure on taking them on like the Lone Ranger? He had Tonto, at least."

"Hey, who sent you, Berk?"

"Mr. Benjamin, I'm just trying to add a touch of realism to this conversation."

"Don't do me any favors."

"Forget it. You want to stay, you've got my blessings."

"Thanks a lot, buddy."

"No, I mean it. To hell with Berk. Let them build their houses around you. He comes calling, tell him Stuart Gordon backs you a hundred percent."

"Stuart Gordon?"

"Yeah."

Benjamin grunted, squinted at me, shrugged, and closed the door.

Mr. Ward leaned heavily on a cane, peering at me near-sightedly as if I were a purchase he was examining at the local grocery store. He had a large, round head fringed by tufts of white hair and an overweight, squat body. A pair of thick glasses rested on his ample nose. He wore a maroon cardigan over a white striped shirt. The walk to his door had left him panting.

"Yes?"

I told him who I was and what I wanted.

Ward mulled over this information for a moment, then invited me in.

I stepped into his kitchen/living room. An overpowering odor of mothballs enveloped me, seemed to come from every corner. If mutant killer moths ever attacked this house, Ward at least would be safe. Slowly, as if wading into frigid water,

Ward lowered himself onto a kitchen chair. I took a seat across the table from him.

"Yes," Ward said, "the building manager was here to see me." He spoke slowly, deliberately, as though each word were cast in bronze and slated for immortality.

"Five hundred?"

"That was the figure." Ward gave an added puff for emphasis. "It was inadequate. I told him as much."

"How'd he take it?"

"He urged me to look at some other apartments he had."

"Did you?"

Ward nodded slowly as though he were about to make a telling philosophical point. "Yes."

We regarded each other thoughtfully. "What were they like?" I finally asked.

"They were good apartments in nice neighborhoods. The rents were very steep."

"So what are you going to do?"

"I will wait."

"For the money to go up?"

He shook his head. "That will not happen."

I asked him how he knew.

"My friend Dropkin was in a similar situation."

"With Primrose?"

"No. But it is bound to happen here, too. Already, Mr. Riskin and his wife have heard the same thing."

"And that is?"

Ward leaned across the table. "We will be put in hotels."

"Hotels?"

"Yes. While these houses are being torn down." He sat back in his chair as though he had just given me the inside track on tomorrow's stock prices.

"Then what?"

"They will build new houses *here*." Ward pounded the table. "And we will move back in."

"At the same rents?"

"Of course."

"Why," I asked, "would they do that?"

"Because this way their renters remain happy. It gives the company a good reputation."

"Aha," I said.

"Also, if no one will move out, what are they to do?"

"Nesbit," I said, "thinks they might stoop to harassment."

Ward laughed. "Companies do not do that. For forty-five years I worked for I.F. Fox. You have heard of them?"

"No."

"They were very big. Educational materials. So I know something about business. And this thing that Mr. Nesbit has been saying is not about to happen. Who would rent their houses if people were treated in such a manner?"

"Maybe," I said, "they'll just give us more money to move?"

"No," Ward said firmly. "This five hundred was for those who already want to move. For the rest of us, those who show that they are determined to stay, there will be very nice apartments, right here." Again Ward pounded the table, glaring as if expecting me to contradict him. Not on your life.

I nodded, rose, and thanked him for his time.

Ward heaved himself up from his seat and saw me to the door. "Anytime you want to know what the situation is," he said, "come to me. Do not let them confuse you."

I promised I wouldn't, asked that he tell Berk we had chatted, and beat it. The mothball fumes drifted after me as if anxious to save me from an onslaught of frenzied wool eaters even here in the hallway. Good old mothballs, man was not alone.

CHAPTER 11

THE PHONE STARTLED ME OUT OF A YEAR'S GROWTH. I REACHED FOR it gingerly as though it might snap at my hand. "Hello."

"Hi," a cheery voice said.

"Honey, you've lit up my entire room."

"You're sitting in the dark?"

"Actually, I am."

"Why?"

"If you saw the room, you'd know."

"But surely," Daphne said, "there is a Beethoven, Schubert, or Mozart handy to lift your spirits? Or at least Irving Berlin?"

"Irving wouldn't've liked it here. And the other guys are dead, too. Their music, of course, lives on. But right now, we're between numbers."

"You're ill?"

"I'm *thinking.*"

"Doesn't that hurt your poor little head?"

"Only when I think hard. I went calling today," I said, "got to meet some of my neighbors. Eighteen, all told; nineteen if you count the seven-year-old kid whose mama wasn't home."

"And?"

"They're weird."

"All of them?"

"Some of them. I talked myself blue in the face getting the

59

facts out. For all the good it did, I might've been speaking Turkish."

"Those were *tenants*, dear."

"Now she tells me."

"You'll recover."

"Don't count on it."

"You visit Code Enforcement, or just spend the day gabbing?"

"Sure, earlier."

"So what happened?"

"Nothing special. Ever hear of an Edward Jenkins?"

"No."

"Seems to own Primrose. How about Lipsky Management?"

"No, again."

"Works for Jenkins and Gerald Munsy. Munsy's the guy who built a tower on Twenty-ninth Street after the mysterious Lacy ran off the tenants."

"Munsy's big league. King Enterprises, right?"

"Yeah. They shifty?"

"Not that I know of."

"Check around, okay?"

"Sure. All three?"

"Yeah. I put your Ms. Lathem on the payroll sifting old records. We'll know more presently. Thing is—"

There was a knock on the door.

"Company," I said. "Don't go away."

I went to the door.

Tom Berk, in overcoat and hat, stood in the hallway. It seemed a bit premature for him to have gotten word of my visits, but you never know.

"Working late?" I asked.

"Just passing."

"Something I can do for you?"

"Wanted to see if you were home."

"And not at one of my other mansions, eh? Camp here by my door, Berk, I'll loan you a pillow."

"That won't be necessary," he said frostily. "Good night, Mr. Gordon."

"See you around, pal."

I returned to the phone. "Old Berk checking up on me."

"We building managers are a suspicious lot."

"So I see."

"You spending the night there, sweetheart?"

"Not if I get a better offer; the inspector's just come and gone."

"Look no further."

"Thank God for telephones."

"And Daphnes."

"Amen to that, honey."

CHAPTER 12

THE NIGHT WAS CLEAR AND COLD, THE STREET EMPTY. I PUT THE collar up on my padded Lee jacket, stuffed my hands into pants pockets, and started up the rise toward Third. The houses fell away, their place taken by a scraggly weed garden protected by a high wire fence. The six-story Chinese laundry across the street was dark. Behind its boarded-up windows, hand-washing for part of the city's countless Chinese laundries went on, an around-the-clock assault on dirt. If someone had to do it, I was just glad it wasn't me. My tour of the tenants had given me a jolt in more ways than one. Another forty years and a couple dozen business flops and, I figured, I might very well be one of them. A nice moment to start fretting about my prospects. The thing to do was get out of here fast, before I came down with the blues and loused up my otherwise splendid mood. I hummed a snatch of Beethoven's violin concerto—an upbeat piece, to my way of thinking—and put on the steam.

I had just about reached the top of the rise when I heard the shout. It came from behind me. For an instant I thought that Berk had been lurking behind a trash can, after all, and had caught me red-handed. I'd gone AWOL and now I'd be restricted to base for the next fifty weekends.

I turned. And got an eyeful.

There were two guys back at the houses, both wearing

leather jackets. And they were chasing Mr. Nesbit. The old duffer didn't have a prayer.

No sound reached me now, no cry for help; Nesbit needed all his breath for running. In the dim lamplight, it was like watching a silent movie, jerky and unreal. As he ran out into the street, the old man's long coat flapped around his legs like broken wings. The leather jackets were right behind him.

"Hey!" I yelled.

No one paid the least attention. As if I were a spectator at some sporting event whose participants were too busy to heed applause.

One of the guys shot out a foot and Nesbit went sprawling.

I was still trying to figure out my next move when my legs kicked into high gear and charged down the rise. So much for well-thought-out strategy.

My downhill sprint brought results: I was noticed. The taller of the two goons, a stocky guy in a peaked cap, finally glanced my way, stopped aiming a kick at his fallen victim, and reached into a jacket pocket. A short length of pipe appeared in his hand. A cheapo thug's weapon, but effective, for all that.

By then I was almost on top of the guy. Momentum kept me going. I did a nice imitation of a bird, took to the air, flattened out, and tackled him just below the knees; he couldn't have been more surprised than me.

The guy hit the pavement first, with me on top. My right fist was ready, even if I wasn't; it popped him in the kisser twice. The old fist must have known what it was doing. The guy's head lulled sideways and the pipe slipped from his hand. I rolled off fast, jumped to my feet, hunting for his buddy. All I saw was his back. He was halfway around the corner on Second Avenue. I couldn't be sure, but he didn't look much older than a kid. He could always try for track and field if he couldn't make it in strong-arm; he knew how to move.

My attention returned to the other guy. He was scrambling up on hands and knees like some oversize canine. He looked wild-eyed and amazed in the lamplight as if it were the old man who had toppled him and not me. Then he was up and dashing down the center of the street. He, too, went around the corner. I felt like Mike Tyson scoring endless one-round knockouts. With pushovers like these, being Sir Galahad was a snap. Aunt Bessie was right: buy cheap, get cheap.

I turned to Nesbit. He hadn't moved, was lying facedown on the pavement like a discarded blanket. It gave me a start. I wondered if he was dead. That would certainly put a crimp in the evening. I went over carefully as though treading on broken glass. Kneeling, I gazed at a long, lined profile under a wide hat. Behind thick glasses miraculously still intact and perched on his nose, gray, bloodshot eyes peered back at me and blinked.

"Mr. Nesbit," I said, "you okay?"

"Dear me, I don't know."

"Come on," I said, extending a hand. Nesbit gripped it in both of his and I slowly pulled him to his feet.

"Are they gone?" His voice was even more quivery and high-pitched than usual. Now at least he had a good excuse.

"Yeah," I said, "run off."

"They tried to mug me." Nesbit was shaking like a man just learning to walk a tightrope. I kept a tight hold on him as we started for his house. I helped him up the stoop. Thank God his flat was on the second and not the sixth floor, or I'd have had to carry him piggyback. We didn't win any medals for speed, but I eventually steered him through his door and into his bedroom. I helped him get out of his overcoat, eased him onto the bed.

"Use a drink?" I asked.

"Oh, dear, no." His face was full of alarm as though I'd suggested a nice shot of Drano. Gingerly, he began feeling his ribs.

"Any damage, Mr. Nesbit?"

"The coat, you know, it saved me. They kicked me, but the coat is padded—it's made for winter. And then you came along before they could do more harm. It was all my fault, of course."

"How's that?"

"When they came at me, I should have stopped."

"And then what?"

"Why, given them my wallet. There was only a few dollars in it."

"Think that's what they were after?"

"Don't you?"

"Mr. Nesbit," I said, "you're the one who first alerted us to Primrose."

He nodded uncertainly.

"And you're still talking against them, aren't you?"

Another nod.

"So what makes you think this wasn't their work?"

Nesbit sat on his worn green quilt staring up at me from behind his thick glasses, his mouth half open, his face with its folds of loose skin, looking crumpled.

"It never occurred to me," he said. "You really think so?"

"It's a possibility."

"At Twenty-ninth Street, you know, conditions were already frightful when the muggings began. Nothing has changed here. . . ."

"Yeah, except we've got Mr. Berk now."

"Lacy."

"Whatever you call him. They could have wanted to make an example of you, Mr. Nesbit. I may be way off, but I'd watch my step if I were you. Stay indoors at night."

"I was only going to the pharmacy."

"Don't open your door until you know who it is."

"I don't."

"Fine. Maybe they were muggers, plain and simple. But let's not take any chances."

"I'm quite sure I won't sleep a wink tonight."

"Want me to call someone?"

"Oh, dear, no. Thank you. I'm fine now. I wouldn't want to bother anyone. My niece lives in Connecticut, you know. What could she do?"

"How about a neighbor?"

"I really couldn't."

"You sure?"

"Oh, yes."

"Is there anyone you could phone?"

"Phone? I've never had a phone here. At work, you know, before I retired, I had to answer the phone *all* the time. It kept *ringing*. I never want to hear that sound again, ever."

"Uh-huh," I said as though Nesbit had made perfect sense. "If you're certain there's nothing I can do, I'll be on my way."

"Yes, thank you."

I left Nesbit sitting on his bed staring at the wall. The old guy had me worried.

I stopped at a door on the ground floor and knocked. It opened presently to reveal a short, squarish, white-haired woman in her late sixties. She wore a faded brown bathrobe. Her feet were stuck into a pair of men's slippers.

"My name's Gordon," I said, "I live two houses down. You know Mr. Nesbit from upstairs?"

The woman nodded, tight-lipped.

"He was mugged," I told her.

"When?"

"Just now. I got him home all right, but he's still kind of shaky. I thought maybe you could look in on him a bit later, see if he's okay."

"Maybe," the woman said. The door closed.

Maybe would have to do. There were, of course, other doors I could try; the building was full of them. There were Hawks and Kazmir next door, if no one else. But Nesbit had said he was all right, and I decided to take his word for it. It had been a long day.

I went back into the night and this time no one shouted.

CHAPTER 13

THE REST OF THE WEEK DID NOT ESPECIALLY DISTINGUISH ITSELF. I divided my time between the office, neighbors, and waving at Berk. The building manager stayed out of my way. The tenants, most of them at least, heard me out, then gave me their slant on the new owners, life, and the world in general. Very uplifting.

Ms. Lathem called on Tuesday to tell me the owner who had sold the Twenty-ninth Street brownstones to King was one Manny Gretz. I didn't know any Manny Gretz and neither did Daphne.

That night, after putting in my usual session at the tenements, I dined out at the Pumpkin Eater—an Upper West Side vegetarian eatery—with my brother Danny and Uncle Max. Among Danny's teaching stints in the Comp Lit Department at Columbia was an occasional course in Yiddish lit. He was an expert. But more like Admiral Byrd touring the Antarctic than some Eskimo hanging out in his igloo. Max—in his seventies now—was the genuine article. He'd trooped through the Lower East Side with some of its leading lights—the poets Glatstein, Greenberg, and Iceland, the novelist Opatoshu, a herd of journalists and actors—and had even been on a first-name basis with a nice sampling of Yiddish gangsters who ran the local rackets. Danny always used these occasions to pump Uncle Max about yesteryear.

And Max always obliged with a slew of anecdotes that made his old ethnic hunting grounds sound like an Errol Flynn swashbuckler. Just to keep my end up, I told them about Primrose, which might, or might not, be a real case, and all the other goings-on at the office that had once been Max's. We all had a fine time.

Wednesday night I continued interviewing renters and caught up with my neighbor, the hard case, Caloney, who invited me in with a broad smile and told me to make myself at home.

Where I had a bedroom, he had a den. The kitchen/living room was sparsely furnished and looked unused. I figured the guy for a fast-food junky, a type sadly beyond help. His bathtub was concealed behind an oriental screen that looked as out of place as a sumo wrestler in the City Ballet. The small, airless room next to the water closet served as his bedroom; it takes all kinds.

I followed Caloney into the den. "Beer?" he asked.

"Sure."

"Bud okay?"

"Fine."

I plopped down in an armchair. My host returned with two mugs full of golden liquid and seated himself opposite me.

"So?" he said.

I took a swallow of Bud. "Just wanted your take on this whole business."

Caloney grinned. "The new owners?"

"Yeah."

"You at the meetin'?"

"Uh-huh."

"Then you know. This private eye stuff is shit. You see this fuckin' guy round here? What's he gonna do anyway? We dealin' with landlords, for chrissakes, not some fuckin' gangsters. Get my drift?"

"Got it."

"Okay. So I got a petition for you to sign. Askin' for a new committee."

I shrugged. "They may be on the right track. Nesbit says the landlord's a crook."

"Nesbit's an asshole. There ain't no landlord born that wasn't a crook. An' that, my friend, is *exactly* why we gotta have legal counsel."

"Got someone in mind?"

"Sure." Caloney reached for a half-smoked cigar in a black glass ashtray and relit it. "Know this guy, name's Tanner, gotta lotta experience in cases like this. Handles himself real good."

"Grateful for the business, too, I bet."

"Grateful my ass. Come on, Stu, think I give a shit who they get? One shyster's like another, right?" Caloney puffed on his cigar. "Listen, this place is okay. They want me out, that's okay, too. Only it'll cost 'em, my friend, that's the bottom line. Another round?"

"Thanks, no."

"So, I sold you?"

"You got the right idea, Ed."

"Okay. You'll sign?"

I held up a hand. "Not so fast."

"What is it?"

"Well, I like the lawyer angle. But I think we ought to give the gumshoe a chance."

"To do what?"

"Find out who we're up against."

"C'mon."

"Look, Ed, your pal the lawyer, what's-his-name . . ."

"Tanner."

"Yeah. He may be great in court, or at the bargaining table, but for street smarts, Ed, you can't beat a pro."

"*Jesus.* Listen, my friend, all we gotta do is pay the rent; that's all. Let that fuck Berk do the worryin'."

"You're wrong, Ed, it's not that simple."

"The hell it ain't. Your fuckin' pro ain't gonna do a fuckin' thing—*if* he ever shows. Wait an' see."

"So *then* we get Tanner."

"Yeah, then."

Caloney saw me to the door. I thanked him for his hospitality.

"Stu, you change your mind, you come see me, right?"

"Right."

We shook hands and I left. Caloney was the friendliest neighbor I'd gotten to yet. There was probably a moral in that, but I was too dumb to figure it out.

CHAPTER 14

MENDELSSOHN'S SEXTET IN D CAME OVER THE RADIO. THE LIGHTS were off. I lay stretched out on the bed, my eyes closed. Mendelssohn, of course, was no Bach, Mozart, or Beethoven, but who was? Schubert, maybe, if he'd lasted a bit longer. Haydn had topped Felix in some ways and Brahms in others. But music isn't sports, and when you listen to Mendelssohn, you get something unique. The maestro didn't hit the heights of passion. He didn't chew up the scenery. He never made you want to cut your throat in despair, either. No storming the barricades. No swooning with nostalgia. He was *solid*. There was poise, class, and balance. There was elegance. And after a while, he took you home.

Home, of course, was where I wasn't, an inescapable fact even with my eyes closed. I was beginning to wonder why. All this chitchat with neighbors was probably great practice for a budding politician, but not so hot for a tired gumshoe with other cases on his mind. It was far from certain that Berk would rise to the bait even if he was the evil Lacy. So what the hell was I doing here? Pretty soon, I'd start worrying about my neighbors during my off hours, and then I'd really be a goner. It might, I figured, actually be smart to become a traveling salesman right about now and blow this joint. No one could say I hadn't put in my time. It was a thought, and as thoughts went, not half bad.

I must have dozed, for the next thing I heard was the phone ringing. Mendelssohn was gone and a commercial had taken his place. I lowered the radio and picked up the phone.

"Yeah?" I said.

"Mr. Gordon?" A woman's voice, a young one by the sound of it.

"Speaking."

"I may have something for you," the voice told me.

"Yeah, what?" I wondered if the something was magazine subscriptions, or home delivery of the *New York Times*. Whatever it was, I hated it already.

"Information," she said.

"You're selling encyclopedias?"

"This is about the houses."

"Yeah?"

"You *are* Stuart Gordon of two forty-two East Ninety-fourth Street?"

"Uh-huh."

"I wake you or something?"

"Perish the thought. You a neighbor?"

"No."

"So who are you?"

"You can call me Lila."

"That your name?"

"Like yours is Gordon." She laughed.

The lady had done it, I was wide-awake now. Next thing, she'd be telling me this was a real case and not a throwback to my days at the welfare department. She'd have to do a lot more than telling to convince me. "I don't think I follow," I said.

"Forget it. Look, I know you've been active on this housing thing. Well, let's say maybe I can help."

"Fine. Let's say that. What happens next?"

"I call again."

"Again?"

"See, it's too early now."

"For what?" I asked reasonably.

"A deal. Things gotta happen first."

"Such as?"

"Things."

"I'm supposed to understand?"

"No."

"Just checking. So what's the point of calling?"

"See if we could get together. Like discuss things later."

"Things again."

"You know what I mean."

"Sure, I'm a mind reader. Lila," I said, "I'll meet you anywhere, anytime. How's that?"

"Super."

"Anything else?"

"I guess not."

"Okay. Call me."

We exchanged byes. I turned the radio up. Something that sounded like Bartók was on. A bit astringent, but pleasant enough. I lay back in the darkness. My case now had a mystery woman. I sighed. What was a case without one? I went to sleep.

I sat up in bed, suddenly wide awake. The luminous dials on my clock said one-thirty. I smelled smoke. At first I thought it was coming from outside. I climbed out of bed, fumbled for my robe and slippers. I went to the window, opened it all the way, and stuck my head out. The air smelled fresh enough. I turned on the light. Nothing was smoldering in my flat. That left the rest of the house. I went to the door, threw it open.

Thick, acrid smoke filled the stairwell, darkening the dim light bulb in the ceiling. I stared at the smoke stupidly. Down the hall a door opened, and a neighbor tumbled out trying to run and get into his pants at the same time. Down below, a voice screamed, "Fire!" The voice didn't lie.

I beat it into my flat, wet a towel, held it up to my face, and ran back into the hall. Two more apartments were on the floor. I ran the length of the hallway, pounding on doors. "Fire!" I yelled.

I started up the stairs to warn the others. People—half dressed, barefoot, coughing—came toward me through the smoke, Mrs. Kazmir in the lead.

"Is landlord!" she screamed at me.

"Everyone out of there?" I yelled back.

"I knock on doors."

Another wave of disheveled tenants poured past me.

"See," Kazmir yelled, "Mr. Nesbit right!"

The old girl was getting set to make a speech. I grabbed her shoulder, propelled her in the right direction.

The upstairs, I figured, was cleared; no one could sleep through this racket. I turned and did the prudent thing, followed Kazmir down.

The smoke grew thicker. Through it a lone figure emerged, moving up. He held a hanky to his face, coughed, and bawled, "Fire!" I recognized Ned Hawks.

I caught his arm. "It's okay," I yelled. "Let's get out."

Hawks didn't have to be told twice. We plunged down the stairs. The smoke on the ground floor was so dense you could cut it into squares.

I stumbled over something. A woman's voice down near my knees cried, "Help me." Hawks and I scooped her up and lugged her outdoors.

We were the last to leave. A coughing, shivering, red-eyed crowd greeted us on the street. There wasn't a happy face among them.

Carlos, the super, joined me. He wore a plush red bathrobe and green slippers. At least his hair wasn't combed; otherwise he looked unrumpled. "The cellar," he said, "fire is there."

"What the hell is it?" I asked.

He shrugged.

Hawks said, "Had my window open, smelled smoke, and

stuck my head out." He shook his head now as if in disbelief.

"Is landlord," Mrs. Kazmir shrieked. "He do this!"

Lights were coming on in windows, people from other houses were out in the street, too.

We all stood and watched the smoke billow through the front door.

It took the fire engines eight minutes to arrive and twenty to go away again.

"Nine mattresses," the fire chief said. "That's what it was." He was a red-faced, jowly man.

I remembered the mattresses. The basement was full of junk: old furniture, bedsprings, even pots and pans. Things people had left that were stored for no good reason at all.

"Accident?" I asked.

The chief shook his head. "No way. Matches all over the place. It was arson," he said, "plain and simple."

CHAPTER 15

THURSDAY, MIDMORNING, UNCLE MAX CALLED THE OFFICE AND asked if I was free for lunch. When Max was in town and not basking in Florida, we usually got together every month or so. But the pair of us had dined out with Danny only a couple of days ago. Despite being in his seventies, my uncle has the energy of a man in his early fifties and the interests to match. So I knew it wasn't boredom.

"Sure," I said.

Max asked where.

"Game for Living Springs?"

Uncle Max allowed that he might be able to stand it.

Living Springs is near Lexington Avenue and Sixtieth Street, a few blocks from the office. The front part is a health-food store; the restaurant is in back. Split level. The buffet downstairs, the main dining room above.

"Where are the hot dogs?" Max asked.

"Two blocks over."

"This is one of Danny's places?"

"Found it on my own."

"You too have become a health fanatic, ah?"

"Must be the old faddist gene at work again. Seems to run in the family."

I filled my tray with a variety of vegetarian dishes ranging from baked potatoes to bean sprouts with tofu dressing. The soup was thick barley. I took a double helping, and two slices of whole-rye bread. Fruit salad, whole-wheat muffins, and herb tea topped it off. If mom were watching from cloud nine, I knew she'd be pleased.

We went upstairs and found a table. My uncle's tray contained two plates, one for the hot stuff, the other, items from the salad bar. Max glanced down at the latter.

"A weed garden," he said.

"That's the alfalfa-bean sprouts. As long as they're not crawling around, you're probably safe."

My uncle and I dug in.

Max Gabinsky had an oval, suntanned face, high cheekbones, and a pointed chin. The top of his crown was as bald as a grapefruit, but a fringe of white hair still remained in back. His white mustache, slightly waxed, was turned up at the ends. He was five foot four and no matter what he ate, seemed to remain lean. No use hoping his genes had rubbed off on me; he was my uncle by marriage. On the other hand, I wouldn't have gotten much kick out of being five four. His tweed winter coat, sporting a fur collar, was neatly folded on the empty chair next to him. He had on a three-piece, midnight-blue pin-striped suit, a red, blue-dotted silk tie, with a three-cornered matching silk hanky poking out of his breast pocket. His black shoes, I knew without looking, were polished to a high gleam. Max would have been the idol of the *Police Gazette* had that venerable publication still existed.

We chatted as we ate, I extolling the virtues of Daphne at some length, one of my favorite topics. Max held forth on a lady friend he had in Florida. The fact that the old boy still had a sex life was heartening, to say the least. Danny, my brother, had half a dozen girlfriends, so we talked about that. A guy from my mother's hometown, Keshinev, Max said, used to fall down in front of trolley cars and pretend he'd been hit. This was during the Great Depression when *everyone* was broke. He collected the first couple of times. The last time he did it, only a few blocks from here, they hauled him off to jail, another man undone by too much of a good thing. Max also told, how as a kid, he'd seen the great Jewish lightweight champ, Benny Leonard, fight. All the Jews used to come to his fight and yell, "*Zetz im in de kishkes, Benny,*" which means, "Whack him in the guts, Benny." I asked what he thought of Dempsey and Louis and he said they were tops; he put Sugar Ray Robinson in the same class. Tyson had yet to face a major challenger, but he could be up there, too. Al Jolson, Max remembered, speaking of great ones, used to perform in the old Winter Garden, on Broadway, and sometimes, after the show, he'd remain on stage and keep singing for two more hours. The audience would go wild. Jolson paid the orchestra out of his own pocket. Max asked if anything new had happened with my Primrose case and I told him about the fire. By then we were on the herb tea. "They won't be able to pin it on anyone," I said, "but a couple more incidents and Berk might be in trouble."

"This Lipsky you mentioned last time," Max said, "his first name is Leo?"

"Right."

"And he is what?"

"Guy runs a management outfit," I said. "Primrose is a client."

"How many buildings?"

"For Primrose? Two."

Max nodded. "There was something else."

"Uh-huh. The West Twenty-ninth Street brownstones where the tenants were run off a couple years ago was replaced by a residential tower. Lipsky's the manager there, too. So far, that's the only connection."

Max looked thoughtful. "This landlord who owned the brownstones, his name was Gretz?"

"Manny Gretz."

He nodded. "You know, Jimmy, there were plenty Jewish racketeers on the Lower East Side before the First World

War, and after, too. Some, in their own way, even became famous. Lipke Buchalter, Gurrah Shapiro, Lefty Louie Rosenzweig, Gyp the Blood Horowitz, Arnold Rothstein of Murder Inc., the papers were full of their pictures; everyone knew about them."

"Even me. I remember your stories."

"You enjoyed them, ah? Well, by the forties, not so many of the old crowd was left. Times were different. The neighborhoods changed. Still, some remained. On Broome Street there was a gang of lowlifes who shook down the storekeepers. Also, they did a little loan-sharking. I myself had nothing to do with this bunch; they were a problem for the police, not a private detective. But I heard stories. One was about a man called Lieb Lipsky."

"What happened to him?"

"Who knows? By the fifties there were no more Jewish gangs."

"They all retired?"

"What retired? They remained crooks, only now they went into business for themselves. Some of them were already buying up houses."

I grinned at him. "And Lieb is Leo in English. A bit skimpy, but has possibilities," I admitted.

"There was someone else, another man with whom this Lipsky was associated. Only the name wasn't Gretz."

"So what was it?"

Max sighed. "That, unfortunately, is what I don't remember. But I will find out, Jimmy. If you are dealing with Lipsky and his crowd, you should watch yourself."

"Not nice guys, eh?"

"Not even for gangsters."

CHAPTER 16

FRIDAY MORNING I SPENT IN THE OFFICE. HARRY WAS OFF IN THE field, and I held strategy sessions with Dick Hanks and Bob Perry about some of their cases. They left and I gave Carl Springer the address of Lipsky Management, asked him to drop over, size up the joint, and see if the boss had horns and carried a pitchfork. Then I tore into a pile of paperwork and let the work ethic triumph over my idea of the good life for at least a little while.

I took a two-hour lunch break at noon and spent the rest of the afternoon doing more paperwork, which was so dull, I actually felt I'd accomplished something. I got to answer the phone six more times and left early before it could ring again. I had dinner at home with Mozart's Twenty-first Quartet in D for company. Mozart was ill at the time he composed it, and in debt, too, but you'd never know that listening to the music. It braced me for what I had to do next, which was hop a crosstown bus and head back to the tenement. I hopped, and was carried away.

The first thing that caught my eye when I stepped into the building's dank, narrow hallway was that the super's door was wide open. That was peculiar enough to warrant further inspection. I went over and looked in. No more Carlos.

Another guy was in the living room/kitchen, moving furniture around. He was big—well over six feet—and broad shouldered, dressed in jeans and khaki work shirt. His head, set on a wide neck, was small, with small eyes, a flat nose, wide lips—the upper one protruding—and high cheekbones. His hands were very large, maybe to make up for the small head. I put him in his late thirties, but it was hard to tell.

It took him a while before he looked up and noticed me.

I said, "Hi, Carlos gone?"

The guy glared at me as though my having spoken somehow violated a clause in his union contract. He began lumbering toward me, his small, dark eyes measuring me as if hunting for defects or trying to guess my coat size. He didn't seem especially happy with what he saw. He pulled up a few feet from me and his lips moved. "Yeah," he said. It came out a guttural sound.

"You the new super?" I asked.

The guy eyed me again as though searching for some trap in my question. "Yeah," he finally said.

"Moving in?"

He nodded. I wondered if "yeah" had used up his entire vocabulary.

"Name's Gordon," I said, holding out a hand.

He looked at it as though I were offering him a dead fish, or maybe a bag of rotting garbage. He finally shook it. Once. "Luke," he said.

"As in saint."

Luke peered at me as if I were an escaped madman from some lunatic asylum. He hesitated as though convinced an admission might incriminate him. "Yeah," he finally said.

"Hope you like it here," I told him earnestly.

"Shithole."

"Eh?"

"Fuckin' shithole."

"Well," I said brightly, "it's home for some of us."

"Home?" The word had a mean ring to it as if what he really

84

meant was that my toilet had backed up and was seeping down to the apartment below.

"Sure. Lots of us love it here. Roof keeps the rain out, walls keep the heat in. What more can you ask?"

Luke's stare now said that I was a *dangerous* escapee from the lunatic asylum. "Pipes in these fuckin' buildin's ain't worth a shit. Won't last t'winter. I seen 'em. Fuckin' roof's fulla holes. Walls got cracks in 'em a yard wide. Fuckin' place ain't fit for rats."

I put a concerned look in my face. "Does Mr. Berk know that?"

Luke shrugged a massive shoulder.

"You should tell him," I said primly. "He's the manager, after all. It's his duty to get it fixed."

"Fixed? These buildin's ain't worth fixin'."

"But people live here."

"Let 'em move."

"Look," I said, "it's the owner's *responsibility* to keep this property in good repair. That's the law. You tell Berk that Mr. Gordon said so. Most of us, you know, have no intention of moving."

A dim light began to appear in Luke's small eyes. "What's your fuckin' apartment?"

"Three-C."

He took a step toward me, balled up his fists. "You the fuck's been shootin' off his yap."

"If you mean my efforts on behalf of the tenants," I said with great dignity, "you are quite correct."

He was glowering now. Another step brought him even closer. I adjusted my weight, ready to block and counter what I figured was coming next. Instead, the big palooka smirked. "Shit, you don't even live here."

"No?" We stood there eyeball-to-eyeball, except that I had to look up. Not quite an advantage.

"Hey, I'm gonna be watchin' you."

I shrugged. "Suit yourself." I turned and started up the stairs. A guy can't take off a weekend without its being a federal offense. During the next couple of hours I saw some more neighbors, then locked up again and went away. I was a big boy now and mother let me stay out overnight.

CHAPTER 17

DAPHNE AND I WENT TO LINCOLN CENTER SATURDAY NIGHT. THE Tokyo String Quartet was doing Mozart, Shostakovich, and Dvorak. I'd cut my eyeteeth on Dvorak's "American Quartet." Half the works I'd learned as a teenager had grown stale for me over the years. The other half, for no reason I could think of, still knocked me cold. The "American" fit into that category. The piece had to be done just right, of course. And the Tokyo had an inside track. Here were four guys who played like one, with a lush, passionate tone that swept you away. They gave what had to be hundreds of concerts a year, popping up all over the map, yet their playing stayed fresh, vibrant, and utterly beautiful, as if they'd just discovered Dvorak or Mozart for the first time. Me, that kind of repetition would have done in. But not these guys. Here was a sure sign that the higher powers were still on the job.

Sunday we just hung around, mostly in bed. Before leaving the next morning, I remembered to ask Daphne if she'd managed to run down any of our landlords. She hadn't. I told her to keep trying.

Monday morning, Lucy Samler called in sick and I took her place in the field. I spent the day in the Bronx trying to get a line on an arsonist who might, or might not, have been spotted running from the scene. Like all good things, this, too, came to an end. I had dinner at home, then caught the *MacNeil/Lehrer Newshour* on TV to see if the world had improved any during my stint in the Bronx. No dice. I packed more clothes, socks, and underwear in my blue shoulder bag, and left.

It was after ten when I reached Ninety-fourth Street. I climbed the three concrete steps, pushed open the street door, and a wave of sound rolled over me that almost knocked my socks off. It wasn't Haydn, Brahms, or Mahler. It wasn't even Cole Porter. The sound was rock music. The house was all but jumping up and down just like in those 1930s Disney cartoons. I could imagine my crow-footed bathtub joining right in.

I juggled open the inside door, withstood the onslaught of volume, and grimly marched up the stairs. The racket was coming from 2C, the apartment directly below mine. Miss Downy lived there, a tiny, prim, white-haired lady in her eighties who wore lace gloves even in summer. For Miss Downy to be playing rock at this or any hour, the world must have come to an end. I wondered how I'd managed to miss it.

I continued up to my flat. Things weren't much better inside. The floor was actually vibrating, the kitchen table and chairs hopping around as if they'd been given hotfoots. I tossed my coat and shoulder bag down on the bed and went down again. No answer came from 2C when I pounded on the door. I could feel my teeth pulsating in time to the beat. I rattled the doorknob. Shackled tight. I kicked at the door, adding to the clamor. I was about to put my shoulder to it when I heard the lock turn. The door came open. A fresh blast of sound escaped through the doorway, almost blowing me away.

An overweight, bearded, thirtyish guy in solid undershirt and patched jeans stood barefoot frowning at me in obvious annoyance. His hair was long, there were dark patches under his eyes, and his face was white and puffy. He wasn't exactly an improvement over Miss Downy. It was too late, I figured, to use reason and logic; this guy was obviously too far gone. I put a palm against his chest and shoved hard. He stumbled back into the room and I followed. The place had been cleaned out. No furniture. Just three bare queen-size mattresses on the floor. Four people were sitting on them, a pair of youngish guys and girls. What they were smoking wasn't Carltons. A couple of empty wine bottles were on the floor. One of the girls giggled.

If the furnishings were sparse, the mini entertainment center made up for it. The speakers were man size. There was a twenty-eight-inch TV and a VCR. The stereo components could handle tapes, records, or CDs. They probably cooked meals and cleaned house, too.

A few strides brought me to the tape deck. I switched the knob from on to off.

Blessed silence. I didn't get to bask in it for long.

"You fuckin' crazy?" my host screamed.

Good question. I often wondered myself. I said, "Too loud, pal."

"Hey, man, we do what we want!"

"Not at this hour."

"Says who?"

"Me."

"Who the fuck are you?"

"The guy upstairs."

"Yeah? Well, we live here."

"You murder Miss Downy?"

"What?"

"Look friend," I said, "even at high noon, you'd want to play this thing so only you could hear it. That way you keep out of trouble."

"Don't tell us how to fuckin' play our music."

I shook my head sadly. "Hardly music. More like torture. What you've got to do is learn not to inflict it on others."

"You gonna get your fuckin' mouth busted."

A man true to his word, he came right at me, belly bobbing

under his T-shirt, hand clenched into fists, his feet only a bit unsteady under him, as if someone were gently shaking the floor. He launched a sizzling roundhouse right that maybe a blind man couldn't have avoided. I blocked it easily. The stomach was an irresistible target. My right sank into it— another blow struck at overeating. The guy made the appropriate sound and doubled over. I was going to hit him again, but he fell down too fast.

The two lads on the mattress had risen now and were swaying toward me as though wading knee-deep in a swamp; by contrast, their fallen buddy seemed a model of sobriety. One was tall, well built, in striped polo shirt and cords. The other, stocky, medium height, had on a plaid shirt and gray pants.

"Guys," I said, "you don't want to do this." Immanuel Kant, the eighteenth-century philosopher, could have put it no better. But this pair was beyond pure reason.

The stocky one, bearlike, tried to grab me in a headlock. A right to the cheek put that idea in its proper perspective; he went down.

His taller pal flicked two jabs past my head. I slammed my shoulder into his chest and he toppled over backward.

My host, half up on his feet, made a run to butt me. I stepped aside and watched as the guy tripped over himself and landed on the floor.

If I were ever tempted to become a dopester, this trio put the notion permanently from my mind.

"Guys," I said, "enough. If I kill you, I won't even be able to plead self-defense."

My three victims stared up at me as if my words were coming from some vast distance behind the clouds.

These pickings were a mite too ripe to bring much pleasure. I strode over to the tape deck and twisted the knob from tape to FM. Lowering the volume, I turned the dial through the usual wasteland of sound till I hit an oasis: Schumann's Cello Concerto. I'd have preferred something more tangy, but this didn't seem the time to go station hopping.

I nodded at my captive audience. "Better, eh?" The floored trio didn't look as if it were better, but their faces hadn't been very expressive to begin with. I told them what they were listening to. "You'll find, guys, that real music like this won't fuck up your minds, make you deaf, or turn you into homicidal maniacs. A little of this and you'll even be able to give up dope and booze. No kidding."

Schumann, meanwhile, thick as syrup, kept pouring from the speakers. Hearing him in this setting was like being served a six-course dinner from the Ritz in a welfare shelter.

"But that's not really the issue," I said, "is it? Noise is. You're making too damn much of it. You've got to learn, guys, no matter what you play, not to infringe on the rights of others. Especially mine. It's for your own good, because if there's any more racket, I'm gonna come down here with an ax and chop your fucking speakers into splinters. You got that?"

I reached over and yanked the cord out of the tape deck. Schumann vanished in midphrase, no doubt thankful to have escaped this place.

"You guys may be too befuddled to listen to reason, so I'm taking this with me." I waved the cord at them. "You'll thank me later. Remember what I told you."

The girls waved good-bye as I headed for the door. I left the guys still sitting on the floor and followed Schumann out of there.

I slept okay that night. If my new neighbors made any noise, I didn't hear it.

CHAPTER 18

THE SUN WAS MAKING BROKEN RECTANGLES ON MY WALLS WHEN I
awoke. I could hear birds in the backyard chirping it up. The
little tykes had no idea they were in America, where citizens
actually shelled out good money for birdseed. I stretched out
a hand, flicked on the radio. A late Haydn quartet added some
voltage to the sun. I climbed out of bed, shaved, showered,
and had breakfast.

I put on a pair of midnight-blue slacks, open-necked
navy-blue sports shirt, blue-gray Stanley Blacker sports coat,
and went to see the building manager.

Berk did not greet me with much joy. He complained I'd
been seeing the tenants. I pointed out they were my neighbors. We chewed that over for a while. I mentioned the *new*
neighbors below me, the ones in Miss Downy's flat. Berk
stared at me as though I'd been speaking in tongues. Then his
hand went to the desk drawer and out came the green ledger.

He nodded, a forefinger on the entry. "Elizabeth Downy.
Two-C was vacated last week. The lady had more sense than
you do."

"She was older, she'd been practicing longer."

"The apartment is empty."

"You lead a rich fantasy life, Mr. Berk," I told him.

I explained about last night. Berk listened grimly and
finally said, "Squatters!" in a tone that would ordinarily be

used for lice. He assured me he would talk to them, ask them to leave, even threaten court action. He warned me that all that might take some time. What didn't these days?

I asked about burning mattresses, and Berk said, "Vandals." I asked who Jenkins was, and Berk hesitated, as though thumbing through a mental Rolodex before saying, "The owner."

"But Rensler runs the show?" I asked.

"I report to him."

"Okay," I said. "Tell him by the time I'm done, every tenant will be wise to his game."

I got up and left. The only thing missing was the sound track. Next time.

"They'll kill you," Harry said.

"Uh-huh." I put my feet up on his desk. "If they can remember any of it. The term 'snootful' doesn't really do justice to their sorry state."

"They part of a conspiracy?"

"Probably. Berk says he'll go to court on my behalf to get rid of 'em."

"Congratulations."

"May be premature. The wheels of justice grind slowly. Gotta phone my big brother, make some plans."

"The Mt. Everest of brothers?"

"That's the one. My motto is, 'Big brother knows best.'"

"Hell, no wonder we're poor," Harry said. "By the way, Carl Springer called in. You ask him to snoop around Lipsky Management?"

"Yeah."

"He says no one's there."

"Ever?"

"Place is locked tight."

"Funny way to run a business."

"A howl."

"Tell him to keep snooping," I said.

* * *

Ninety-fourth Street looked sleepy in the late-afternoon sun. The power cord was gone from in front of 2C, where I'd left it earlier, on my way out. An ear against the door brought nothing. In my flat, I pulled off my trench coat, scanned my makeshift tenants' list. So far I had managed to reach about two-thirds. Not bad, but no great shakes either. Some were never home. Others wouldn't talk to me. A few knew no English but babbled away anyway, figuring me for a linguist, no doubt, or a fellow national in disguise. I decided to take one last stab at irritating the management, see a couple more tenants, and then pack it in. The rest was up to the opposition. It took two to play.

I was fooling with the radio, hunting for a moment of bliss, when a knock sounded on the door. I killed the music, straightened up, and went to the door. Remembering my pals from 2C, I asked who it was before flinging it open.

"Hawks."

I opened.

"Saw you coming home from my window," he said. "Got a moment to spare?"

"Sure."

Hawks stepped in and looked around. I could tell he wanted to say "Nice place" out of sheer politeness, but what he saw had him tongue-tied. I was actually embarrassed. I kept myself from explaining that I really didn't live here—which was far from easy—and said, "Get you something? Coffee?"

"Thanks, no."

I escorted him to the next room and waved him to the easy chair. Hawks stretched out his long legs. His large-knuckled hands lay peacefully in his lap as though dozing between jobs. He wore a checkered green-and-blue flannel shirt, Levi's jeans, and scruffy work shoes.

I perched on the bed. "Fire away," I said.

"Well," Hawks said, "I hear you been talkin' to some of the tenants."

I nodded.

"See Caloney, too?"

"Yeah."

"I'd be much obliged, Mr. Gordon, if you'd tell me what happened."

"With Caloney?"

"With all of them."

"Checking up on your constituency, Mr. Hawks?"

"Politician's *got to* have it easier than this."

"Tenants acting up, eh?"

"Nothing but complaints," he said. "Knew I couldn't keep them all happy when I took the job, but I never figured it would be this much trouble."

I smiled. "First try at public office, Mr. Hawks?"

He shrugged. "Was a shop steward once. Back in '52 when I worked for Ford."

"Detroit?"

"Yep. Grew up on a farm in Michigan. Still be there, I guess, if the bank hadn't took it all. Kids had to fend for ourselves. Younger brother enlisted in the navy. Another just up and went; never heard from him again. Me, I served four years in the army. That was during the Second World War. All stateside, though. After that, it was Ford. Had a wife and daughter, too. Lost them both in an accident." He sighed. "Changed my life; just about finished it. That was later."

"I'm sorry," I said.

He shrugged. "Was a long time ago. Water under the bridge now, I guess. Anyway, being shop steward was nothing like this."

"You can quit, Mr. Hawks."

"Suppose so. Thought about it. Only it don't sit right with me. Leave everyone in the lurch. Lots of old people here."

"Lots," I agreed.

I briefed Hawks on my chat with Caloney and the others. He ran a large hand over his face, knitted his brows, bit his lip. At least he didn't get up and start hopping from foot to foot.

When I was all done, he nodded his large head and said, "About what I expected. Look, Mr. Gordon, any chance I can interest you in joining the committee?"

"Me?" It seemed a quaint idea. I could vote myself a raise and no one would be the wiser. "Wouldn't I have to be elected first?"

"Whole thing was a joke. You think anyone voted?"

"I hope so."

"Not on your life. Maybe three, four per house. Had to go around, beg them to do it. You'd be more than welcome on the committee. I could use a strong shoulder."

"Mr. Hawks, I can't just show up and take a seat."

"Guess not."

"How about you appoint me as adviser or something. That possible?"

"Don't see why not."

"Adviser to the chairman, let's say. No one should object to that. And if I skip a few sessions, it won't matter."

Hawks nodded, smiled. "Done," he said. "I'll tell you, Mr. Gordon, I'll feel a lot better having you around. Folks on the committee are well meaning enough, but some of them aren't too sharp, you'll pardon my saying so. Most are immigrants, you know. Some been here maybe forty, fifty years, still don't know how things run. That's the truth. Mrs. Kazmir's all right, but she can hardly speak the language. Times I can't understand a word she says."

"Need a translator more than an adviser."

"That's a fact. Don't even know how I got myself roped into hiring this detective. Had Mrs. Kazmir jabbering away at me, her friend dishing out more gobbledygook, and then Mr. Nesbit chiming in, and the next thing you know, we've got a detective. And I've got to defend the cockeyed idea in public. Man hasn't even bothered to show up."

"Probably working undercover," I said.

"More likely gone off on a drunk. And laughing all the way. You're not going to believe this, Mr. Gordon, but we paid that man close to three thousand dollars. And I don't even know his name."

"How," I said earnestly, "did that happen?"

"My fault, I guess. First they rammed through this detective fellow. Then somebody said the treasurer should handle the money part. And I never did think to ask how much that was going to be. Not till later, and by then they'd already given him the money. Three thousand, almost."

"Kazmir says most of it goes back if there's no case."

"Think the fellow's going to hand over that money? Not on your life. We can kiss it all good-bye. When Mr. Caloney finds out about that, there'll be the devil to pay."

"Well," I said, "Kazmir may speak funny, but she's no fool. Detective turns out to be honest, you've got yourself a good deal."

Hawks shook his head. "You're an optimist, Mr. Gordon. This detective ought to be checking out that fire right now."

"Maybe he is."

"Sure. Like the invisible man. You know, ten windows were broken on Ninety-third Street last night."

"Uh-uh."

"Well, they were. Berk says more vandals. Police say the same thing. We need a hands-on detective, Mr. Gordon, not some damn spook."

It took a while, but I managed to get through to Captain Rogers at the Twenty-first Precinct.

"What is it, Shaw? I'm busy."

"It's about the fire on Ninety-fourth Street."

"What?"

"Mattresses. Someone set fire to them a couple of nights ago, rousted the whole house. And last night windows were broken on Ninety-third."

"What's it to you?"

"I'm back in my old flat, using the name Gordon again."

"What the hell for?"

"It's your fault, Captain. When that old lady, Kazmir, asked about me, you shouldn't have given her my real name. Now I'm back here wrangling with the new landlord."

"About what?"

"Relocation."

"You called so I could put in a good word for you with the landlord?"

"Your man handling the fire and windows, Captain. A good word with him. It may not be vandals. Landlord here has a lousy record. I think we need some cops riding by from time to time. A visible presence, sort of, to keep the peace."

"You're right, Shaw, I shouldn't have given her your name. Now I've got you back in my district."

"Captain Rogers, I did you a favor once, cleaned up a mess in your own backyard. Don't make me beg."

"I'll be hearing about that for the rest of my life, won't I? Listen, Shaw, broken windows and burning mattresses aren't exactly a crime wave. Get back to me if something serious happens and I'll give it all the attention it deserves. We don't have any cops to spare for this."

"The house could've burned down," I complained.

"But it didn't."

"No, not yet."

"Good-bye, Shaw."

CHAPTER 19

DUSK BEGAN TO SLIP OVER THE CITY. I STROLLED SOUTH ON SECOND Avenue, crossed Eighty-ninth. On my right, properties were at least as developed as Arnold Schwarzenegger. And maybe a mite richer. Look-alike towers stood tall, with enough inhabitants to make up a small country. Creaky six-story houses squatted across the street, a mute testament to rampaging obsolescence. I left it behind, ambled on. The whole neighborhood here had been German about half a century ago. *The House on Ninety-second Street*, a movie about Nazi saboteurs, was set in Yorkville. That was back in '45. You could still pick up a nice iron cross in a shop over on Third. But mostly the Germans were gone. What remained of their tenements—now occupied by others—was part of a bygone era that had somehow neglected to fade away on schedule. Now, good Samaritans like Berk were giving it a hand.

I crossed Eighty-sixth. West was a maze of neon lights. The fast-food chains had clobbered the ethnic eateries on the main drag and sent them packing. But Second Avenue south of Eighty-sixth still had its share of Old World charm. Every other block, right into the Sixties, sported a couple of Old Country shops, such as Paprikas Weiss with its open barrels of grains and spices. Step through the door and the fragrance hit you. You were back in history. Kids in knickers. Els running past upper-story windows. Clotheslines dangling wash in backyards. Dad out of work. Uncle Max opening a private-eye agency on Manhattan's Lower East Side. Danny and I still waiting in the wings. The world hadn't improved much since our arrival, either. But then, we hadn't been around all that long.

I ate dinner in a small Hungarian joint in the Seventies. Shunning the counter and stools, I chose a bare table near the window. I ordered cherry soup, beef goulash, and palacsintas for dessert, washing it down with a cup of decaf and leaving a two-buck tip for the waiter, who had a gimpy leg. He probably owned the joint, too, but what the hell.

It was dark by the time I got back to my neighborhood. Most of the stores had shut down for the night. The streets had emptied out. Only the traffic gliding by on the avenue showed any signs of life. But it belonged to another time and place, had nothing to do with the sagging houses that had somehow become my problem. I wondered how that could have happened. I hadn't sinned enough against the higher powers to deserve a headache like this, one that seemed to wipe out all the intervening years and plunk me down again in my childhood slum. Maybe that was it. I'd begun to see my dottering neighbors as part of my family, an extension of the old Yiddish community I'd grown up in. If injustice was afoot, old gumshoe Shaw would save them from it. Old gumshoe Shaw was in big trouble, his mind had sprung a leak.

The workingman's bar was open, of course. Dried-up codgers held down stools and tables, looking yellow-faced in the dim light as if they had been pickled by too many shots of cheap booze. I turned the corner. Ninety-fourth Street was empty. Lit streetlamps climbed the rise, dwindled at Madison Avenue; they made lousy company.

I ascended the three stone steps, entered the alcove, and juggled open the inside door. The distant whisper of TVs from above spoke of gaudy drama even here. I went up the stairs. Nothing stirred behind 2C. Had Berk actually driven off the squatters? It didn't seem likely. But if he had, it just might mean the landlord was on the up-and-up, after all. Who would believe it?

I paused before my door, used my keys, and pushed it open. The flat was dark as I had left it.

Entering, I reached for the dangling light cord. Weak light spilled over the kitchen. I started for the bedroom.

"Hey, motherfuck," a voice said behind me.

I turned.

They had been waiting in the darkened storage room, the three guys from below. The tall one held a baseball bat. His shorter pal wore a pair of brass knuckles. It's not every day you see brass knuckles outside of a comic book. Potbelly, with the beard, was the real menace, though. He was waving around a kitchen knife just like one of the heavies on the tube.

They had moved into the living room, were blocking the hallway door so I couldn't make a break for it. But had they forgotten the window?

A quick glance in that direction told me they hadn't.

He was about six feet tall, husky and bearded. I searched for signs of dissipation and didn't find any. His hands were empty. No weapons for this guy; he didn't need any. Great. The Three Stooges looked pissed off, but this guy didn't look anything. He was just lending a hand. What were friends for?

The foursome moved toward me slowly, closing the vise. I was being given time to contemplate my doom.

"Hey, big mouth," brush-face snarled. "Say something smart."

"Your mother still changing your diapers?" I asked with interest.

That didn't sit too well with old bristle puss. I was supposed to fall on my knees and beg, not be sassy. The guy lunged at me, already off balance. The knife began low—a textbook thrust—rose swiftly toward my midriff where it would explore the contents of my dinner. My left clamped down on his wrist; my right caught his elbow. I yanked, stepped aside, and he sailed past me, another sad case of textbook learning undone by practical experience. His friend, by the window, stopped him, shoved him aside like so much excess baggage, and began purposefully moving toward me. He held his arms wide so that I couldn't dodge around him and crawl out the window to safety. His eyes, cool, steady, and patient, seemed to pin me to the spot. From the other direction, Baseball Bat and Brass Knuckles moved in for the kill. I didn't bother reciting the prayer for the dead. Or try to will myself into becoming invisible. What I did was far more reasonable. I opened my mouth and let out a holler that Tarzan would have envied.

Results were instantaneous. The hallway door was almost ripped off its hinges as it banged open.

The figure who darted through the doorway was six six with huge shoulders, a narrow waist, and muscles to spare. No red cape or giant S on his chest this night. He wore a Columbia U gray sweatshirt, fashionably faded jeans, and black Rockport walking shoes. Full lips, a straight nose, and large brown eyes were set in a longish face. While the body was that of some fanatical health freak, the wide forehead under the tousled hair could have belonged to a college professor. And did, in fact.

The professor slammed a large fist into Brass Knuckles' unguarded side, which made the lad twist sideways like a pretzel and fall down.

The other guy managed a half turn before the bat was wrenched from his hands. He was now facing the professor, which was a bad mistake. It allowed the professor to drive the bat into his stomach. The guy bent far over as though eager to examine his shoelaces. The professor, master of six languages, ladies' man supreme, and possessor of a much-used card to the Columbia gym, which I sometimes borrowed, sliced down hard on the guy's neck, flattening him. The professor seemed a bit miffed, no doubt, at the thought that someone might want to harm his kid brother. I couldn't blame him.

104

The athlete with the wide arms sized up this new situation instantly, turned, and dived headfirst through the open window. I could hear the fire escape shake as he landed and scrambled down.

Potbelly, unmolested so far, stood frozen as if trying very hard to sink through the floor. He still held the knife. He stared at it uncertainly as if wondering how it had managed to sprout in his hand. He dropped it as if it were suddenly red hot.

I said, "Who had you move into this building?"

"No one," he said, "we're squatters."

"Were," I said.

CHAPTER 20

THE TAXI PULLED AWAY FROM THE CURB. IN IT WERE MY THREE former neighbors and their home entertainment system. They had claimed to the last that they were only squatters. A friend had spotted the moving van carting off Mrs. Downy's belongings and passed on the word. The trio had expected to get booted out sooner or later, but not quite this soon. They had no plans to return, they assured me, and Danny, who despite having replaced his horn-rimmed glasses, still looked more like King Kong's smaller nephew than Clark Kent.

We returned to the building, retrieving Danny's leather jacket where he had left it at my call, then went out again.

The place was dim and noisy. One of the last old-line German eateries left on Eighty-sixth Street. We had a small table in the rear. German band music filtered through the audio system. I thought of Hegel, Goethe, Beethoven, the Weimar Republic, but it didn't do any good. I still felt like getting up and goose-stepping all over the joint.

Danny was having a bowl of homemade potato soup with black bread. I dug into a plate of sausage and sauerkraut. I had a mug of dark beer. My fourth meal today. A couple more daring adventures, I'd have to join Weight Watchers Anonymous.

I drank some beer. "You still seeing Linda?"

Danny nodded, finished his soup. "One in a million, Jimmy."

"That's the redhead who paints?"

"Member of the Prince Street Gallery, a collective in Soho. She's having a show this spring."

"Nice. I won't even ask about the other belles in your life."

"Being phased out."

"Just don't tell 'em. And remember to duck."

On the audio system the band had marched off into infinity and Marlene Dietrich began to sing something in German. The record was old and scratchy, but the ditty sounded so nostalgic, it almost brought a tear to my eye for the old fatherland. In Marlene's heyday, the Nazis seemed to be just a bunch of dumb cranks.

"Your former neighbors," Danny said, "didn't appear to be professionals. Your terrible Mr. Berk couldn't do better?"

"Against the average tenant, Danny, they'd have been perfect."

"They could," Danny said, "have really been squatters."

"Sure looked like squatters."

"You seem dubious, James."

"That's high-class private eye training. Also, I had some help from Berk. The guy sits there in his storefront office all day reading his paper. He's not being distracted by heavy thinking. Nothing much is happening. He's offering peanuts and there're only a handful of takers. I drop around and after one visit, he knows me by name. I ask about two-C, the guy's stumped, he's gotta look it up. Miss Downy, he discovers, has moved out. Whaddya know? He's finally gotten someone to vacate the premises, probably talked to her till he's blue in the face, done all the paperwork in duplicate, put in for her check, and it's *totally* slipped his mind. It's a wonder the guy remembers to come in for work. But he does. He's there every damn day, except Sunday. So he must be doing something to earn his pay."

"That's your case?"

"There's more. Old Berk keeps an eagle eye on the buildings. He's got his own guy in there, too, the new super. But the first he hears of squatters is when I tell him. Not to mention a fire in my building and broken windows across the way."

Danny nodded. "Impressive."

"Yeah. Trouble is, our real-estate maven, Daphne, tells me there's this gray area between legit and dirty. Three squatters and vandals don't quite add up to dirty."

"So all this may have been for nothing."

"Give it time, big brother. We private eyes are mavens, too. Odds are, our Mr. Berk is just warming up."

CHAPTER 21

A COUPLE OF MY NEIGHBORS TOOK TO THE ROAD NEXT DAY. THERE was talk that they'd pulled down a hefty settlement, but no one knew for sure.

Someone during that night had broken the door locks in six buildings and bashed in some mailboxes. Berk denied all involvement. There had been no witnesses. Someone said a street gang from Spanish Harlem had been seen in the neighborhood.

During all this I trotted off to work every morning and returned each night. I made sure that either Berk or Luke saw me. Apartment 2C remained empty. Nobody bothered me.

Luke, for his part, hulked around the buildings and glowered at the tenants. But that seemed to be his natural demeanor. Carlos had had a couple of assistants from neighboring blocks to help out with the chores. There was no sign of them now. The steam and hot water kept coming, though, and none of the houses caved in.

The phone rang Thursday night.

I put aside the *Times*, lowered Mozart, and went to answer.

"Mr. Gordon, this is Lila."

It took me a second to remember who she was. "My mystery woman," I said.

"Uh-huh. We should meet."

"About the houses?"

"Kind of."

"Just kind of?" I still had the feeling this was some kind of scam. Only *what* kind, I couldn't figure out yet.

"It's complicated," she said. "Know Carl Schurz Park?"

"Yeah."

"You free now?"

I gave her a yes.

"In half an hour?"

"Why not?"

"Take a bench on the walkway. I'll find you."

There was plenty of fog. An icy wind blew off the water. I heard a foghorn, but couldn't see any boats. There weren't any people around either. I wore a sweater and scarf under my trench coat, but my goose bumps were working overtime. I was starting to have second thoughts about this outing. Nothing was worth freezing to death for.

A hand touched my shoulder.

I almost fell off the bench.

I turned, and a blonde who looked to be somewhere in her twenties smiled at me.

"You shouldn't do that," I said.

"Scare easy?" Her voice was low and husky.

"Damn right."

She sat down beside me. Unlike Daphne, her blond hair was straight and the color of straw. She wore plenty of lipstick, eye makeup, and rouge.

"Let me be honest," she said, only half turning toward me.

"That would be nice."

"I'm not sure we can do business."

I shrugged. "Try me."

"I've got to know who you're working for first."

"That's easy. No one."

She turned wholly in my direction now. "We aren't going to get anywhere if we're not up-front with each other, are we?"

"Right. Why should I be working for someone?"

"I followed you. You were real active around the houses. I wanted to know who you were, what you did."

"And who am I?"

"Harry Canfield or James Shaw."

"That gives me a choice. Of course, I might be the office boy, too. So who are *you*, Lila?"

She shook her head, looked off toward the fog-covered water.

"Fair's fair," I said.

"I've got to protect myself, and it's not important."

"What is?"

She turned my way again, put an arm on the back of the bench, crossed one leg over the other. "Let me tell you a story."

"Shoot."

"No names."

"Anything you want." What *I* wanted was an electric blanket. I could have used some sense from this woman, too, but why ask for the impossible?

She took a deep breath. "I was going with this guy, let's call him Frank; he was kind of in your line of work."

"Office boy?"

"Cut it out. He found out things."

"A researcher?"

"Uh-uh. More like a private detective."

"Licensed?"

"No."

"Go on."

"About seven years ago, he was on a job. There were these people dealing drugs, like preparing it for sale. And Frank was in a house across the street from them, taking pictures. Some friends of his wanted a piece of the action and figured this was a good way to go about it."

"And was it?"

"Uh-huh. He could have sunk the whole operation with

those pictures. Only they were all busted a couple months later."

"Frank, too?"

"Uh-uh. He wasn't part of that. They paid him his money and he went his way. Thing is, Frank kind of witnessed a crime. While he was on the job."

"Must have shocked him."

"Cut it out, huh? Two guys ran by while he was taking his pictures. Turned out they killed someone."

"This have anything to do with the houses?"

"I think so but it's kind of tricky. Frank figured the guys he'd snapped were in the rackets. He asked around and got a line on them."

"Old Frank planned to turn 'em in, eh?"

"Quit kidding. He was going to shake them down, only they were dirt poor."

"Tough luck," I said.

"That's what Frank said. Their bosses had plenty of money, though, and that's where Frank hoped to cash in."

"Your Frank was an enterprising guy."

"Uh-huh. Except he got nailed for mail fraud first. They gave him eight years. Third offense."

"He in the slammer now?"

"He's dead."

"Sorry."

She shrugged. "No big loss. Frank was in a fight and lost. This was maybe six months ago. By then it was long over between us. He'd left a suitcase with me, and when I heard the news, I dug it out of the basement and went through it. The pictures were there."

"You remembered Frank's scheme?"

"Sure. It was going to make us rich. Just like all the others."

"And you're carrying on the good work."

"I've got to look out for myself. I have the pictures. And I know who's involved."

"It's got to be someone at Primrose or you wouldn't be here."

"Maybe. Maybe not. Thing is, I'm not crazy enough to go up against any of those guys alone."

"Smart thinking."

"I waited around," she said, "to see what was going down at the houses."

"You mean the burning mattresses and broken windows? Stuff like that?"

"I don't know about any mattresses, but I don't think the smashed windows had anything to do with the new management."

"What then?" I asked.

"Look, I learned something real early in life. No free rides. I asked you who you were working for. That's important. See, what I want from you is kind of a straight business deal."

I nodded.

"Only, I've got to develop it first."

"You've lost me, Lila."

"Okay. I think your new landlords are going to shaft you. They've got their pieces in place now and they're playing their old game. That's what I needed to know. But for you to know, it'll cost you."

"How much?"

"Twenty-five thousand."

I smiled. It was all I could do to keep from rolling off the bench with laughter. "Lila, if I'm what you think I am, I must be working for the tenants' committee, right? You see them shelling out twenty-five grand? Even three would leave them prostrate."

"I kind of figured it wasn't just them."

"Who else? Someone who has it in for the landlords?"

"Something like that."

"Wishful thinking."

"You've got an office on Madison Avenue."

"So does Joe's Shoeshine Parlor. Don't kid yourself."

115

We both sat in silence and stared at the fog. I shivered.

"No deal, huh?" she said.

"No money," I said. "Why not give me some time to see what I can raise."

"It doesn't sound very promising."

"You never know," I told her.

"Think you can move fast?"

"I'll do my best, Lila."

"You do that."

I called Harry before turning in and told him about the girl.

"She thinks we're the Pinkerton's," I concluded.

"Even the Pinkerton's wouldn't have that kind of money, kid."

"True. But their clients might."

"You have a plan?"

"My guess is, we can dig this stuff up ourselves."

"We can? I didn't know we had it in us."

"Sure we do. Provided it's there. And Primrose is as rotten as she seems to think."

"Okay, what if the latter is correct and the former unattainable?"

"Bite your tongue. But if worse comes to worst, the lady's given us time to come up with the dough."

"A generous spirit."

"My feelings precisely."

"We rob a bank?"

"We use our wits. She calls. We get together and I stall her. One of our lads tails her home. And guile and cunning take it from there."

"I hope they have more on the ball than we do," Harry said.

"How can they fail to?" I asked.

CHAPTER 22

FRIDAY MORNING WAS GRAY AND OVERCAST. I ATE BREAKFAST BY THE window and let Bach's Third Suite in D Major convince me that the world made perfect sense, after all. I was scanning yesterday's edition of the *Times* for any juicy tidbits I might have missed, and I was just about ready to start for the office when a knock sounded on my door.

I went to investigate.

Berk stood in my ill-lit hallway in hat and gray overcoat, his face under the hat brim looking pasty like a hurriedly slapped together hunk of dough.

I stepped aside and the building manager waddled in. A guy who walked like a penguin couldn't be all bad. I said, "If you've come about the faucet, it's too late: it died yesterday. I buried it in the backyard."

Berk didn't crack a smile. He glanced around my dump tight-lipped, as though it confirmed his worst fears about my character. "How can you live like this, Mr. Gordon?"

"It's not easy," I said truthfully enough.

I waved him toward the easy chair in the next room—the royal seat of honor—but Berk chose a kitchen chair instead, a man who shunned comfort while on duty. The hat went on his lap, the coat stayed put.

I leaned up against the sink, my trusty bathtub on its claw-feet, by my side: we were both standing tall.

"You're still running around pestering everyone, aren't you, Mr. Gordon?" Berk sounded sad, as if this was yet another blot on my already besmirched record.

"Informing them of their rights," I said.

"There's a committee for that. Can't you let them handle it?"

"I'm their new adviser."

"You said you weren't part of that crowd."

"That was then."

He shook his head. "I thought you were a reasonable man, Mr. Gordon."

"Someone gave you a bum steer, pal."

"You've harassed the people below you, too."

"The squatters? I did more than that."

"Don't they *also* have rights?"

I shrugged. "Sure. Let them sue."

We exchanged glances like a pair of cardsharps who both had extra aces up their sleeves.

Berk said, "There are some people want to see you."

"Yeah, who?"

"They are with Primrose."

"They have names?"

"They'll tell you themselves."

"That's nice. What's it about, Mr. Berk?"

"They would like to make my job a little easier. I don't think you deserve this, but my firm is about to do you a big favor. I hope you will be smart enough to take advantage of it."

"I know how to take advantage," I told him.

"Mr. Gordon, let's be serious, shall we? Frankly, I was against this. I don't believe in rewarding troublemakers. But the firm felt differently. You're going to come out ahead."

Berk eyed me closely as if to see if I was about to fall over from sheer ecstasy.

"I'm open to persuasion," I said.

"That's all we ask."

He rose, came toward me, a card in his outstretched hand.
I took it.

The address was on East Broadway.

The name, Lipsky.

CHAPTER 23

THE HUGE *FORVERTZ* BUILDING LURKS OVER THE SQUARE AT ESSEX, Canal, and East Broadway like some ever-watchful guardian angel. Back in its heyday, in the early twenties, the *Forvertz* was the largest Yiddish daily in the world, with almost a quarter million circulation. That included my parents, of course, and most of the Shaw clan—who had been called Shumsky in Warsaw before an Ellis Island immigration clerk found their name too tough to write in English and summarily changed it to something more convenient. It included Uncle Max, whose detective agency in those days was on East Broadway, and who used to specialize in tracking down missing husbands. When a guy lived in a slum, had a bunch of kids, an exhausted wife, and a job in a sweatshop that kept him hopping ten hours a day, six days a week, the shrewdest move often seemed to be to become missing. The *Forvertz* ran a section called "The Gallery of Missing Husbands" containing photos and descriptions of guys who had skipped out on their families. Uncle Max knew all the *Forvertz* writers and used to hobnob with them in the corner Garden Cafeteria. As a kid I used to leaf through the *Sunday Forvertz* rotogravure section, which my parents left lying around. It was all in brown and had English as well as Yiddish captions under the photographs; English I could read. Today the building houses a group of Chinese businessmen.

A few doorways up the block is the converted townhouse that used to be the home of the rival *Tog-Morgan Zhurnal*, which, along with most of its readers, now resides in heaven. Farther up the block, at 197 East Broadway, is the Educational Alliance, "instructor to the millions," still open for business. These days its adult classes are given mostly in Spanish, not Yiddish.

There are still lots of Yiddish signs on walls and storefronts, and some of the shops are still run by Yiddish speakers, but the neighborhood belongs to other cultures now. The current inhabitants must have been doing all right: it took me ten minutes to find a parking space.

The building was old; a guy that old would have been either retired or dead. The tenants' directory in the musty lobby held only a few names. Lipsky wasn't among them. His business card directed me to 6H. A rickety wire-cage elevator that had been converted to self-service took me up. The ghosts of countless elevator operators seemed to look on disapprovingly. The wide hallway was a dim, faded brown like the pages of some ancient volume of Yiddish poetry. My brother Danny's apartment was stacked with them. No lights shone behind many of the frosted-glass windows as though the offices themselves had packed up and gone off to live in Florida, along with their former owners.

Six-H bore no name, but light shone through the window. I turned the knob and stepped inside. A sagging black vinyl sofa, an empty end table, and a thick layer of dust that looked as if it dated back to the Hoover administration. For all I knew, dust that old was worth something. I tried not to disturb it and I went into the inner office.

A table, a phone, some hardbacked chairs, a Playboy calendar from the seventies, and a curtainless window that looked out on an airshaft made up the amenities.

The three guys in the room weren't a bundle of laughs either.

The one behind the old battered desk was slender, medium

height, with bags under his eyes and receding gray hair. His nose was long, his cheekbones high. Thin lips seemed to be twisted in a perpetual sneer, like Raymond Massey playing Robespierre. I put him somewhere in his sixties. He wore a gray sports coat over a white shirt and striped tie. A short man with plenty of gray, curly hair was lounging against the wall. Bushy salt-and-pepper eyebrows sprouted over heavy-lidded eyes. His nose was ample, his face lined. A cleft decorated his chin, which must have been the devil to shave. He wore a light blue jacket and open-necked navy-blue shirt. His hands were jammed into the pockets of his dark trousers. He was in his sixties, too. He didn't appear very chipper either. I'd seen full-grown lemons that looked less sour.

The third one, however, was the scene stealer. Perched on a hardbacked chair next to curly, he was a hefty two hundred plus, about six two, sixtyish, and still muscular as far as I could tell. His nose and lips were thick, his eyes small. Light glistened off his balding scalp. His brown sports coat was wrinkled, his gray shirt, unironed and missing a button. His pants had lost their crease somewhere in another era. The guy looked as though he was either a retired wrestler or the building's handyman. He didn't seem as out of sorts as his pals. He didn't seem very friendly either. He stared at me impersonally, as if I were something the tide had swept in during the night that might just begin to rot.

It would be an exaggeration to say I felt right at home.

I used the one name I knew. "Lipsky?" I said to the room.

Curly grunted.

"You asked to see me?"

He inclined his head toward the desk. "Him."

Him said, "You Gordon?"

"Yeah. And you?"

"Your landlord."

"I call you Mr. Landlord?"

"Jenkins."

123

"What happened to Rensler?"

"He works for me."

The fat guy spoke. "I hear you moving out." His voice was deep and rumbling.

"You hear wrong, pal. Who're you?"

"Moisha Pupik."

Great. We were back in vaudeville. Moisha Pupik was a Yiddish gag name, something like Sam the Sap. Literally, it meant Moses Belly Button. This big lug was a landsman. In fact, they all looked and sounded Jewish, including Jenkins with his goyish moniker. I wasn't impressed. Mother would have told me not to play with them anyway. You couldn't fool mother, she was a tough cookie.

"You my landlord, too?"

"Don't make no difference," Pupik rumbled, "since you moving out."

"Sure," I said. "If conditions are right."

"Conditions? *What* conditions?" The word seemed to outrage him.

"A square deal," I said in my best Henry Fonda voice, as though I'd just stepped out of *The Grapes of Wrath*.

Pupik stared at me as if I'd suddenly broken into Chinese.

"For me," I added, "*and my neighbors.*" I nodded, waiting for applause. It would have to come from heaven; these crackers didn't look impressed.

"A Bolshevik," Lipsky said. "Go back to Russia. There they'll give you deals."

Jenkins squinted at me. "You look out for the whole world," he said, "or for you, too, sometimes?"

I shrugged. As if I hadn't quite made up my mind yet.

"Worry about *you*," Pupik said. "You got plenty worries."

"Meaning *what*?"

"He don't know," Lipsky said, "ain't no use telling him."

"That pigsty," Pupik said, "it's gonna come down on your head."

Lipsky nodded. "Ain't safe no way, mister."

124

"So fix it."

"*Pisher* like you," Pupik said, "ain't safe on the street even. Car comes and hits him, what's he gonna do?"

Pisher meant "pisser," not a compliment.

"You threatening me?" I demanded.

"What threatening?" Lipsky said. "It's the neighborhood. There a man plays with his life."

"Sure," Pupik said. "Something from a roof could fall on him." The idea brought a smile to his thick lips.

"Or a crazy man shoot him," Lipsky said. "Plenty crazy men around there. From East Harlem. Got knives, guns, what ain't they got? We don't want no accident should happen to you, mister."

"That's real sweet of you."

Jenkins nodded earnestly. "Want to help yourself, Gordon? Move somewhere else. You better off."

I looked at them. "You guys don't really expect me to fold my tent and fade quietly into the night for a measly five hundred, do you?"

"Ah," Lipsky said, "so *that's* it." And grinned at me knowingly, as though we both shared some dirty little secret.

"All right," Jenkins said, "five hundred isn't enough. So tell me, what is enough?"

Three pairs of eyes were fixed on me. This was my big moment. I had their full attention. I could recite the soliloquy from *Hamlet*, although something from *Macbeth* would have been more apt. I could sing a snatch from *Tannhäuser*. Or just give my version of Sandburg's *The People, Yes*. Actually, I'd been doing that all along, hadn't I? No matter what I did, though, I knew I could never measure up to these guys; when it came to performing, they were tops. The creeps had obviously missed their calling by becoming landlords.

"Well?" Jenkins said.

"Fifty grand."

Jenkins's lips tightened, his nose wrinkled; any second he'd

125

reach for the bug spray and I'd be a goner. "You trying to be funny, Gordon?"

Lipsky said, "Mister, you think we're Rockefellers?"

"Come on," I said, "you guys are gonna clean up on this. How about giving the little guy a break?"

"You mean *you*," Jenkins asked, "or everybody?"

"Let's start with me."

He nodded. "You sure?"

"Uh-huh."

"Fifty's crazy."

"Forty-five?"

"Ask for the moon better," Lipsky said.

"Why haggle?" I said. "Let's say forty and call it a day."

Pupik rumbled, "We talking to you, but you don't hear."

"You come here to make fun," Lipsky said, "or *what?*"

"I came because you asked me to."

"This forty is a joke," Jenkins said. "Give us something we can live with."

"I'll go down to thirty-five," I told him, "but that's rock bottom."

"You can go more," Lipsky said. "You can go. Because you are not a fool and know what's in your best interest."

"My best interest is not to leave with empty pockets."

"Who said you should leave with empty pockets?" Lipsky asked.

"I haven't heard a serious offer yet."

"Sit down," Jenkins said.

I pulled up a chair, sat.

"Ready for business, eh?" Pupik rumbled.

I nodded, ever eager.

"Good. You ain't got no problems," he said. "One hand washes the other, eh?"

Jenkins reached into a desk drawer, withdrew what looked like a legal form. "This paper," he said, "says you agree to vacate the premises in one month. In return we agree to give you three thousand dollars the minute you show up with your new lease. *Real* money, Gordon, not pipe dreams. Listen, from us there are no names that go to the tax man. In our books we lump all the payments together. So what you tell Uncle Sam, that's your business. Look, you come here, talk like a gentleman, that counts with us, we take it into consideration. So we give a little extra; more than a little. All right, no complaints. We understand each other. Only one thing: Keep this to yourself. So our business don't go crazy. Do us that favor. Find yourself a nice place, Gordon, take this money and let us wish you good luck and good-bye."

From outside, far away, I could hear the sound of traffic. Kids were yelling somewhere. The real world was out there. But these jokers had all but made it vanish. I wouldn't have been surprised to see them all break out in song. They do that in never-never land all the time. I sat back, took a deep breath. "Mr. Jenkins," I said, "if this were the turn of the century, I'd grab your offer. Three thousand went a long way then. You could almost retire on three thousand. Today, it's good for a quick vacation somewhere. Gentlemen, I didn't ask you to buy my building. I don't see why I should get out and screw up my life just so you can make some big bucks."

"You'll never get thirty-five thousand," Jenkins said, "even if you should sit there for a hundred years."

"Not even five," Lipsky said.

"So I'll stay put," I told them. "What you guys are dishing out is crap. You can keep it. And that, pals, is what I'm going to tell the tenants' committee."

"You look smart," Lipsky said, "but you're dumb, mister. Some people, they always learn the hard way. After it's too late."

I glanced from one creep to the other, waiting for more words of wisdom. There weren't any.

Jenkins nodded toward the door. "Go on, beat it, Gordon. We got nothing more to discuss."

"If that's how you want it," I said with some dignity. Nobody denied wanting it that way. I got up and left.

CHAPTER 24

I SAT AND WAITED. THROUGH MY CAR WINDOW I SAW FADED storefront lettering advertising YIDDISH BOOKS, but the store itself was empty. Kosher Caterers was a Chinese laundry. Even Feingold's Hosiery was gone, turned into a Korean grocery. A couple of Hasidim strolled by in their long black coats. The Amish of the Yiddish world. The last remnants, too. Years ago, when East Broadway was a center of secular Yiddish culture, poets, actors, journalists, social activists, were all over the place. But the secularists, wanting their kids to get ahead, had failed to teach them Yiddish. The Hasidim still spoke the language, but had nothing to do with secular culture. Leaving the likes of Danny to read the books. Guys like me who could still understand some Yiddish. College kids who wanted to. Old-timers like Uncle Max—a vanishing breed. And a scattering of turkeys like the rotten trio I'd just left. When I thought of Yiddish, I saw my family, not a bunch of rogues. Guess again. It takes all kinds, right?

The three guys in question presently hit the street. Lipsky headed left on foot. Jenkins climbed into a red Olds and drove away. Pupik walked downtown for another block and turned a corner. I pulled out and went after him. He was getting into a black Pinto when I cruised by. I waited around the next corner till he drove past, then fell in behind him. Lipsky and

Jenkins were listed in the Multiple Dwelling forms. I had their number. But Pupik was a question mark. That made him interesting.

It was a nice tree-lined street in Brooklyn. Lawns were wide. Two-story houses were separated by hedges and driveways. No factories, high rises, or tenements defaced the neighborhood. Here was an oasis far removed from sordid reality. I parked down the block, gave Pupik some ten minutes to get comfortable in his domicile. I climbed out of my car, ambled up the block, turned in at Pupik's front walk, and marched up to the door. I didn't use the ornate knocker, a brass band with a lion's head, to announce my presence. I merely glanced at the black, square-shaped mailbox next to the door. It told me a lot more than Pupik ever would. It told me his real name was Manny Gretz. Although, Pupik, for my money, fitted him a whole lot better.

The Rent Stabilization Association is located at 1500 Broadway, a few blocks north of Times Square. They are probably in one of the no-nonsense high rises and not some crummy joint housing an all-girl nudie show. But I wouldn't bet my last dollar on it. I've never been there. There are close to a million rent-stabilized apartments in the city, and dozens of tenant groups take up their cause. The Association, however, is not exactly one of these. They are a group consisting of most New York landlords. It's only fair that the other side should be heard from, too, no?

I dialed from my office. They picked up on the first ring.

"Hi," I said, "this is Mr. Shaw from Daphne Field's office at Ajax Management."

"Yes, Mr. Shaw?" A woman's voice.

"We're trying to track down one of your members, Manny Gretz."

"I'll check. One moment please."

One moment was all it took. A triumph of computer efficiency.

"Mr. Gretz is with Continental Equity."

"Where's that?"

"Fourteenth Street and Third Avenue."

"He the boss?"

"Mr. Gretz is listed as chairman."

"Who's president?"

"Jake Sandler."

"Any other brass?"

"A vice president, Leo Lipsky."

"That it?"·

She said it was.

I thanked her and rang off. Next, I called Mrs. Lathem at Code Enforcement, gave her Gretz and Continental to pry into, and promised her another slice from the old expense account—whatever that was. Then I went into Harry's office. I waited till he put the phone down, then asked, "Want the latest on Primrose?"

"I'd rather be drawn and quartered."

"Who wouldn't? Jenkins, its big boss, just promised me three grand to fade. Naturally, I refused."

"Had a fit of idealism, no doubt."

"Greed, probably. Game's barely begun."

"How'd he take it?"

"Poorly. This happened in Leo Lipsky's so-called office, which looks like it's used at least once a decade. He's the guy who manages properties for both King and Primrose. Another guy calling himself Moisha Pupik sat in. Means something like Joe Shmoe in Yiddish. Literally, 'belly button.' Are you getting the full flavor of this?"

"Too much flavor. Sounds like a laugh a minute, kid."

"At least. I tailed this Pupik home. Guy's name is Gretz. He's chairman of Continental Equity, real estate."

"We are wallowing in landlords," Harry said.

"Market's glutted with 'em. This Lipsky's a Continental VP.

A sure sign of evil, but probably not enough to put him away yet."

"Too bad."

"I told them, death before I'd desert my neighbors."

"I'll send flowers."

"The only thing I didn't do," I said, "was insult their mothers. I was working up to it when they asked me to leave."

"If they don't come after you now, Jim, they never will."

"Uh-huh. I can live with it either way."

"Let's hope."

CHAPTER 25

LANDLORDS DIDN'T FIGURE OVER THE WEEKEND BECAUSE I DIDN'T stay at the tenement, but at Daphne's. I deserved two days of self-indulgence and took them. Monday, I put in a day at the office, taking time off to visit a couple of stores, one of them army surplus. I had a leisurely dinner at home, serenaded by Brahms, dug up some gear from my war chest, put on suitable clothing, and went east.

Some thirty minutes later I was hiking down the block from Third Avenue. My "Flying Tiger" leather jacket kept the cold at bay. Countless fighter pilots had worn this jacket into combat during World War Two, and some of them had even lived to tell about it. A pilot's jacket is nothing without goggles and I had those on, too. So as not to attract undue attention, I wore my peaked leather cap low. Jeans and New Balance running shoes rounded out my attire. If it came to running for it, I was all set.

Nothing much happened as I neared my house, and I was starting to worry. The thought of getting dolled up like this for the next two weeks didn't fill me with wild enthusiasm. In chess, what I was doing is called a prepared variation. It means setting a trap for your opponent. Without an opponent, of course, you're out of luck; that was the catch. There was still the hallway and my flat, but could I count on it?

I half turned to start up the stone steps when two guys

stepped out from behind a parked car. I heard a noise behind me and caught sight of the third guy. Full deck. Theory had become reality. Now that I had my heart's desire, I wasn't sure I wanted it.

Nine P.M., and for all the people around, I might have been on some country road. Cars were scooting along on Second Avenue, all right, and there were lit windows on both sides of the street. But cops, pedestrians, and neighbors had packed it in for the night.

The trio didn't look especially like thugs, but what do thugs look like? The tall, broad guy was black with the flattened nose and scar tissue of a pug. Gray sideburns sticking out from under his wool cap put him past his prime; I was glad to see it. He had on a navy peacoat and jeans. The guy by his side was even broader, but a good head shorter. He wore a peaked cap, gray down vest over a flannel shirt, and jeans. He was Hispanic. The third guy was younger, on the skinny side. He was dressed in a faded burgundy parka and worn corduroy chinos. A black-jack in his right hand made up for his lack of brawn. This guy was white. Under other circumstances I might have applauded their equal-opportunity employer. Right then, I wasn't in the mood.

I began backing up slowly toward the building. A brick wall at my back seemed preferable to the guy with the sap.

"Something I can do for you guys?" I asked.

None of the three answered.

My back met the wall. I'd run out of space. Time to take a stand. If Custer could, why not me?

The black guy was in the lead, flanked on either side by his two cohorts. They moved in measured paces, simple work-men out to do a workmanlike job.

I had nothing against a fair fight. But three against one didn't fit the definition. And no referee was in sight. What I needed was an equalizer, a little something to even the odds. Fortunately, I had remembered to bring one along. Not a gun, but something a worried amateur might pick up after being threatened by his landlord. The black was so sure I was a pushover, he was taking his own sweet time to measure me. One solid punch would deck me, then he and his pals could finish the job, put me in the hospital for a nice long stay, an object lesson to other troublemakers. Fine idea. But hardly a cinch.

I reached up my sleeve. The canister was about the size of an eight-ounce can of V-8 juice, but not nearly as good for you. I caught the pug square in the face with a full blast of Mace and ducked. His swing was a bit off the mark. I kicked skinny away with a well-aimed foot to the ribs, sprayed the hefty guy who looked like more of a menace, then turned my attention back to skinny. I didn't discriminate. My thumb kept the nozzle depressed so that all three could get the product's full benefit.

By now there was plenty of coughing and choking going on. I'd used enough juice to topple an elephant. I kept my lips sealed and head averted. My eyes were protected by the goggles. I almost felt sorry for these guys, but even beating up on hapless tenants has its risks.

The empty canister fell from my hand. I made a fist and aimed a haymaker at the pug's jaw. He let me nail him twice before falling down. He was too busy gagging to worry about appearances. I poked the Hispanic on the side of his noggin. He staggered back across the pavement, was stopped by a parked car; he turned, coughing, and began stumbling up the block. The black guy had beaten the count, was up on his feet and heading toward Second. I let them both go. The skinny white one wasn't going anywhere because I had him up against the wall. I hoped he was amenable to reason. While he was busy gagging, I used one hand to pull the goggles from my face; the other had kept my catch from falling down. When he looked as though he might recover, I steered him toward my building and up the stairs. His sap was in the gutter; without it he came willingly enough.

I sat the kid down at the kitchen table, flicked on the radio, and caught Bach's first Brandenburg Concerto. Prolonged exposure to classical music will often unnerve primitive minds. Next I poured us both a shot of Scotch.

"Bottoms up," I said, raising my tumbler.

The kid, still gasping, looked at me as though I'd offered him a shot of lye. I set an example by taking a swallow of mine. That convinced him; the Scotch went down the hatch in a couple of gulps.

While he was still reeling from Bach and booze, I played my trump card and put two twenties and a ten down on the table.

"All yours, pal," I said, "for the right answers."

The kid glanced from the money to me and back again. It took some time for the idea to sink in. "Whaddya wanna know?" he finally said.

"Your name for starters."

"Billy Hall."

"May I see your wallet, Mr. Hall?"

The kid hesitated only a second, reached into his pocket, and put his wallet on the table. I pulled out six credit cards, all under different names, fifty bucks in tens and twenties, a driver's license made out to an Edmund Clark, and a social security card in the name of William Hall.

I gave the kid a long, hard stare.

"Those belong to my friends," he said. "They loaned them to me."

"Nice friends," I said. "You were hired to work me over?"

He nodded. "Sorry, mister—"

I held up a hand. "No harm done, Billy."

"No?"

"Uh-uh."

A canny grin crossed his face that said the pair of us were going to be friends. Bach and Scotch were doing their work. I refilled his glass. Billy raised it in a toast and downed its contents.

"What was that stuff?" he asked. "Tear gas?"

"Mace. Works wonders, doesn't it?"

He nodded his admiration. "How come you had it?"

"Because I'm smart."

Billy grinned as though I'd said something sensible. I poured him a third shot.

"Ready to earn that dough?"

"Ask me something."

"Who hired you?"

"Bugs."

Ask a question, get an answer. The image of my childhood chum, the famous rabbit, flashed through my mind. I fought it down manfully. "One of the guys with you?"

"Nah."

"So who's this Bugs?"

"Guy hangs around the upper Nineties on First Avenue."

"You pals?"

"Shit, no."

"What does he do?"

"Nothin'."

"Beats working, eh?"

Billy grinned.

"How come I rate a beating?"

"'Cause you was annoyin' his friends."

"Which ones?"

"He didn't say."

"You and your two pals do this for a living?"

"We ain't pals."

"A one-shot deal?"

"Yeah."

"How much?"

"Fifty each."

"I'm hardly worth it."

"Bugs said it'd be a breeze."

"Bugs was guessing."

"He didn't say nothin' about no fuckin' Mace."

"They rarely do. How'd they recruit you, Billy?"

"Off'n the street."

"The other guys, too?"

He shrugged.

"Who are they?"

"Mike and Leroy. That's all I know."

"They work?"

"Hang around."

"Black guy a boxer?" I asked.

"Guess so."

"He's Leroy?"

"Yeah."

"Describe Bugs."

"Short."

"A midget?"

"Five six. Heavy, like one ninety. But the fucker's *strong*."

"Strong."

"Yeah, uses a bat."

"What for?"

"Fights."

"Who," I asked, "does he fight?"

"Anyone."

"Uh-huh."

"Got lotsa hair."

"Like an ape?"

"That's good. On his fuckin' head."

"You guys supposed to report back?"

"Yeah. Leroy is."

Billy obligingly gave me Bugs's address. I didn't even have to ask.

"Do this before, Billy?"

"Maybe."

"Where?"

"Around."

"Twenty-ninth Street, three years ago?"

"Shit, I was just a kid then."

I recited my lists of landlords, one by one. He'd never

heard of them. Their descriptions didn't ring a bell either. I asked if he knew Bugs's last name.

"Rocca."

"How come they call him Bugs?"

"He's weird."

"Like crazy?"

"Yeah, a psycho."

I pushed the money toward him. "Think you can use some more?"

Billy thought that was a possibility.

"Okay," I said, "we'll keep in touch."

CHAPTER 26

I DIDN'T ESPECIALLY WANT TO DO IT. I HAD ALREADY MADE MY POINT: You can't mess with star tenant Gordon. My point had gone over well. I wasn't missing any teeth. No bruises marred my boyish features. Neither my legs nor my arms required a cast. The thing to do was quit while I was ahead, before something bad happened. But intrepid manhunter Shaw never let reason and logic interfere with a job. Or miss a chance to hammer home a point, once and for all. Good old Shaw was probably as loony as poor Bugs. But a helluva lot better looking, I was willing to bet.

The stairs were bent and scraped as if through the years their users had born them a personal grudge. The smell of dried urine mingled with that of dead rat, creating its own overpowering urban scent, one that wasn't sold across the fragrance counters at Bloomingdale's.

I hit the fourth-floor landing. Four-D came into view. I stood before it, raised my knuckles, and rapped. That was my first mistake.

The guy who opened the door was all he'd been stacked up to be, and then some. He was short, maybe no taller than five five. But he made up in width what he lacked in height. His shoulders were at least a third wider than mine. His belly, under the striped T-shirt, was perfectly round, as though he'd swallowed a globe. His hair, long, fuzzy, and sticking out at all angles, resembled weeds.

What I should have done was excuse myself and tell him I had the wrong apartment. What I did was make my second mistake. I shoved him. I put my hands on his chest and gave him the old heave-ho. It had worked perfectly well on the rock creep in the flat below mine. It didn't work now. This guy seemed welded to the floor. I got him to back up half a foot by sheer effort, then squeezed into the flat. By then, I was already regretting it. By then, it was too late.

The guy swung. He didn't stop to ask what's what, who's who, or anything like that. He just swung. I'd have probably done the same thing in similar circumstances. The round-house right came from left field. The fist couldn't have been as big as a beach ball, but that's what it looked like. I raised both arms and blocked it. The force sent me crashing back against the wall.

"Okay, punk—" I snarled.

That's all I managed to say. Bugs literally flew at me as though he'd been shot out of a cannon. I dived sideways, rolled over on the floor, and came up gripping a hard-backed chair by the legs. I had time to swing it once. It connected solidly enough, but Bugs merely peeled himself off the wall and charged again.

The chair stopped him. For about half a second. A sweep of his arm knocked it from my grasp. He was growling low in his throat. The last time I'd heard that growl was in a zoo, but the animal was safely behind bars.

He swung and I ducked. A pattern that was becoming all too familiar.

I came out of my crouch, saw an opening, and without thinking, planted a hard right square on his chin. I felt the jolt all the way up my arm and shoulder. It would have given a charging bull second thoughts. Not Bugs. Bugs was obviously one step below that on the evolutionary scale.

142

He reached for me. And this time I didn't get out of the way in time.

I was locked in a pythonlike embrace, one I wasn't likely to survive. *Here lies James Shaw. He gave his all for the tenants' cause.*

I went over backward, pulling my knees to my chest. Bugs came with me.

My shoulders hit the floor, almost knocking me silly, but my feet, all on their own, pressed against Bugs's chest. I straightened my legs and flipped him over my head. He let go of me, too. They usually do, even the crazy ones.

I was up before him. Only one problem. He was between me and the door.

I glanced around frantically, hunting for an escape hatch. There were windows, all right, but I wasn't about to jump four stories to the ground. Probably a fire escape was attached to one of them. By the time I found out which, I'd be beyond caring.

Bugs hurled himself at me and I ran. I dodged behind a table. It wasn't very big. Bugs reached across to grab me. I upended it on top of him, shoved hard, and ran for my life. The racket behind me, I figured, was Bugs tossing the table off him. I didn't bother to look. I shot through the doorway and down the stairs as if this was my one chance to make the Olympics team.

Thudding sounds came from behind me on the staircase. Olympic competition.

I hit the street and kept going.

I was halfway up the block before I dared glance back.

Bugs was chugging after me on his short, stubby legs. He was making good time, too, for a little fat guy. Maybe he was indestructible in hand-to-hand combat. But when it came to track and field, he was a novice. I put on a burst of speed, turned a corner, and gave it my all. My New Balance running shoes, which had cost a bundle, were finally proving their worth. I turned some more corners. It took a while, but presently, when I looked back—maybe for the tenth time—I saw I had the field to myself.

My plan had been simple. I was going to identify myself, take a poke or two at the guy, and bust up his place some—maybe with his own bat. The power of irate tenants would strike again! Thank God I hadn't had time to give him my name. Maybe he'd never find out.

I went home to my West Seventy-seventh Street penthouse. Enough was too much already. At least I knew why they called him Bugs. It had hardly been worth the effort.

CHAPTER 27

NEXT DAY AT THE OFFICE, SOMETHING STRANGE HAPPENED: SOME OF our cases began to really simmer. By Wednesday they were boiling over. I could hardly believe it. I forgot about Bugs, slumlords, and my tenements. I was busy seeing dollar signs just then, a truly inspiring sight.

Uncle Max called in to remind me of the case. He had finally tracked down the name of Lieb Lipsky's Lower East Side buddy. It was Yankel Sandlovitch.

I skimmed my Primrose notes. Sandlovitch didn't figure in them. Which, of course, meant nothing. What's in a name? I asked Max if he wanted to nose around some more. He did.

Ms. Lathem, of Code Enforcement, called with a list of Gretz/King properties. I took everything down, thanked her, put this list in the drawer, and wrote her out another check.

It took all of eight days before I thought about the case again. I dropped into the office at noon that day. Harry was out. Our stringers were all in the field. There were a number of messages at our answering service, including one from Mrs. Kazmir. It said I was fired.

I looked at the old girl, turned down the glass of tea she offered, sat back in the lumpy easy chair, and said, "All right, let's hear it, what's the problem, Mrs. Kazmir?"

"Is no problem. Everything good now. You sure no tea?"

"Yeah. How's it good?"

"They give lots of money. Is okay."

"Who's they? Berk?"

"Sure."

"What's lots?"

"Three thousand."

"To whom?"

"Mrs. Priznovsky."

"Just her?"

"No, Mr. Bullchik, maybe twelve others. Mr. Hawks know, he tell you."

"They all satisfied?"

"Sure. What you think?"

"I think they could've gotten more."

"How?"

"By holding out. You got this offer, too?"

"No. Others must wait. Is okay, Mr. Shaw."

"Gordon. Why's it okay?"

"Mr. Berk say *everyone* get soon."

"When soon?"

"Soon."

"No more complaints, eh?"

"Sure, someone always complain."

"But most think everything's just hunky-dory?"

"They happy. You want coffee, maybe? I got home-baked pie. Is peach."

"Thanks, I've eaten."

"Committee, it want money back, Mr. Shaw."

"Gordon. The vote unanimous?"

"Mr. Nesbit, he say landlord is crook, still need detective."

"What about Hawks?"

"He vote you go."

"And you?"

"I vote with rest. No want trouble. They all say I give too much money, detective never come. Now you give back money, is okay."

"Mrs. Kazmir, when I first took this job I wasn't sure you needed me. Primrose didn't look any worse than any other landlords. Even when squatters took over Miss Downy's flat, I wasn't convinced. That could've just been the breaks. The fires, broken windows, and locks are something else again. I met with Berk's bosses a couple weeks ago and gave them some back talk. Last week three thugs tried to jump me."

"You hurt?"

"No."

"Then everything fine."

"Not quite. Sending goons to beat up tenants isn't cricket. Guys who do that can do a lot worse. And probably will."

"But they give money."

"Just three grand, and only to a few."

"They give everyone soon."

"Maybe."

"Is nothing I can do, Mr. Shaw. Committee want money."

"Mrs. Kazmir, try and remember I'm Stuart Gordon."

"Okay. Why I should remember now you not detective here?"

"Because I'm still going to be around. I'm keeping seven hundred as fee plus expenses. You'll get the rest back tomorrow, in cash. No checks. I want everyone to go on thinking I'm Gordon."

"I no understand."

"I'd like to be here if things heat up. And the best way to do that is to hang on to my apartment. You folks need a guardian angel."

"That you, Mr. Gordon?"

"That's me, Mrs. Kazmir."

"Fourteen, all told," Hawks said.

"Same going rate?"

"Three thousand."

"Out by month's end?"

He nodded.

"You talk to them?"

"Some."

"Tell them to go slow?"

"Mentioned it."

"No takers, eh?"

"Three thousand's big money to some of these folks, Mr. Gordon. Lots are on welfare. Others are pensioners. Old folks on social security, fixed incomes. Berk done real good by some of them."

"Slipped 'em an extra fifty?"

"Found them cheap apartments."

"No kidding? I'm impressed."

"Me, too. Maybe things'll work out after all."

"Maybe, Mr. Hawks."

I glanced around. The place was pretty much like the man, clean and neat. His furniture, sturdy bargain-basement stuff. The patchwork quilt on his bed looked like a family heirloom, a bit worn but probably good for another hundred years. Plain window shades held off the outdoors. One black, straight-backed armchair was opposite the thirteen-inch TV set; a small yellow pillow rested on its seat, a sure sign that my host was giving in to the good life. A gilt-edge-framed photograph of a younger, black-haired Hawks hung on the wall. A plain-faced woman and a little girl of about three were beside him. The deceased wife and daughter he'd mentioned. They were grinning as if to say being dead wasn't half bad.

Hawks and I were seated around a small plastic-topped kitchen table. I had already nixed the obligatory drink offer.

"What I don't get," I said, "is why just these fourteen? How come Berk stopped?"

"I asked. Says he fell behind with the paperwork. Soon's he catches up, we start rolling again."

"What paperwork? The contract? He's got a desk full of 'em. The check's routine."

"Give the man a chance."

"Yeah, but it doesn't add up. Here they are, busting their

chops to start things moving, they gain a little momentum, and stop dead."

"Only temporary. Don't pay to make a federal case out of it."

"Those fourteen," I asked, "they from one house?"

"Scattered around."

"Any two from the same building?"

"Don't think so. Why?"

"Funny, that's all."

"Just the way it worked out, Mr. Gordon. Ask me, the last ones to leave, they're the lucky ones."

"Think the price will go up?"

"Sure do."

"As one of the last ones," I said, "I hope you're right."

CHAPTER 28

I GOT BACK TO THE OFFICE AROUND FOUR TO FOLLOW UP ON SOME paperwork. Harry had been in and out. He'd left a note on my desk: *Call a Detective Drummund. The jig's up, kid, head south.* I dialed the number on the pad, reached the Twenty-fourth Precinct, asked for Drummund, and identified myself when he came on the line.

"Know a Norma Windfield?" he asked.

"No, should I?"

"Maybe. Captain Rogers says you like the name Stuart Gordon."

"Crazy about it. Can't understand how I missed out on it at birth. Why?"

"This Windfield had it on a slip of paper in her purse. Along with your agency's name and address."

"Describe her."

"Midtwenties. Straight blond hair. Pale complexion. About five three. Nose a little crooked. Eyes gray-green."

"Yeah," I said, "I know her. She called herself Lila."

"Well, her name's Windfield and she's in the city morgue. Come and take a look."

"The icehouse" always lives up to its name. I stuck my hands into my pockets and would have crawled in after them given half the chance. It wasn't just the temperature. The

morgue gave me the creeps. Formaldehyde, as if the rest
wasn't enough, made the air almost unbreathable. The temporary residents didn't seem to mind.

Drummund pulled back the sheet. I looked down, then
away.

"Still gets you," he said.

"Always will."

"That her?"

"Yeah."

"Not very pretty."

"Strangled, eh?"

"Uh-huh."

Drummund was a lean, muscular man of about forty. He
had very black hair and eyebrows, a long slanting nose, brown
eyes, and narrow lips. We sat in his parked car and I told him
what I knew about Norma Windfield, which was practically
nothing. I gave him the entire story including my recent stint
as Captain Tenant, defender of the poor. He heard me out
silently, frowned, and said, "Never even hinted at who was
killed or why or where?"

"That was her ace. She wasn't showing her hand till she saw
the money was right."

"What about the men in the photos?"

"Mum's the word. You find the photos?"

"Nothing like that."

"Frank's notes, his belongings?"

"We found a suitcase with some shirts, underwear, pants, a
couple sweaters. No notes."

"Who was she?"

"A waitress. Worked in a joint on First Avenue. Think she
tried to peddle her stuff to the wrong parties?"

I shrugged. "Your guess is as good as mine."

"Thanks for the ID," Drummund said.

"Can't say it was a pleasure."

CHAPTER 29

I VISITED MY BANK THE FOLLOWING DAY, WITHDREW A PILE OF money, carried it across town, and traded it to Kazmir for a receipt. Then I dropped in on Berk. The building manager seemed glad to see me, explained that the jackpot had shot up to a scintillating three grand, admired my fortitude in holding out for the big prize, and predicted that lucky days were here again, if not for everybody, at least for me, and fourteen other of the chosen—although he failed to mention the latter point. I waited for the band to burst in and the building manager to hop on his desk and start tap dancing. When reality held firm, I told him I'd already turned down that sum from his bosses. Berk admitted hearing something to that effect, but said he had a surprise for me. I told him I liked surprises. Berk gave me his best smile and offered me a walk-up on Avenue C at seventy a month, every inch as good as my present abode. I could believe it. Avenue C was dopester turf. The rents were dirt cheap, but the bodyguards needed to maintain life and limb came a mite high. I told him I appreciated his generosity and would always think kindly of him, but that I liked being where I was. Berk nodded grimly as if I'd told him the black plague had been spotted heading this way from midtown. His friendly smile was only a faint memory now.

I said, "I've landed a job that'll keep me on the road for a while. You can reach me through my boss, Ralph Clinton."

Ralph had fronted for me before. Last night, a phone call had brought him on board for another round; he hadn't seemed to mind, at least not too much. I had almost married his daughter some years back, and I think we were both grateful it had stopped short of the altar. I gave Berk the address of Clinton Tools, handed him next month's rent, collected my receipt, and left.

I stopped off at my flat, packed my radio, some stray paperbacks, and most of my clothing into a canvas suitcase. The cheap dishes stayed, along with some cut-rate work clothes. I'd failed to spot my resident mouse this time around, but someone was eating the cheese I left out, so I put another wedge on the floor and filled a small dish with milk. I knew I wasn't acting irrationally, because the thought of carrying the mouse home to Seventy-seventh Street as a house pet never even crossed my mind.

More than a full month later, three-thirty on a Tuesday afternoon in the first week of February, the temperature was pushing fifty-two degrees as I hiked down Ninety-fourth Street toward the clump of sagging houses at block's end.

I carried my blue-and-yellow shoulder bag, which contained a change of shirt, underwear, and socks, some Mozart and Beethoven tapes, my Aiwa portable, and a small flask of cognac. I was going to drop in on Berk with the month's rent, catch up on developments with Kazmir and Hawks, and spend the night. Tomorrow I'd be off to my make-believe stint at Clinton Tools, my tenant's credentials intact. All I had to do was get through the night.

My first sight of the buildings gave me a start. Usually, there were few loiterers about. The elderly and infirm—the only ones around at this hour—had better places to hang out: the Ninety-sixth Street public library, a nice bakery serving tea and coffee, Carl Schurz Park if the weather was right. But the turf now was crowded, as if a fire drill were in progress and the occupants had been shooed out of their homes. I didn't know any of them either. There were blacks, Hispanics, whites, even a few Orientals. The women, mostly in their twenties, looked like hookers: leather miniskirts, skintight pants, six-inch heels, and glitzy makeup. A few guys, done up in chintzy finery, could have been pimps. The others looked like scraggly down-and-outers. A couple of blaring ghetto blasters tuned to different stations gave just the right accompaniment. The talk was loud and slurred.

A couple of heads turned my way, glazed eyes blinking dully. I stepped around four parties sprawled across the stoop, who ignored me as if I were invisible, and opened the front door.

Inside, I kicked some empty bottles aside and started up. I halted on the second landing. Someone was in the apartment below mine again, another rock buff. Only this time 2C wasn't alone. The whole house had become one giant party.

The door to my flat was ajar, both locks busted. The old clothing I'd left behind was gone, the closet bare. No food was in the fridge, but some benefactor had left me a six-pack and a gallon of cheap red wine. The sheets were still on the bed, only slept in. Cigarette butts, empty wine bottles, and beer cans cluttered the floor. I found a syringe in the water closet, but no toilet paper.

I had expected a guest or two during my absence, but nothing quite like this.

I opened the window, cleaned some of the junk off the floor, and still clutching my canvas bag—which I had no intention of losing—climbed two flights of stairs to rap on Mrs. Kazmir's door. I had some questions to ask. Like Tonto, the old girl knew the real me was the Lone Ranger. So how come she hadn't called when the shit hit the fan? No one answered my knock. I turned, started down. Company found me on the second floor. My pal, the bearded, big-bellied squatter, stood in 2C's doorway, a young blonde peering out over his shoulder.

"Better keep goin' fuck-face," he told me.

I took a step toward him and the door slammed shut. A lock clicked. Pea-brain had grown cautious, if not wiser. I continued down. The milling druggies and drunks were still living it up. I tried Hawks but he was out, too. I went around the corner to see Berk. Clean sweep. He wasn't there either. Another guy sat behind the lacerated desk talking to a tenant. I sat and waited. Berk's substitute had a square jaw, crooked nose that tilted to the left, and thin lips. His hair was black and cut short. Medium height and build. He wore a black-and-gray-checkered jacket, and a black knit tie. I never saw him smile once. The tenant, an old codger, shuffled out after fifteen minutes; he wasn't smiling either. I took his seat.

"Where's Berk?" I asked.

"He's moved on."

"Another site?"

"Forget him, buddy, what's your name?"

"Gordon. Berk and I were working out a deal."

"You deal with me now. Name's Pitts." He didn't offer to shake hands. Pitts found my card. "You're the traveler."

"Yeah." I handed him the rent, received a receipt in return. "In the future, buddy, mail this to the main office. This place is part-time now."

"What's going on here?"

"What you see."

"I see a lot of strangers."

"The boss," Pitts said, "don't like empty apartments."

"Those people look like trouble."

"They're your new neighbors; you don't like it, move."

"Berk mentioned three grand."

"That was the deal?"

"Yeah."

"Forget it."

"So what's your offer, Pitts?"

"Five hundred. Take it or leave it."

"Thanks. I'll pass."

"Suit yourself, buddy."

156

I said, "Some squatters below me are back."

"What apartment?"

I gave him the number. Pitts looked it up, shook his head.

"Ain't squatters."

"Been promoted, eh?"

"They got the money, we rent."

"Where'd they get it?"

"Go ask 'em."

"Maybe I will."

"Fuckin' shit," Caloney said. "Wake up one mornin', it's a fuckin' zoo. Fuckin' whores, spades, spics. Listen to *that!*"

"What's Hawks doing?"

"Runnin' to all the agencies he can think of. Big brother's gonna bail him out. I told the asshole, get Tanner."

"Your lawyer."

"Guy calls in the fuckin' Mafia, they clean up this shit."

"He said no?"

"What the fuck's *he* know?"

"Kazmir or Nesbit around?"

"Nesbit? Look under his bed. The old dame I hear's in the hospital."

"What happened?"

"Fuck knows. Something fell on her."

"Hurt bad?"

"Listen, my friend, I got my own problems. I work the swing shift now. Only way I can get some fuckin' sleep around here."

"Anyone bother you?"

"Let 'em try. Gotta fuckin' baseball bat here, carry it to and from the job. They get in my fuckin' way, I'm gonna kill me a few."

CHAPTER 30

I BOUGHT MYSELF A COUPLE OF DAYS' WORTH OF GROCERIES AT Grand Union and some cheap locks at a hardware store. Dusk was darkening the streets and lights snapping on by the time I got home.

I chopped up a salad, broiled a batch of steak burgers, steamed some whole okra and baby potatoes, and sat down to dinner. The tomatoes under the olive oil were a bit waxy, but you had to hand it to a product whose shelf life would far exceed yours. The steak burgers were delicious; the cow had not died in vain. The radio, volume turned way up, was playing Brahms's Fourth Symphony. It didn't help. Not even Wagner could drown out the noise. I didn't like being here. But now that push had come to shove, maybe I could actually do something for the old tenants. It was a startling idea. After dinner I installed the new locks, replaced my radio in the shoulder bag, hefted it, and went.

"Can't say I don't envy you," Hawks said. "Got a job keeps you on the road."

"What's happened here, Mr. Hawks?"

"We were invaded. First they dished out that three thousand, then went right back to five hundred next week. Big fuss at first, sure."

"Those fourteen vacancies," I said, "they stay empty long?"

"Filled overnight. 'Long with the other empty apartments, 'bout two dozen in all. Pretty soon, folks started to take what they could and run."

"Old tenants being threatened?"

He shook his head. "Not to speak of. Prostitutes bringing men into the buildings. Noise round the clock. Place turned into a shooting gallery. Drunks lying around in their own piss and vomit. Not much need to threaten anyone, is there?"

"Not much," I had to admit. "Muggings? Burglaries?"

"Couple. Police came, looked around, couldn't tie any of it to the new bunch, and left."

"Cops do anything about the racket?"

"Drop by every now and then, tell them to keep it down. Never makes a bit of difference. They drive off, damn thing starts up all over again."

I asked, "What's with Berk?"

"Wasn't here, beginning last week. Storefront shut down. Then, midweek, this Pitts showed up. Don't matter none, I guess; they both take orders." He sighed. "Seen an assistant DA. No crime in renting to hoodlums; they have to live somewhere, too. Said to call the police if they got out of line. Went to the mayor's office. They sent me to Rent Control. They said I needed something called The Division of Housing and Community Renewal. They said it didn't sound like harassment yet, and to come back if services were stopped. Or if these new people got physical. Cops can handle noise, they said."

"How about a lawyer?"

"Got one. Morton Feld. He's been to see the landlord himself."

"Which one?"

"A Mr. Rensler. Said he'd fix what violations there were. Only good plumbers, carpenters, were hard to find. Said he'd ask Berk to keep things quiet. Don't know what Pitts'll do. Berk did nothing."

"What does Feld say?"

"Got to give the landlord time to do right by us before we go to court. Thing is, a lot of judges come down on the landlord's side, according to Mr. Feld."

"Uh-huh. The committee on your side?"

"What's left of them. You hear about Mrs. Kazmir? Window box on the third floor came loose. Wind, maybe. She was just leaving the building. Lucky, I guess. Could have been killed real easy. Hospital says she's in for a stay."

I nodded, trying to digest this latest bulletin. "Whose apartment was it?" I wanted to know.

"No one's at the time. Empty. Got some of *them* in it now."

"Kazmir up to her old tricks," I asked, "agitating and all?"

"Sure. Gave Berk a piece of her mind. Was trying to organize everyone, keep them from running out. Wanted to bring back this private-eye fellow of hers. We vetoed that one real quick. Lawyer's expensive enough." Hawks shook his head. "Lots of folks threw in the towel when this happened to her."

"What about Nesbit?"

"Gone. Didn't even claim his five hundred."

"Come into money?"

"Said he plain couldn't stand it anymore; think he's with his niece somewhere." Hawks stared off into the distance as if trying to see if Nesbit was happy now. "Mr. Ward died, you know," he said.

"The old guy?"

Hawks nodded. "Heart attack, the doctor said. I say the noise got him. Lost a couple more from the committee, too. Don't blame them, either. I'm about fed up myself."

Hawks and I sat in silence. We were the only bastion of silence in the vicinity. Aside from the omnipresent boom boxes sounding through the walls, floors, and ceilings, there were the shouts, screams, and raging arguments. The new neighbors showing off their lifestyles.

"Don't let them beat you, Mr. Hawks."

He shrugged.

I said, "There just might be a remedy."

"If you mean those damned agencies—"

"Uh-uh. Me."

He raised his brows. "I don't follow, Mr. Gordon."

"That detective, the one never showed up? He did. In fact, he's here right now."

"Where?"

"Sitting across from you."

Hawks stared my way as though trying to see if someone were hiding behind me. "You, Mr. Gordon?"

"Me, Mr. Hawks."

"But you've been living here a long time."

"Not so long. Three months, maybe. I was on a case here, doing surveillance. My rent was still paid up when Kazmir roped me into coming back."

Hawks shook his head. "You joshing me?"

"No."

"Hard to believe."

"Believe it. You people wanted me to work undercover, so I did. When I began organizing, Primrose tried to bribe me. When that didn't take, they hired goons to work me over. That showed their hand. Only, just then, you folks gave me my walking papers. Couldn't have picked a worse time, either."

Hawks seemed embarrassed. "Didn't know it was you."

"It would have made a difference?"

"Guess not, Mr. Gordon."

"Shaw. Not Gordon."

"Shaw?"

"Yeah. Gordon in public."

"Take some getting used to."

"Well worth it," I said. "Listen, we can give them a run for their money, Mr. Hawks, take on their goons and maybe restore some hope and peace to everyone. We can try to nail them with a felony, too. We do that, we can either pry them loose or make them pay top dollar."

"You can do that?"

"I can try."

"How much will it cost?"

"Less than caving in."

CHAPTER 31

TWO BLACK GUYS WERE BUSY ON MY LOCKS WHEN I GOT BACK TO MY flat. They only had a screwdriver between them, a real handicap.

"Uh-uh, guys," I said, "that's not the way. Watch." I withdrew my keys and opened the locks. "See? Nothing to it."

"There some mistake, brother," the short guy in the billed cap told me. "We lives here."

"You don't say?"

"Yeah," his friend with the screwdriver said. "That's a fact."

"Got a lease?" I asked.

"Ain't signed one yet, brother; gonna do that tomorrow."

I unzipped my bag, reached into one of its handy pockets, and fished out my document.

"You mean something like this?"

"What that, brother?"

"My lease. For this apartment. Never make a move without it."

"Don' mean shit," the guy with the screwdriver said. "We tol' you, this *our* place now."

"Who rented it to you?"

"The super."

"Wrong guy. Better take it up with him, he's two flights down."

"Why you talkin' to this man?" Billed Cap asked his friend. "He ain't no one."

165

The guy opened my door, stared in.

It was the noise that did it, of course, the so-called music pounding in on me. It made me edgy, got in the way of achieving a reasonable dialogue with this pair. The noise was entirely to blame.

I dropped my bag, grabbed the guy's shoulder, spun him around, and belted him in the beezer. His friend lunged at me with the screwdriver. I chucked Billed Cap at him, stepped in, and hammered a right cross at Screwdriver's head. I got a jab in, too, before Billed Cap grabbed me. I could understand why: I'd been neglecting him. I put a fist in his rib cage, making him let go. My shoulder collided with his chest. He tumbled down the stairs. His pal was just standing there, clutching his screwdriver. I slammed him in the belly, latched on to his shirtfront, yanked, and sent him flying down the stairs after his friend. Noise, lots of it. And then a satisfying silence. The pair got to their feet slowly, cautiously. Neither of them came charging back. These were squatters, not fighters.

"Seems we was in error, brother," Screwdriver said from the staircase.

"No problem, right?" Billed Cap said.

They began edging down the stairs. I watched them go, resisting the impulse to say I was sorry.

I went into my flat. My hands were shaking. I sighed. No one could say I hadn't defended my castle manfully. The racket, I noticed, hadn't abetted any. I did what any law-abiding citizen would do under the circumstances: I called the police.

The two uniformed cops who showed up some forty minutes later did not look happy. They were both young and probably had little experience with volcaniclike noise.

"It's coming from everywhere," the blond-headed cop said. He had a small mustache that had begun to twitch.

"Sure seems that way," I said cheerfully.

"Christ!" the other cop said. He was a tall, pale-skinned guy of about twenty-five.

"Only four or five music buffs doing that," I said. "Rest of the building wants to sleep."

"We'll talk to them," the tall cop said.

"They may be beyond language," I told him.

"We can give them a summons."

"This has been going on for weeks," I said. "Whatever you do, don't forget to write it up. There's a court case in the works."

He nodded.

"You might try the other houses, too. Same problem there."

"How many?"

I told him.

"Shit," the blond cop said, "we'll be here all night."

"Call in," I said, "get some backup. This thing spreads, the whole city could be inundated."

It took the cops a while to restore law and order. I listened to the silence, remembering what Hawks had told me. I sat in my easy chair, waiting. I didn't have to wait long. At first, only one boom box started up. Pretty soon, another joined in. Then, a third began to party. We were back in whoopee land.

I reached for the phone.

It took the cops only ten minutes to arrive. The same two cops; they had still been working the buildings on Ninety-third when the call came in.

"What the fuck's going on?" the blond one asked.

"Exactly what you imagine," I explained.

The cops looked grim. Again they did their thing. This time when they finally left, it remained quiet.

CHAPTER 32

EIGHT-THIRTY. I WAS SITTING ACROSS FROM NED HAWKS AT HIS kitchen table, sharing a cup of instant coffee. It was to real coffee as Bible Comics is to the Good Book. I spared Hawks this vital piece of knowledge, but cued him in on some other matters.

"This guy Feld, your lawyer, is either a jerk or he's been bought off," I said.

"We don't know that."

"It doesn't matter, Ned, get rid of the guy."

"Don't seem right, Mr. Shaw."

"Jim, we're going to be in this together awhile. Look, the guy isn't doing his job, he's dragging his tail, that's all you've got to know."

Hawks drank his coffee as though it were alive and tasty, a sad delusion. "Who do I hire in his place," he asked, "this Tanner Caloney's been pushing?"

"That's all we need, Caloney's Mafia lawyer."

"So what do we do?"

"You have confidence in me, right, Ned?"

Hawks nodded as though he couldn't quite trust himself to say yes with conviction. I'd been hoping for a statement signed in blood, but this would have to do.

"Leave everything to me."

"Mr. Shaw, the committee hasn't even met about *you* yet."

"Jim. You expect trouble there?"

"Guess not."

"Good. Call an emergency meeting for tonight, get that squared away. Then, a general one as soon as it can be arranged. My partner, Harry, will give them a pep talk they won't forget. I've got a plan they should hear about."

"What's that?"

"I call it 'the resistance.'"

"Sounds like guerrilla warfare."

"You got it, Ned."

I brewed some good Colombian coffee at the office, unwrapped four whole-wheat doughnuts I'd bought, and called Max. "Didn't wake you?"

"I get up at five, Jimmy."

"That's uncivilized. Max, remember when I asked you to run a check on Leo Lipsky and his pals?"

"Of course."

"Anything ever come of it?"

"Some headway, yes."

"You never got back to me."

"You were away, Jimmy. I called Harry and he told me the case was closed."

"It's open again. I'd like to hear what you've got."

"When?"

"Now."

"One month I am sitting on this and now suddenly he is in a rush. All right, Jimmy, are you free later this morning?"

"Yeah, sure."

"I will make a call and if everything is in order, we will take a short trip."

"Sounds good to me," I told him.

Harry wandered into the office around nine-thirty. "Smells like a coffee shop," he said. "Have some for me?"

"On the house, pal."

I shoved the napkin with two doughnuts toward him across

the desk, poured another cup. Harry seated himself. "Should have opened a coffee shop, kid, never miss a meal that way."

"Never have any fun either."

"Who's having fun?"

"The fun, partner, is about to begin. You are going to become a big-shot private eye."

"About time. Do I get a nice expense account to go with the honor?"

"I'm working on it. Hawks'll put the squeeze on the tenants."

"Back to that, huh? I was hoping Trump had hired us to guard his fortune."

"He will," I said, "when he hears what a swell job we've done on these buildings. Primrose has called out the heavies, filled the houses with lowlifes; they loiter all day, party all night."

"Now *there's* a job."

"Got to be a lowlife first; your mother wouldn't like it."

"You're right."

"I got Hawks to bounce his lawyer. We got anyone halfway decent?"

"Shields?"

"Guy's a shyster."

"Resnick?"

"Another shyster."

"How about Wendy Lewin?"

I munched the last of my doughnut. "At least she's cute. Is she cheap?"

"Depends on the cause."

"Rarely has right and wrong been so clearly defined."

"I'll line her up, kid, you give her the pitch. I don't think I can do it with a straight face."

"Deal." I poured us both second cups. "Last night I was attacked by rock and rap. Right through the walls."

"The mob obviously knows your weakness."

"There are limits. I'm starting to take this personally, Harry."

"They hear that, they'll quake with fear."

"Think they won't? Am I old, helpless, senile? Do I have 'victim' written all over me? That's their speed, Harry. Show a little gumption and they'll head for the hills."

"That's what you're going to do, show a little gumption?"

"Actually," I said, "that's what *you're* going to do. And rouse the tenants to new heights."

"Glad you told me."

"Harry, you're going to be the mysterious detective Hawks hired."

"The one that never showed?"

"That's you."

"They'll eat me alive."

"Tell 'em your agents were all over the place."

"They'll never buy it."

"You forget your boyish charm. Besides, they're desperate. You'll have them at your mercy."

Harry sighed. "When do I do this wonderful thing?"

"Hawks is setting it up."

"And you?"

"I'll be there to cheer you on, pal. What are partners for?"

Harry returned to his chores and I rummaged in my desk hunting for my notes. I laid them all out on my desk top and pretended I was Sherlock Holmes. The gods were not deceived.

I reached for the phone, dialed Code Enforcement.

"Ms. Lathem," I said, "Jim Shaw. Stand some more work?"

Lathem thought she might be willing.

I reeled off all the real-estate outfits my investigation had touched on so far. "What I'd like to know," I said, "is who they bought from and sold to."

"That's all?"

"Yeah."

"It's quite a job, Mr. Shaw."

"Big job, big check," I said breezily.

"How far back do I go?"

"All the way."

"A very big check, I'm afraid."

"Have no fear, Ms. Lathem, big checks are the American way."

"Registration unit's only been active since '71. Have to go to rent control for anything before that."

"A problem?"

"Not really. I have a friend there."

"Where would we be without friends?"

"When do you want this?"

"Yesterday."

CHAPTER 33

UNCLE MAX COLLECTED ME AROUND ELEVEN AND WE DROVE OFF TO Riverdale, which is almost in the suburbs.

"If I'd known we were going that far," I told him, "I'd've brought a picnic lunch."

"There is no place to picnic, Jimmy. There is more country in Central Park."

He was right, too; our destination was a red-brick apartment house with a blue awning, the kind you find all over Manhattan.

"Olinsky," Max told the doorman.

The doorman checked, verified that we were expected and not the noted miscreants he'd been guarding against for twenty years, and let us in. We got as far as the sixth floor.

The man who answered our ring was short, round shouldered, and in his late seventies. His brow was furrowed, his face deeply grooved, but his hair was jet black; he had it parted straight down the middle. The mournful expression he wore was undone by the numerous laugh lines around his eyes and mouth. He had on a striped white shirt. Red suspenders held up gray beltless slacks.

"Olinsky," Max said, "this is my nephew, Jimmy Shaw, the detective."

Olinsky eyed me deadpan, raised his hands over his head, and agreed to come quietly.

Max said, "Olinsky, act your age."

"If I did," Olinsky said, "I would have to stretch out on a table with candles at my head and feet."

We shook hands, and Olinsky turned his back on us and shuffled into his apartment. We trailed after him.

There were floral drapes on the windows and deep-pile carpeting on the floor. A bookcase held classics from the last century, literature going into the 1940s, and best-sellers from the fifties on, as if the reader had finally lost patience with art. Or maybe a new reader had inherited the bookcase. There were lots of photographs of smiling kids and adults in Woolworth frames on the shelves, too. The place had a faintly musty odor as though it had been stored in a warehouse for the last few decades and just recently unpacked.

"You will join me for lunch, of course," Olinsky said gravely. "With my own hands I have prepared for you a feast. Cat burgers." He shuffled off into the kitchen. "I will miss the little darling, but nothing is too good for friends."

"Where did you find him?" I asked.

"Usually," Max said, "I found him trying to swindle some old woman out of her life savings. I only helped arrest him twice."

We ate in the study. Pastrami, roast beef, and corned beef. A sliced loaf of onion bread. Plenty of Chinese mustard. Two large bottles of Dr. Brown's Cell-Ray soda.

"Nice spread," I said. "I'd've come more often if I'd known about the meals."

"You are always welcome."

"Just stop off at the Carnegie Deli," Max said, "and pick up the food first."

"I was going to tell him," Olinsky said, "only I didn't want he should have heartburn so soon."

"You guys had an act once?"

"More like a sporting event," Olinsky said. "I ran, he chased."

"Those snapshots," I asked, "family?"

176

"Two grandsons, two daughters, nephews, nieces, their children. My wives, too. The girls were from Rita, the first one."

"He had four wives," Max said.

"Never at the same time," Olinsky said.

"Only because he was afraid they would catch him," Max said.

"True."

Dessert was canned peaches in heavy syrup. We lingered over coffee and a tin of assorted cookies.

"Remember Lou the Jinx?" Olinsky asked Max. "Every time he went to rob someone, he got caught. Once a policeman was in the store. Another time a card game was going on in the back room, and all the toughs ran after him with guns. Once he held up a restaurant and took a thousand dollars. But the car wouldn't start."

"Where did he get a car?" Max asked.

"He stole one, where else?"

"Izzy Spaghetti," Max said, "they never caught."

"He liked, after a nice job, to have a plate of spaghetti," Olinsky told me, "along with plenty of wine. A habit."

"He did stickups?" I asked.

"He was a burglar," Olinsky said.

"Remember Rosie Fine?"

"Mother Fine," Olinsky said. "Best madam who ever lived."

"Died a millionairess," Max said. "Owned property all over the Lower East Side."

"Abe the Gimp used to shake down storekeepers," Olinsky said. "He would sell raffle tickets. You wouldn't buy, your store would have an accident."

"They bought," said Max, "every month."

"It was for the poor," Olinsky pointed out.

"Right," Max said. "Abe was never a rich man."

"Didn't even come close. He played the horses and won

177

once in a blue moon. He would ask you should buy an extra ticket on account his leg hurt from going block to block."

I said, "Anyone ever win the raffle?"

"Sure. Abe, every time."

"Some lucky son of a gun, ah?" Max said, grinning.

"Once," Olinsky said, "he wasn't so lucky. Remember? He was still a young man then. He was playing around with a married woman. She had, I think, three children, too, all young. The husband, he comes home, finds them in bed together, and throws Abe down the stairs. That's how he got his limp. His leg never healed right."

"Strongman Moe," Max said, "could carry a safe away on his back."

"Irv the Ox," Olinsky said, "was also strong."

"They called him Ox," Max told me, "not because he was so strong, but because he was dumb like an ox."

"Horse Rosenfeld," Olinsky said, "used to collect from the peddlers."

"In those days, Jimmy," Max said, "peddlers had wagons. Some bought junk, scrap iron, others sold fruits and vegetables. Horses pulled all the wagons. Rosenfeld would poison the horses if they wouldn't pay him. It was a good business. Even when he went into another line they still called him Horse. He died only last year."

Olinsky gave me a wink and a grin. "Your friend Lieb Lipsky, who I am told you are interested in, was one of them, only younger. He began as a thief. He stole packages from delivery trucks; also he rolled drunks, picked pockets, good things like that. This, when he was still only a teenager. Soon he was with a gang that did shakedowns, like Abe the Gimp, only a few blocks over. Sometimes they would just point a gun and take the money. They did other things, too. They fixed elections, bought votes, and beat up voters. *Shtarkes*, they were called—strongmen. Lipsky wasn't a *shtarker*, he was the one who gave them orders.

By then this was no longer such a good way to make a living. First, the police were more active in the neighborhood. For years they did nothing, then Governor Lehman, he hired Thomas E. Dewey for special prosecutor. Dewey was such a good racket buster, he went on to become governor himself, and also twice, the Republicans, they ran him for president. Both Roosevelt and Truman beat him. Someone said once that Dewey, he looked like the little man on top of the wedding cake, and this stuck. It didn't help in the elections. Anyway, the Lower East Side, by this time, wasn't so Jewish anymore, because the Jews, as soon as they got some money, they moved to better places. Others moved in and their people started to take over. More coffee?"

Max and I said yes and our host shuffled off to the kitchen to get the pot. Outdoors the sun was shining. Riverdale seemed as far away from the Lower East Side with its crowded tenements as Ford's Model T was from the Honda 500.

"So," Olinsky said when he was seated again, "your friend Lipsky went on to other things: loan-sharking, fencing, the labor rackets. This last one was a fine business. You got control, say, of a trucking local. What you did was bribe or beat your way in. The trucks deliver to a baking company, maybe. You call a strike, plenty could be lost. So they pay off in a hurry.

"This was just a step up the ladder, so to speak. What it led to was labor consulting, the best business yet. You could, in this business, work on both sides. The bosses want strikebreakers, you give them strikebreakers, come down to the picket line with baseball bats, brass knuckles, lead pipes, a few guns, too. Pretty soon, no strike. In those days they never posted no police at strikes, so this was easy. Bad enough there is no money coming in, you are on strike, but also you took your life in your hands. But the union bosses aren't so dumb

179

either. What's good for the bosses is good for them, too. Buying thugs is a two-way street; they, also, can hire labor consultants. Now, the *shtarkes* show up for the union, protect the workers. So what you got lots of times is two outfits sending their boys to break each other's heads. Which side wins depends on who has hired the best consultants.

"From there it is only a small step before you are part of the union or part of the company; by then they can't do without you. That's how the racketeers got into the unions and businesses. Once in, you couldn't get them out. Lipsky never went that high. This was for big shots.

"By the forties we still had Jewish gangsters, but no more Jewish gangs. The rackets themselves were in trouble because of Dewey, and in Brooklyn, the new district attorney, O'Dwyer, who did such a good job they later made him mayor of New York. And still later, when he showed he had learned maybe a little too much from crooks, they chased him from office.

"Lipsky, meanwhile, he went with the times. What happened to the consultation business, I don't know. But the next thing I hear, Lipsky has bought himself some small houses in Sea Gate and become a landlord. Anyway, that's what people said. From then on I hear nothing because the old crowd does not exist anymore and everyone has gone his own way. Except once, maybe twenty years ago, someone said they heard one of Lipsky's houses has burned down and a woman died. Right away, I think of the insurance. But who knows?

"Anyway, that's the story of Lieb Lipsky, who Max tells me now calls himself Leo. You saw him?"

"I saw him," I said.

"What does he look like?"

I described him.

"So, he has not lost his hair?"

"No, but it's turning gray," I said diplomatically.

"He was, of course, sarcastic."

"That's what I'd call it."

"And now he manages buildings?"

"He's supposed to have a firm. The place I was in looked unused."

"With Lipsky you should pay no attention to what it says on the door," Olinsky said. "Tell me about the two who were with him."

I told him.

"Well, I have never heard of this Ed Jenkins," Olinsky said, "but names mean nothing. In Lipsky's circle they change names like you change shoes. From what you say, it could have been Yankel Sandlovitch. About him, if that's who it was, I don't know much. He was a *macher*, a big shot in the garment industry. He worked for the bosses. He was, I think, a manager or something. For a time he ran a shop himself. What I remember is, he was the one did business with the consultants. If union people were making trouble, Sandlovitch, he would see someone fixed it. He handled also the payoffs to union bosses, to make sure everything went smooth. Lieb and Yankel, they probably met in the line of work. But then they became friends. What happened after that, you have to ask them.

"Your Manny Gretz, I know better. He used to be Moisha Gretzberg in the old days when for a living he was beating up people and setting houses on fire. Then later, when he bought some tenements of his own, he was already calling himself Manny Gretz. Maybe because under his real name, he had been arrested a few times, and once almost went to jail. Usually, when it came time for the trial, the witnesses against him, they would suddenly get cold feet. But this once, when a house burned down, there was a witness and he came forward. For Moisha, this was a new experience; it did not look so good. But on the stand, the witness changed his mind and said he had made a mistake. What can I tell you? Gretz walked out of court a free man.

"He was one of Lipsky's *shtarkes*, but he rose, and soon

they were equals. It's interesting that they now work together. I didn't know they were close.

"About Gretzberg, you should remember this: he is a
violent man, a slugger. Always he was unpredictable. Watch
out, you cross him, he will make you pay."

"Think he burned down Lipsky's building for him?"

"Him, or someone like him."

CHAPTER 34

O'NEAL'S BALOON IS ACROSS FROM LINCOLN CENTER. IF YOU LISTEN
hard and hum a bit, you can convince yourself that you're
being serenaded by the great artists who've trooped through
its doors. Only it takes a bit of doing. I sat at a square table for
four in a glassed-in section that jutted out onto the sidewalk
and sipped a whiskey sour.

Harry was the first to show up. He hung his tweed topcoat
on the rack, seated himself beside me, and ordered a hamburger rare, french fries, coleslaw, and coffee.

"According to Danny," I warned him, "rare hamburger
could have all kinds of dangerous parasites crawling around."

"What I say," Harry said, "is if Sam Spade wasn't afraid to
eat it, neither am I. Gotta live up to the tradition, right?"

Harry wore a blue blazer over a pale blue shirt and paisley
tie. His blond hair was mussed and he looked as though he'd
just registered for his first undergraduate course at NYU.
While he ate, I gave him a rundown of the day's doings. I
dipped into my whiskey sour as we planned strategy.

"Boys," a voice said.

I looked up and there was Daphne.

"Hi, cookie," I said.

"Daphne." Harry smiled, raising his coffee mug.

Her curly straw-colored hair had a red ribbon in it this day.

183

She was clad in a powder-blue suit, and cream silk blouse. Large, red-rimmed aviator glasses gave her a dashing look as though she were about to take off for high adventure on the China coast. But maybe I was imagining things.

She sat down across from us.

"Eaten?" I asked.

She said yes and ordered a gin and tonic.

I gave her some of Olinsky's dope on our landlords.

"Well, you've done better than me," she said. "Primrose is the new boy on the block. They've only been around a couple of years. Same with Continental Equity. At least under those names. Their leaders don't seem to have any track records at all. Which means they kept a low profile and hid out behind underlings."

"Should have tried the police blotter," Harry said.

"I had better luck with Munsy," she said. "I asked around. Marcy Bromely has a friend, it turns out, who crossed swords with King real estate. His name's Peter Wakefield, a lawyer. He specializes in representing tenants. I called him. He says Munsy plays a mean game of hardball."

"This Wakefield speaks in metaphors?" Harry asked.

"He was a little more specific," Daphne said. "Naturally, Munsy warehouses."

"That's keeping empty apartments off the market," I told Harry.

"I thought it was collecting warehouses," he said.

"*Everyone* warehouses," Daphne said, "including my firm. Munsy bought a row of ancient brownstones and tried to get rid of the tenants. He did not stoop to assault the residents. He sent out Xerox copies of dispossess notices."

"Put the fear of the law in them," Harry said.

"Exactly. Especially those who couldn't read English and had someone tell them the news. These were low-income tenants, and not very wise to the ways of justice. A lot were scared out."

"This was before Wakefield?" I asked.

"Before. The dispossess notices had been typed by King itself. They were worthless. But to know that you had to know the law."

"Whole thing sounds illegal," I complained.

"Ah, but it's not," Daphne said. "The tenants were merely being asked to leave; they didn't have to."

"That's nice," Harry said.

"Munsy offered them a thousand if they went before the month was out. By the time someone thought to question the bona fides of the documents, the damage was already done. Next, Munsy went after the holdouts and took them to court. Thirty-five tenants received eviction notices."

"These were real?" I asked.

"Real. Most were based on trumped-up charges, or obscure technicalities in the housing law."

"And the rest?"

"Two families were behind in their rent."

"Had they no shame?" Harry demanded.

"The criminal personality," I explained, "delights in withholding rent. Next thing, they take to killing people in the street."

"Boys," Daphne said, "this is the serious part now."

"Sorry," I said.

"It's his fault," Harry said. "He encourages me."

Daphne shook her lovely head. "You guys deserve each other."

"Proceed," I said, "*please.*"

"These people showed up in court," Daphne said, "but Munsy's lawyers didn't." She took a taste of her drink and looked at us as though she'd made a telling point.

Harry said, "Some arcane legal strategy, no doubt. These lawyers are full of tricks."

"The cases against the tenants," Daphne said, "were dismissed."

"Now that's really tricky," I said. "So tricky, in fact, I don't understand it. Am I missing something, or has the side of virtue and honor just won one?"

"You're missing something. What this is called is harassment."

"Could have fooled me," Harry said.

"Look," Daphne said, "these people didn't know *what* was going to happen to them. Would they be evicted? Would they maybe even go to jail? They were simply terrified. Sure, the cases were dismissed, but the damage was done. A lot more tenants got out; they didn't want the aggravation."

I said, "No more eviction notices, eh?"

"On the contrary. That was their major tactic. They kept coming."

"Where was Wakefield?" Harry asked.

"He's on his way," Daphne said, "hold your horses. Someone was smart enough to contact the West Side Tenants Union. They steered our victims to Wakefield."

"Enter the hero," Harry said.

"Not quite," Daphne said.

"Doesn't this story have a happy ending?" Harry asked.

"Munsy won. It took seven months, but he did it."

"Gretz uses brass knuckles," I said, "and Munsy, kid gloves, but the results are the same."

"They always were," a voice said.

I looked behind me and there was Uncle Max, grinning.

"How long you been eavesdropping?" I asked.

"Long enough to hear most of this beautiful woman's story. I didn't want to interrupt."

"He can't resist playing detective," I said.

"Mr. Gabinsky," Harry said, rising. They shook hands.

I introduced Daphne. Max stepped around the table, took her hand.

"I've heard so much about you, Mr. Gabinsky," she said, smiling radiantly.

"And I about you. Please call me Max. Jimmy forgot to mention your beauty."

"I did, too."

"Like a Miss America," Max said, beaming.

"You'll make me blush," Daphne said, actually blushing. Satisfied, Max seated himself next to her. "This Munsy," he said, "sounds like a good partner for our East Side friends."

"That's what I figure," I said. "How'd it go?"

"Well, the old precinct house has not changed much. It still smells the same. The hooligans are different, of course. So are the police." Max grinned at Daphne, his audience. She beamed back. The waiter turned up and Max ordered tea and cherry pie. It was getting dark outside, so I decided to order a bowl of chili and onion soup. I figured, with some luck, they'd find a way to squeeze past Olinsky's repast.

"Know anyone at the precinct?" I asked.

"A few. They were no more than children when I was on East Broadway."

"Must've looked funny in their little blue suits," Harry said.

"I will tell you what's funny," Max said. "They have become old men."

"Sidesplitting," I said. "Max, you'll outlive us all. It's me I'm worried about."

"You look in great shape, Mr. Gabinsky," Harry said.

"Thank you, Harry. I manage, somehow, to keep schlepping along."

"Jimmy says you have a girlfriend," Daphne said. "In Florida."

"In this day and age, even men in their hundreds have girlfriends."

Max pulled an envelope out of an inside breast pocket, laid it down on the table.

I took another forkful of chili and reached for it. Inside were three rap sheets. The name's were Lieb Lipsky, Moisha Gretzberg, and Jake Sandlovitch. Their offenses against society ranged from disorderly conduct to suspicion of arson and outright conspiracy. Sandlovitch had only run afoul of the law once, when he had tried, unsuccessfully, to bribe some strike leaders. The matter had never reached court. The other two had been arrested a dozen or so times, mostly misdemeanors, with the exception of the arson charges against Gretzberg, which had been dismissed. The last entry was dated 1946.

"This citywide?"

"Statewide. We live in the age of computers, Jimmy."

"Now he tells me. After '46 the boys went straight?"

"They moved upstairs," Max said, "where they could hire others to do their dirt work for them. I have more." He removed another envelope from his pocket. It contained three Xerox copies of mug shots.

"They are the ones?" Max asked.

I nodded. "Jake has hardly changed at all. Moisha has hair here and is less fat. And all Lieb's done is pick up a couple of wrinkles along the way. Guys must be living right. Yet just looking at them makes you wonder about the perfectibility of the human species."

"They have been perfected," Max said, "only in reverse."

"You're a philosopher, Mr. Gabinsky," Harry said.

"This beautiful lady inspires me," my uncle said, beaming. "I should only have met her when I was younger."

"You say the *sweetest* things, Max," Daphne said.

"He means when he was seventy," I explained.

"That's almost a baby," Daphne said.

Max smiled and winked. "She learns fast."

"From you, Max," I said, "we all do."

CHAPTER 35

IT WAS ONLY EIGHT-THIRTY SO I COULDN'T COMPLAIN THAT A PARTY was in full swing somewhere in the building. The fact that there actually seemed to be *three* parties going full tilt only added to the merriment. No one had busted my locks yet, which, if not a sure sign of respect, was at least a hint. On the other hand, the evening was still young.

A tour of the houses failed to add much joy to my life. If anything, our side had lost ground. Bottles and beer cans had multiplied as if by binary fission. They seemed a step away from taking over the entire neighborhood. Bums lay passed out in hallways and stairwells. Junkies had taken over the basements of two of the houses, living testaments for their version of the good life. Hookers roamed the pavements pursuing customers. In a half hour I'd gotten more offers to party than in all of the last five years. A nice brawl had broken out on the top floor of a house on Ninety-third Street; you could hear the screams, shouts, and banging all the way up the block. Boom boxes served as a nifty accompaniment. Some of the drunks I ran into were friendly to a fault, others, indifferent or belligerent, and one guy was outright menacing. He had a knife, but I didn't hang around long enough to find out what he wanted to do with it. None of the old residents were in evidence. Who could blame them?

I went back to my flat and called the cops. By now I knew the number by heart.

Rogers was long gone and I ended up speaking to a Sergeant Garluchy. I explained our problem in some detail. Garluchy acknowledged that a thing like that might get out of hand. I suggested a flock of cops. Garluchy thought he might be able to spare a squad car or two. I asked him to hurry.

In due course the cops appeared on the scene—four of them. I sat on the stoop and watched them enter two of the houses. They must have bumped into some rowdies straight off, for presently two more prowl cars pulled up to the curb.

Behind me, the door opened, and Luke, the super, stepped out. "What t'fuck's goin' on?" he growled.

"A bit of noise in the houses," I said. "Someone must have complained."

"What noise?"

"Heavy sleeper, eh?"

The super's jaw muscles bulged. "You makin' trouble again?"

He rushed past me to buttonhole one of the cops. Just then the paddy wagon rolled up.

I went upstairs, called the *Daily News*, gave them the address and told them a riot was in progress. Then I went down again to my stoop. The *News* has radio cars roaming the city; it didn't take long for one to materialize. The first of the rowdies were being packed into the paddy wagon; their duties, no doubt, didn't include getting pinched, but this crowd was too far gone to know the difference. The guy from the *News* began taking pictures. I joined Luke and two cops who were engaged in a heated discussion.

"Just havin' a little fun," the super was saying, "that's all."

"Yeah," the cop was saying, "in all the houses at once."

The *News* man came over.

"Goons," I told him. "Installed by the landlord to run out the tenants."

"*He's* the troublemaker," Luke growled, pointing at me.

"Who're you?"

"Guy who called in the complaint."

The super waved an arm. "What's he talkin' about? They all lives here. He's the one don't. The fuck's been bad-mouthin' everyone. Get ridda him, there won't be no trouble."

"New super," I said, "the landlord's boy."

"What's your name?" the reporter asked.

"Stuart Gordon. You want to speak to Ned Hawks, our chairman. He's the one over there, in the checked shirt."

The *News* guy went over to Hawks. I strolled up the block. Cops and rowdies weren't the only ones out on the street. The commotion had roused the old-timers. They stood in coats over pajamas and nightgowns, small knots of gawkers exchanging whispers. Yellow and red squad-car spotlights gave the tenements a festive look. Walkie-talkies riding the policemen's hips filled the air with static and chatter. Some rowdies were still arguing as they were led out. Others had to be half carried. A couple of cameras and I'd've figured I was on a movie set.

I spotted Caloney in front of his house. "Fuckin' time the cops came," he said.

"You could've called them, too," I said. "Anytime."

"One thing I don't do, my friend, and that is run cryin' to the fuckin' cops. I fight my own battles."

"Don't complain much when they show up, eh, Ed?"

"Hey, that's what we pay taxes for, right?"

We stood there, taking in the action. "Think this'll do the trick?" I asked.

"Don't kid yourself, Stu, these assholes *like* bein' busted; they like the attention. Soon's they get out, time for another party."

"So what's the answer?"

"Hey, it's a free country. Let 'em raise the roof. We'll see who has the last laugh. You and me, my friend, we'll still be here when this is all over."

"That's what they'll put on our tombstones: 'They lasted them out—but not by much.'"

He shrugged. "You got a better idea?"

"Could be."

"So let's hear it."

"Stick around," I told him.

We didn't make the front page of the *News* the next day. For that we'd have needed a real riot. But there was a nice spread on page five. With any luck there might even be a follow-up.

Hawks and I spent the morning putting up notices in the hallways about the meeting scheduled that night. We knocked on doors, too, alerting as many as we could in person. No ghetto blasters accompanied our chores. The storefront office remained closed all morning. By midday, the first batch of rowdies began to straggle back, looking pale and haggard in the February sun. They walked unsteadily, as if recuperating from some long illness. They didn't meet our gaze. Without dope or booze to back their play they were washouts, as docile as stray sheep. More showed up during the next half hour. I left Hawks to finish the last few houses by himself, went back to my flat, and called Rogers.

"Heard all about it," he said. "The holding pen was full of them this morning. Can't complain now, Shaw, we cleaned house for you."

"Thanks. So how come they're all drifting back here?"

"Not all. We're keeping four. Found them carrying controlled substances."

"What about the others?"

"Well, that's a bit more ticklish, Shaw. We were responding to a public nuisance complaint. Drunk and disorderly. They sober up, we let them go. Civil Liberties Union wouldn't have it any other way."

"Cut the comedy, Captain. You know who these people are."

"You mean prostitutes, pushers, pimps? Has a nice ring to it but hard to prove on the spur of the moment. If they aren't wanted on some previous charge—"

"These people don't belong here. They're interlopers."

"Perhaps. But that's not what the landlord says. Your building manager, a Mr. Pitts, was down here this morning, vouching for all of them. Said they all had leases."

"He show you these leases?"

"No. And we didn't twist his arm, either. This isn't a law court, Shaw. Until they start beating people or burning down houses, it's still your baby."

"Thanks loads."

"Anytime," Rogers said.

CHAPTER 36

THE PLACE WAS LESS CONGESTED IN THE AFTERNOON BUT APPEARED even more frazzled, as though the multitudes who had filed through it had worn down the walls and furnishings. The personnel looked exhausted, too, as if the last hour had finally broken their backs. Lingering cigarette smoke and sweat gave off a sour odor. Overhead, neon light, like some alien sun, glared down impassively.

Lathem wore a green dress. The sash she favored this day was silver. It matched the silver chain around her long neck. "I wanted to show you this myself," she said, pushing five sheets of lined yellow paper across at me. The sheets were full of jottings in a small and utterly indecipherable hand.

"Very impressive," I said. "Just what am I looking at?"

"Some detective. They didn't teach you to read?"

"Not Chinese."

She sighed. "You asked me to check on three landlords. You asked me to go way back."

"So I did."

"I hope you'll think it's worth it." She looked uneasy.

"I've made my fortune padding expense accounts," I said cheerfully. "Why would I begrudge you?"

"This isn't padded. It took real work."

"Uh-huh." I suddenly began to see stacks of dollar bills flying on tiny wings into Lathem's purse. "Better tell me what you found quick," I said, "before I pass out from suspense."

195

Lathem took a deep breath. "These people have been selling to each other, Mr. Shaw," she said. "One buys a property then sells it to the other. Once it's Jenkins selling to Munsy. Another time it's Gretz to Munsy. A couple times Munsy sold to *them*. But mostly it's the other way around. And this has been going on for years since the late fifties. There's a Leo Lipsky whose name keeps coming up. He's managed buildings for all three. And he's owned a good dozen or so himself through the years. Still has three."

"He sell the rest to Munsy?"

"Him or the other two," she said. "This began around '58. But Munsy already owned property by the early fifties. He was doing the same thing then, too. With someone called Moe Gretzberg. That Gretz?"

"The very same."

"There's another one, a Jake Sandlovitch."

"Jenkins. What we have here are four guys. Like the Marx brothers. With a penchant for musical chairs."

"The Marx brothers were three."

"Four. You're forgetting Zeppo, who dropped out. We detectives know arcane stuff like that. You would too if you were a fan."

"I watch *Dallas*."

"There you are."

"I do all right for you, Mr. Shaw?"

"Ms. Lathem, I think you may actually have earned your money."

She smiled. "That's a change," she said. "Around here I don't do beans."

CHAPTER 37

THE BASEMENT WAS LOADED. EVERY SEAT TAKEN AND A STAND-UP audience four deep against the wall. It wasn't just the opportunity to see a real-life private eye, enticing as that might be. Self-interest had given us a boost. I was just sorry we weren't selling tickets.

Hawks introduced Harry. No one cheered. No one threw eggs or booed, either; I considered that a plus.

I had first met Harry in my senior year in high school. And we had both majored in social science at City College together. I had gone on to become a jack-of-all-trades, while Harry had picked up a master's in social work. He had given the racket a run for its money, all right, and for all I know had actually gotten a number of his clients leading praiseworthy lives. Years ago, when I was working for welfare, I had managed to convince two of my clients to check out a rehab center; I don't know what happened to them. The trouble with social work is that you not only have to wrestle with a bunch of recalcitrant clients, but with red tape and a bureaucracy that's a real ball buster. The burnout rate is terrific. By the time Uncle Max handed me the agency, Harry was ready to sign on. He was still dealing with the underclass, only now he got to bash them over the head once in a while. He was earning less but feeling better. Someday he might hit the jackpot, something he could never have done as a social worker. Meanwhile, Harry and I carried on just as we had in high school and college. Now, there were no teachers to complain. The next step was taking our act on the road. The next step was still a ways off. While addressing our collective clients, Harry was as tight with the gags as Scrooge McDuck was with a buck, which was just as well. They'd been through a lot recently and blamed some of it on the old private eye. Harry was *very* earnest. Dressed in a gray herringbone tweed jacket, charcoal-gray slacks, white shirt, and blue-and-purple-striped tie, he was the very model of respectability. He had a lot of explaining to do, and he did it in the same tone he must have used on winos in trying to wean them from the bottle.

Harry said that appearances to the contrary, his team of intrepid bloodhounds had been out on the job. They had taken note of the newcomers and scrutinized every turn of events hunting for illegal acts that might sink the landlords. A few items had come up, and these had been passed on to the new lawyer. More important, he personally had been delving into the landlord's past. The whole operation was broken off at the behest of the committee, but was back on track now. If the landlord had done anything especially bad in the past, Harry and his team could be counted on to dig it up and use it against him. The tenants were no longer alone, Harry assured them. A united front was moving against the landlord, and his days were numbered. I was glad to hear that myself—even if I did know better. Harry admitted that the rowdies had driven out some people, but their days were numbered, too. Carlos, the old super, was back as an employee of the committee. He and some friends of his would be riding shotgun against the rowdies, keeping them in line. Nothing violent, Harry said, just moral persuasion, which can be very effective if presented in the right way. I knew my partner was drawing on his social-work experience, and not that of his two-fisted gumshoe days, but that was all to the good. Who could object to moral persuasion? If we had to use a billy club to achieve it, those were the breaks. Harry asked for volunteers to assist Carlos and his cohorts, and I was the first to jump to my feet. Caloney, Benjamin, and a half dozen others joined me. A few ladies stood up, too, no doubt eager to rescue the rowdies from their moral turpitude. Or maybe administer a well-placed karate chop.

Harry said that even Carlos, a man everyone knew and trusted, one who actually belonged here, could not donate his services for free; he had to buy food and pay rent just like everyone else. As long as he worked for the committee, he couldn't hold down another job. His watchdog pals rated a payday, too. The folks here needed a war chest if they were going to defend their rights. Harry recommended a special finance committee to achieve these worthwhile ends. I seconded his motion and it was carried by a slim majority.

Harry reclaimed his seat, and Wendy Lewin took his place. A short, thirtyish lady, she had large brown eyes, olive skin, and a tapered face under medium-length black hair and looked neat and crisp in a gray wool suit, blue blouse, and black high-heeled shoes. She sounded breathtakingly knowledgeable with the legal facts of life—which was doubtless the idea. The rowdies should have been challenged long ago, she said, and now would be. A complaint can be filed with the enforcement bureau of the state Division of Housing and Community Renewal. The bureau could make things hot for the owners, but fewer than half the complaints were acted upon. Phony harassment charges were too common, and it took a good deal of evidence to get the bureau moving. If they opened a docket, started an investigation, and found against the owners, they could enforce their orders through the courts. That, however, was a big if.

The tenants were asked to report all violations to Hawks. An outbreak of crime and vandalism was also a distinct possibility. Carlos and the defense committee would guard against that, and the DA's office would be contacted at the first sign of trouble. She warned her audience against another tactic the landlord might try: false eviction notices, and hauling renters into court on spurious charges. Lewin asked to be notified at once if any legal papers were served. She would personally accompany the victim to court. The problem was that only the court could decide if litigation was unwarranted: owners could bring totally unfounded charges against each and every tenant and it would not be deemed harassment. If the landlord *lost* such a case and sued again on the *same* charges, then the housing bureau could step in. If the landlord sued on *other* charges, the whole process could start again.

That was what everyone might have to face, Lewin said. The aim was to break their spirit, spread fear and panic. These tactics had worked before. They weren't going to work now. The committee had assembled a team of experts to carry the ball. All the tenants had to do was stick together. *And pay till it hurt*. She forgot to mention the last point, but her audience knew all about that anyway.

I saw myself leading a ragged army of slum dwellers down Fifth Avenue. We were all dressed like characters out of a 1930s movie and were waving red flags around. But instead of looking like someone sensible—Lenin, Stalin, Trotsky, or even Eugene V. Debs—I looked like Charlie Chaplin in *Modern Times*. Any second, I'd turn a corner and fall into an open manhole. Miscast again. I knew there was something wrong with my attitude, I'd been told often enough. What I didn't know was exactly what to do about it.

I was trying hard to pretend I was an adult, and even pay attention to Lewin's spiel, when the lights went out.

An instant of silence. And an eruption of babble. Over the tumult I heard Harry's voice: "Keep seated! Stay where you are! Male volunteers, block the staircase! No one gets by you into the cellar!"

Good old Harry!

I was out of my chair and moving fast—or trying to. Half the crowd, at least, was up on its feet, and the rest, I figured, wouldn't be far behind. When it came to taking orders, this bunch had a long way to go. My guess was that this was only a prelude; pandemonium was sure to follow once the fireworks began.

My guess was right.

The door leading to the cellar burst open. Men, made dimly visible by the hallway light behind them, began pouring down the stairs. They hooted and shrieked as though trying to round up a herd of cattle. The crowd around me doubled its efforts, surging as one; no one was left seated. Folding chairs crashed against concrete, bodies collided with one another, mouths opened to shriek and scream as if in answer to the new arrivals.

I used my shoulders, arms, and legs against the crush. I slugged, clawed, and booted a path for myself. I'd've used my teeth, too, if it would have done any good. I wasn't heading for the stairs but away from them. Behind me I heard what sounded like a first-class brawl. The volunteers taking on the toughs. I hoped they were able to hold the line.

My progress was slow, but steady. Panic drove the tenants. They wanted out, and that meant the stairs. No one seemed to remember the fire exit that lead into the courtyard. As I neared it, the crowed thinned. A final obstacle, a large fat lady, was shoved aside, and I was running down the short corridor that would take me to the courtyard.

I almost ran headlong into them.

A rectangle of gray—the back door ajar no more than a half inch—silhouetted three nondistinct shapes. The blackness made them appear to be melted together. But one shape towered over the rest. The word "Luke" sprang into my mind, and I knew who had shorted the lights. I didn't break stride. I aimed a fist at where his head ought to've been and let fly. I felt the impact shudder through my body. The giant shape fell away, and two smaller shapes were on me. The advantage was mine. Anything I clobbered was fair game, while this pair could be flailing away at each other for all they knew.

I banged heads together, was whacked in the face a couple of times, walloped in the guts, cuffed in the back, shoulders, and neck. I swung, swatted, and chopped back to the left and right of me. I did it rhythmically, leaning into the job. Finally, there was something concrete to pommel.

It didn't take long; the two shapes joined the third on the floor. I left them there. No one followed me into the courtyard. I could still hear the ruckus behind me: it had risen to fever pitch.

I scaled a fence, beat it back to my flat, and called the cops. The cops were starting to feel like part of my agency, a last resort in solving any and all problems.

I heard the first of the sirens as I started back to the cellar, trotting along Ninety-fourth Street, armed with a broom handle, and bent on attacking from the rear.

The cops saved me the trouble. Thank God.

CHAPTER 38

"ACCORDING TO ROGERS, NO ONE KNEW ANYTHING," I SAID. "MORE coffee?"

"Sure," Harry said. "So what is it, a case of collective amnesia?"

Ten-thirty next morning and I was seated across from Harry in his office. I poured him another cup and pushed a couple of sugared doughnuts his way on a napkin. "Some guy who apparently looks like a hundred other guys rounded up a bunch of bums on the Bowery last night, paid them each a sawbuck, loaded 'em into a van, and told them they were going to a party. They were supposed to surprise the guests by whooping like Indians."

"The guests were surprised, all right."

"With the lights out, someone no doubt figured panic would do the job for them."

Harry took a swallow of coffee. "Almost did, too."

I shrugged. "Cuts and bruises, mostly. Only three tenants were kept overnight at Metropolitan. Can't say as much for the bums."

"We thought they were the bad guys."

"Score one for the volunteers. Next time we take on some real heavies."

"Remind me to be out of town."

"Thing is," I said, "I didn't really expect any move by the landlords. Figured they wouldn't want the heat."

"You figured wrong, kid."

"Yeah. Rogers will sweat 'em. But if there's no tie between them and the bums, they'll walk. And that's what they counted on."

Harry helped himself to a third doughnut. "How come we rate sugar doughnuts this morning? I'd just about given up hope."

"Reward for services rendered."

"Valiant services. Took me months to train those boys. Think we lost some tenants last night?"

"Probably. But you and Lewin put on a good show. Most, I imagine, will stick."

"Cops roasting the super?"

"No such luck, pal. Luke claims he was an innocent victim. Heard the racket and rushed to investigate. Someone bopped him. Doesn't know who. Doesn't know who removed the fuses either."

"Man lives in ignorance."

"Alas. No mention of his two buddies who awoke in time to fade into the night. So that's that."

"The old punch must have deserted you, kid."

"Too many doughnuts."

I handed my partner a retyped version of Lathem's list, told him what it was. "I think we ought to pull some of our stringers off whatever they're up to and put them on this for a while. Check out as much as they can."

"It will cost us," Harry said.

"When you're at war, who counts cost?" I said airily.

"I trust that was a momentary aberration, kid?"

"Jeez," I said, "I sure hope so."

CHAPTER 39

CHINATOWN WAS ONLY A STONE'S THROW AWAY. FROM WHERE I STOOD you could see the back of the court complex, white and shiny in the cold February sun. A nice frigid wind was blowing westward and according to the weatherman, was bringing snow. There was no trace of it yet.

I was wearing my gray trench coat, a peaked tweed cap from Dublin, and my multicolored wool scarf. I carried a notebook. I was masquerading as a private eye. Good thing I'd brought my credentials; half the folks I canvassed didn't believe me.

The tenements across the street, by the look of them, had been here before Columbus. A strong wind would probably carry them off. Frayed curtains and soiled window shades peered out at the battered trash cans below on the pavement, which crowded together like homeless derelicts. To my right, about a block and a half over, some dandy middle-class brownstones gave the tenement dwellers something to think about in their spare time. In front of me, as if transported from another planet, was more food for thought: a wide-windowed, white-brick luxury tower, adorned with a uniformed doorman whose outfit was guaranteed to turn a five-year-old, or a five-star general, green with envy. The only thing missing was an automatic weapon to ward off the marauders from across the street. Gerald Munsy owned the tower, and if the agency ever went into the security-guard racket, he'd be the first guy I'd buttonhole.

There was little to be learned at the high rise itself: none of its inhabitants were likely to have antedated their building in this community, not unless they'd won big at the track and kept on winning. The brownstones were too far away to do me much good. Leaving the tenements and the mom-and-pop stores below. By now I should have been used to it.

I began at the coffee shop on the northeast corner. Munsy's tower had been around for eight years. The waitress had been in Greece eight years ago; she couldn't help me. The boss at the cash register knew nothing. The small supermarket next door had changed hands so often during that time that it was having an identity crisis. The cleaning store was run by Koreans new to the neighborhood whose English was only a mite spryer than my Korean. I had no luck in the Chinese restaurant; they'd been in business for fifteen years, and while their English was passable, none of their customers seemed to have confided in them about anything except their orders.

I traveled to the next block.

The old granny behind the candy-store counter remembered the houses, all right; she'd been on this very spot for the past thirty years. "There was bad time," she told me in an accent as formidable as Kazmir's. There had been a fire, an old woman had been mugged. The neighbors spoke of break-ins. No one, she assured me, was left from those days. But like a lot of experts she was a bit off the mark. The shoe repairman up the block knew at least two families who had lived in the houses and were still somewhere in the area. "I see them every few weeks," he said, "out on the street." What he didn't know was their names or exact whereabouts. He remembered more muggings. An old man died of a heart attack during a robbery. Everyone was complaining about conditions in the houses. More tidbits turned up at the liquor store. Thieves had come right through the walls one night and cleaned out an entire apartment. Sledgehammers must have been used, but no one had called the cops.

I had lunch at a greasy spoon, learned nothing from the management. Afterward, I ambled over to the houses directly across the street from Munsy's towers and started going from door to door. It was the kind of drudgery that I knew would convince me, after a while, that I was definitely in the wrong line of work. By late afternoon I'd come up with additional tales of wrongdoing, all of them secondhand and hearsay. I had yet to meet up with a single person who had actually lived across the street. Eight years was a long time.

I pressed another doorbell.

A Mr. Jibbler heard me out, invited me in, seated me in an armchair, gave me a cup of instant coffee to toy with, some Entenmann's chocolate chip cookies, settled into an easy chair, sipped his own coffee noisily, and told me he had lived in the houses.

"Scum," he said. "The old owner was all right, not a prince, but all right. He sold out to scum."

Jibbler was a stocky, white-haired, gravelly voiced man in his midsixties who wore a plaid shirt, gray, beltless trousers, and worn black loafers. The place was sparse and clean.

I said, "Vandalism?"

"And how."

I asked for details.

"Spray paint," Jibbler said bitterly. "Everywhere. Even got into the closets and sprayed the clothes. Walked off with anything they could carry."

I asked about the police.

"Sure, we called 'em. Didn't catch no one. Some of us knew it gotta be the new owner, this Jenkins, but how do you prove it? He came around himself, looked at the mess, and said he'd never seen anything like it. Said the Hell's Angels were in the neighborhood and he supposed they'd paid us a visit. See,

they'd sprayed swastikas and skulls and crossbones everywhere. Said they always came back, too. Had people shitting
in their pants."

"So what happened, Mr. Jibbler?"

"Whaddya *think* happened? Look outside. See that fucking
white monster?"

I forgot myself, took a sip of the by now tepid coffee, and
killed the taste with a chocolate chip cookie. I said, "How did
the super function through all this?"

"He didn't. Fired the old one and brought in this other guy
who started a job and never finished. I mean *never*. Always
had to run off somewhere in the middle, and that was it. You
either fixed it yourself or hired someone to do it for you. Guy
wasn't even around half the time. Lived somewhere else."

"This super," I said, "was a tall, muscular guy called Luke?"

Jibbler shook his head. "Short, dumpy, and his name was
Harvey. No last name, just Harvey."

I tried again. "Jenkins's building manager here was Leo
Lipsky, right?"

"Short guy with curly hair?"

"Right."

"Once, maybe twice, he came around with Jenkins kinda
looking the place over. His man was around all the time.
Opened an office on the ground floor in an empty apartment. He was right there, you know, when we got all that
shit. Said it was plain awful and went around wringing his
hands. Guy said his doctor told him to take it easy, see? So
he asked to be put in the field. But this stuff was happening
was making him sick all over again. A lotta people they fell
for it. Something go wrong, they go running to him. What
he did was get them to pull out. Me, I always figured he
was the worst of the lot. You knew where you stood with
the others, they were scum. Didn't matter what Jenkins
said, you knew he was lying. But this guy was slick, he
could fool you. And before you knew it, he was helping you
pack. Thing is, he didn't look like much. I'd give you his

name, only I can't for the life of me remember what it was."

"Berk," I said.

Jibbler's face lit up. "Berk. That's it, Berk," he said. "Man was a regular devil."

CHAPTER 40

LUCY SAMLER'S FACE WAS ROUND, EYES BROWN, NOSE UPTURNED, lips full. She wore her brown hair in bangs that hid her wide, smooth forehead. She was five three, midthirtyish, and one of the best part-time operatives the agency employed. She looked as much like a private eye as I did a leader of American industry.

I filled her in on Primrose. "Berk was their boy on the spot, but he's gone now. He's one of them, Lucy, and he dates way back. I've been wondering why they pulled him off."

Lucy shrugged a shoulder. "Bigger game afoot, some new takeover that needs his attention, a promotion in the ranks."

"All possibilities," I agreed, "and not much good for us. Then there's the off chance he developed a conscience all of a sudden. Not very likely, but worth checking out. Maybe years of grinding away at the weak and helpless finally got to him? Maybe Ninety-fourth Street was the last straw? Pitts, his replacement, didn't give anything away, so we should take a peek at this guy, just on principle. We know his business address. We have his home number on the multiple-dwelling form. No need to salute, Private Samler, merely bring back a signed confession and we'll see you make general."

"I'd rather get paid my normal salary, sir."

"Poor demented dreamer," I said.

* * *

It took four days and four stringers plus myself to run down a
good part of Lathem's list. We were turning up more abuse
than a body could stand. A systematic search of the records,
I hoped, would produce even more. Carl Springer, meanwhile, had dug up one item that didn't quite fit the pattern of
deaths through heart attacks, fires, and freezings in heatless
winters. A Hugh Bradford had died in a Gretz building. But
this one was more than the "usual" accident.

"Bradford," Assistant District Attorney Bloom said, "lived
with his wife on the fifth floor of a West Forty-seventh Street
walk-up."
"How exactly did he die?"
"He was mugged on the third-floor landing."
"Mugged?"
"Two men pushed him down the stairs."
"Some of the neighbors used the word 'murder.'"
"It's used in the report, too." Bloom waved the pages at me.
"As I pointed out, Mr. Shaw, he was an old man, in his late
seventies."
"Not apt to duke it out."
"Not against these two. They were spotted running away.
The descriptions were at odds. A couple were rather quaint:
One was pictured as 'big as a horse,' the other 'looking like a
gorilla.' Bradford was supposed to be old, but not senile
beyond redemption. He'd have meekly handed over his
wallet, wristwatch, or anything else they wanted."
"They take the wallet?"
"No."
"They take *anything*?"
Bloom shook his head. "Not according to his wife. She said
nothing was missing."
Murray Bloom was a square-shaped, middle-aged man
about three inches shorter than I. He had black hair, sported

a Thomas E. Dewey mustache, and wore a three-piece suit. Captain Rogers had set up the meeting.

"But you called it a mugging," I complained.

"That's what they settled for. Bradford died of head injuries resulting from the fall. No motive was uncovered. He was a retired schoolteacher, led a quiet life, nothing out of the ordinary. So how could it be called murder?"

"Beats me. Gretz have his operation in high gear by then?"

"Wasn't even on the job yet."

"He own the building?"

"Just barely. The papers were signed transferring ownership, but the old landlord still had a week to go. He still had the month's rent to collect and his staff was still in place. Makes the Gretz connection rather tenuous, I'm afraid."

"Maybe. But things go haywire when Gretz and his friends buy something."

I told him about Norma Windfield, the photos she had tried to peddle, and what happened to her. Bloom laced his fingers and waited patiently till I was done.

"Those photos were never found?"

"No."

"She ever come right out and name names?"

"Uh-uh."

"So all we have is unsubstantiated speculation. What do you expect me to do with that?"

"Our landlords have been at their little game for thirty years. And you guys are still talking about *speculations?*"

Bloom gave me a crooked smile. "There are no 'you guys' here, Mr. Shaw, just myself. These four men move around a lot, don't they? With the exception of Munsy's outfit, the business names have a habit of changing. The complaint machinery was cumbersome in years past. Cases were handled on a piecemeal basis, looked at one by one. The overall picture, involving all of an owner's properties, was often ignored. The situation is only a fraction better now. Wholesale harassment of tenants is relatively new, Mr. Shaw, came into its own during the last decade or so with the conversion boom. That caught everyone's attention. There was plenty of harassment before then, but a blind eye was often turned."

"Not by the victims."

Bloom gave me another smile, and I saw Dewey plastered across the nation's newspapers on election eve, predicting certain victory. Truman gave him a shellacking, proving what my dad, the horse player, already knew: There's no such thing as a sure thing. "I don't have to tell you that the real-estate interests are the heaviest contributors to citywide political campaigns. Fact of life, Mr. Shaw. Judges are hardly immune. They run up a nice bill attaining office and value all the help they can get. Not every tenant is a straight arrow either. It's not unknown for tenants to cause housing violations, break walls, locks, plumbing, then go to the State Housing Division and ask for a suspension of rent. Certainly does wonders for the budget if they can swing it. What I'm saying, you need some high cards to win at this game. I don't want to appear hard-hearted, Mr. Shaw, but even now in our enlightened age, with you smack in the middle of these shenanigans, you still don't have enough to bring criminal charges, do you?"

"That's why I'm here."

"All right. We can take a look at this. I'll have some men wade through the Sprint reports, our computerized listing of incidents, see how these buildings you've given us rate."

"Thanks. Who owned the Forty-seventh Street property before Gretz?"

Bloom scanned his report. "Parrick Doyle."

He gave me Doyle's address and a handshake before I left.

"Sure, I sold," Doyle said. He was a sandy-haired Irishman with a beer-barrel gut and friendly grin. "It was good business. Used the money to open this place. Got a couple more just like it in Long Island."

"This place" was the Surf, a seafood restaurant in the West Village off Barrow Street. We were in back in Doyle's office.

"This was just at the start of all this fuss about cholesterol," he said. "I got lucky. Now, I've always had a soft spot for fish, but I wasn't fanatical about them, never. I thought I'd do well, but I never figured the whole world would start eating fish. Going to open another Surf in Queens next year."

Doyle had noticed nothing especially shifty about Gretz the few times they had met. A Mr. Jenkins from Gretz's office had done most of the bargaining. The price had been fair.

"Mr. Doyle," I said, "you still keep the old rent rolls?"

Doyle nodded toward a cabinet by the window. "Keep all my back records."

"Mind if I have them copied?"

"Suit yourself."

Jefferson Wallace was no doubt in his seventies, but he looked a good ten years younger. He was a muscular black man with an almost bald skull, wide nose, and erect posture. We were in his living room. Two stories down was 139th Street and Broadway, otherwise known as Harlem. I wasn't entirely a stranger to the community. My alma mater, City College, was a couple of blocks over on Convent Avenue. There seemed to be more black men on the street than in my day, but I wasn't going to bet on it. I'd paid less attention to such matters in my student years.

"Well," Wallace said, "my title was janitor back then."

"Work for Doyle long?"

"Close to twenty years."

"Remember Hugh Bradford?"

"Surely. I remember them all. Half the folks in that house were clean crazy."

Buildings, I knew, could be like a village, with cultures all their own. What seemed like lunacy to Wallace might be no more than standard Manhattan fare, the high jinks that go on above the Manhattan schist that underlines the island. I let Wallace rattle on, hoping to land an interesting nugget.

Rosea Douglas, pushing fifty back then, Wallace informed

me, had a different boyfriend every few months. Stella Crawford really *was* crazy, and when she wasn't being institutionalized, she was being pinched for shoplifting. Darrel Coles, the only black tenant in the building, was in the numbers game. He was friendly with old man Greenberg, who had been a bona fide bootlegger in the twenties. Mrs. Shepply cheated on her husband. Wing Fu Wong might very well have been a Communist spy, but that was inconclusive. At any rate, his bookshelves were full of Marx and Lenin and indecipherable Chinese tracts. Mr. Kacherginsky had been a gangster, or so it was said, especially by Mr. Kacherginsky himself. Although he had also been a milkman, Wallace recalled. Susan Linger was an alcoholic who lost one job after another. Mr. Linger had been one, too, but he had died. Mr. and Mrs. Berger had been actors on both the English and Yiddish stage. They both had parts in Broadway plays and would troop back and forth on foot between theater and home, even when it snowed. Thousands of dollars were found in Mr. Goodwin's apartment when he died. The money went to pay his debts. Mrs. Nickols had been married six times, people said, but was without a man the whole time Wallace was there. Fred Earl was an ex-convict. He used to be a professional boxer who, it was said, had taken dives more than once, and later when he was a manager, had fixed fights, too. Mr. Friedberg had gotten into trouble passing bad checks when he was a young man. Mr. Boggs was senile. Mr. Richards had been big in vaudeville.

These were Wallace's prize tenants. They hadn't all lived there at the same time—which might have just stretched the limits of credibility, turning the house into a sort of sitcom— but over a period of twenty years. As for the Bradfords, they fell into that larger category of gray, colorless residents between whom the former janitor could hardly distinguish.

"He was retired," Wallace said. "I don't know what his profession was. They were quiet people, very quiet. I wish I could tell you more."

Mrs. Wallace, a short, squat woman, came home just then, loaded down with shopping bags, and I told Wallace he had been very helpful and made my exit.

Back at the office I tried E. Bradfords in the phone book, beginning with Manhattan and going on to Brooklyn, Queens, and the Bronx. I didn't find her. By now she could have been dead and buried, or remarried, or alive and well in any of the fifty states, not to mention some foreign country. Or one of the numbers that hadn't answered. I turned to Staten Island and there was an Emma Bradford. I dialed, the phone was picked up on the first ring, and a woman's voice identified herself as *the* Emma Bradford. I explained who I was. "I'd like to see you, Mrs. Bradford."

"Certainly, when?"

"Would now be convenient?"

"Now?"

"A couple of hours."

Mrs. Bradford said it was fine with her.

I took the ferry.

The house, one of eight frame cottages on a short block, was opposite an empty lot. The weeds seemed happy enough.

A small, mousy, white-haired woman in a black-and-gray dress answered my ring, led me into the living room. The place had a quilted look and smelled of the country. I chose a padded chair across from her sofa.

"He was a good man," she assured me.

"No enemies at all?"

"Not a one, believe me." Her voice belied her appearance. It was firm and confident.

"No problems with Doyle?"

She smiled. "We always paid our rent on time."

"What about the new landlord, Mr. Gretz?"

"We never met him."

"How about his partners?" I gave her about as many names as I could think of, then went on to describe each one.

"No," she said. "I didn't stay long after my husband's death. We weren't wealthy, but we were what you might call well-off."

"He taught?"

"Elementary school. We both did. We have three grown children. They helped out and I bought this house. The area is still mostly undeveloped; it was really quite cheap." She sighed. "Hugh and I had dreamed of leaving the city. After he was gone I just couldn't stay there anymore."

"You left right away?"

"Within two months. So you see, I never did have any contact with the new owner or any of his people. I just sent the rent in by mail."

"Gretz was trying to relocate everyone."

"I know."

"You were never visited?"

"I wasn't there, Mr. Shaw. I stayed with my son, Bill. I didn't want to be alone. We went looking for a new home, and then I moved directly from Bill's to here. I returned to Forty-seventh Street to pick up some things, but my son made all the arrangements with the movers. I don't think I spent more than two whole days at the old place."

"I see," I said. What I saw was a blank wall staring me in the face and a day of wasted effort. Not the first time. "Did your husband seem worried or preoccupied that day?"

"No."

"Nothing out of the ordinary at all?"

She smiled. "There was nothing sinister in Hugh's life, believe me. He was a good and kind man. When he was attacked, he was in the process of helping a neighbor, Mr. Kacherginsky."

"The gangster?"

She grinned broadly. "He did tell people that. He was really a milkman, a very sweet old man."

"He actually delivered milk?"

"In the suburbs, yes, before he retired."

"Doesn't appear ominous. Wallace, your super, made your building sound like the stage of a soap opera, one that specialized in crooks and crazies."

"You saw Mr. Wallace?"

I nodded.

"How is he?"

"Seemed fine. Very robust."

"Mr. Wallace was a character. Our building had its share of eccentrics, certainly, but I doubt if we were in any way out of the ordinary."

"You had an ex-convict who fixed fights, a shoplifter, a man who ran a numbers game, a Communist spy, a bootlegger, a guy who passed bad checks, and a self-styled gangster." I grinned at her. "A regular rogues gallery."

"Or a super with an overactive imagination. Mr. Greenberg, for instance, had worked in a speakeasy for a time during Prohibition. Is that your bootlegger?"

"That's him, all right."

"Your Communist spy was probably our inscrutable Oriental."

"Uh-huh."

"A housepainter. And a very vocal Trotskyite, too. I doubt if he would have made much of a spy. Mr. Kacherginsky loved to tell people he had been a gangster. Why not? He had time on his hands, I think, and this was a way of gaining attention. He was a gentle man who couldn't live without his daily Yiddish paper. My husband was bringing it to him along with some groceries when he was killed."

"Really?" I said, glancing sideways at my watch. I was running out of incentive fast. That is, I was hungry, having foolishly resisted the temptation to snack on junk food on the ferry. My own fault. Now I could die here, an exile from Manhattan. And on my tombstone they'd write: "He held out for vitamins, and so died." The least Mrs. Bradford could do was offer me a cookie. Any kind would do, even store-bought; this was no time to stand on principle. But the idea hadn't even crossed her mind despite the frantic mental projections I was beaming at her. What I was getting was a useless replay of the Wallace scenario from another angle, the inside scoop on a lot of people I couldn't care about less. And whose lives—some, no doubt, long past—would net me no profit at all.

"Mr. Kacherginsky was ill, the flu, I believe. And for a week, my husband and some other neighbors had been taking turns bringing him his paper and food."

"Uh-huh," I said.

"The muggers were waiting on the third floor, almost in front of his door. It was senseless, Mr. Shaw. He was either pushed, or more likely stepped back in alarm and fell down the stairs. He only had six dollars in his wallet and they left that." Sighing, she shook her head, staring into the distance as though picturing the whole scene again. A small mouselike smile crept across her face. "He had a bad limp, you know."

"Who?"

"Mr. Kacherginsky, our gangster. He said the police had shot him making a getaway. His first name was Abraham." She smiled broadly. "He said they used to call him Abe the Gimp."

CHAPTER 41

DARKNESS COVERED THE WATER. I STOOD LEANING AGAINST THE RAIL as the ferry carried me back to the city. Lights from tall buildings twinkled at me in grand good humor. I didn't object. I'd just polished off two franks, some french fries, and a Coke. A stiff wind was blowing, but guys like me and Bogie never paid that any mind. Not when the cameras were rolling, and we had a load of junk food under our belts. I had my trench coat buttoned tight. I hummed a few bars from Mozart's G Minor Quintet, going one up on Bogie, who in the movies, at least, never got much beyond Hoagy Carmichael.

The quintet, except for the last movement, which just bubbles along, is a real heartbreaker. As though Amadeus had figured out he was a goner. The guy was going to kick off at thirty-five, only he didn't know it yet. What he did know was that business was lousy, and making ends meet got tougher each year. His work was a bit too original for his public, packed with too much emotion; he'd sailed out ahead of the crowd. If Mozart had lived to be sixty-five or seventy, he'd have been smack in the era of the mature Beethoven, changing the course of music forever. I was in the process of figuring out how that might have worked—something analogous to Napoleon's conquering Russia and hanging on to his throne—when a voice said:

"Hi, Mr. Gordon."

221

I didn't fall over the side only because the railing was too high. But I came close.

I turned and there was Billy Hall.

The kid was grinning, his narrow face white, pasty, a testament to what a diet of hot dogs and french fries can do to a guy. I wondered if the higher powers had sent him along as an object lesson. Probably there was a better reason. He had on a short tan raincoat. He wore no scarf, and I could all but feel the wind freezing him solid. At least he had his hands in his pockets.

I said, "Out for a breath of air?"

"Jeez, Mr. Gordon, you oughta be a detective."

"I am."

"Yeah, I know."

"I know you know, kid. Bugs put you on me?"

"Sure."

"How long?"

"Coupla days."

"Get everything?"

"Stuck right with you." The kid laughed as though he'd pulled off a grand scam.

I sighed. "Should've looked over my shoulder, eh?"

"What for? You think I'm gonna give Bugs the time of day? I'm with you, man."

"That's nice."

"I figure you're good for it, Mr. Gordon."

The city was drawing closer, the boat gently rocking under our feet as if in anticipation of docking and going out on the town. The kid, I had to admit, had the makings of a private dick: he knew where the money was; in my pocket, that's where.

"Billy," I said. "What I did yesterday was go for a long walk. Say, along Second Avenue."

"I can feature that, Mr. Gordon."

"Shaw. Jim Shaw."

"Yeah, I know. I was waitin' for you to tell me."

"Very considerate. What I did was walk to Fifty-ninth Street, did some shopping at Alexander's, had a bite at McDonald's and took the Third Avenue bus home."

"Yeah, I remember."

"I had a chat with Mr. Hawks, whose name you got off the mailbox after seeing me go into his apartment. Then I went up to my place and stayed there."

"Right."

"Today, I went to the Buildings Department."

"You did?"

"Yeah." I gave him the address. "Spent most of the day there."

"Doin' what?"

"Who knows? You couldn't get close enough to find out."

"Yeah, I remember."

"When I got home, I went calling on a lot of my neighbors."

"How come?"

"Stirring up the sheep."

"Should I say that?"

"Uh-uh. Bugs'll get the idea. Or his bosses will."

I reached for my wallet, counted out five twenties, and clutching them tight against the wind, gave them to the kid. "Down payment," I said. I gave him my office card. "Have an assignment for you. It's kind of tricky."

"Fire away."

"What I want," I said, "is for you to keep an eye on Bugs."

"He knows me."

"Sure. So do I. No trouble in tailing me, right?"

"No." The kid sounded uncertain. I was waiting for him to say that Bugs was much sharper than me. And then throw him over the side.

"Look," I said, "Bugs won't be expecting it any more than I was. Long as you restrain yourself from making small talk with the guy, you'll be okay."

"He's a maniac."

"So?"

"He'll murder me."

"Gotta catch you first."

"Let's say he spots me?"

"Billy," I said. "Put on dark glasses, wear a peaked cap pulled low. Bugs know your car?"

"Uh-uh."

"Okay. Stay in it. Venture out only when you think it's perfectly safe."

"You payin' for this?"

"You're a double agent, Billy. That means more bucks."

"More bucks. All I gotta do is be invisible."

"No sweat. Just do what I say. Call in at the office twice a day, keep in touch. You'll get me, or my partner, Canfield, or my answering service. I'll leave a message if I need something special."

"This mean I'm a pro?"

"It means you're a Dick Tracy junior G-man, kid," I said. "And that's even better."

CHAPTER 42

"KACHERGINSKY, AH?" UNCLE MAX SAID.

"Look," I said, "he was a player when Gretz and his pals were riding high on the Lower East Side."

Max nodded.

I said, "Okay, he knew them. Then years later Gretz buys the Forty-seventh Street property. And right away, during the very first week, there's a killing, literally on Kacherginsky's doorstep. There's got to be a connection."

"Aha."

"Max, this is no time for skepticism. We gotta run this down."

"And what," Max asked, "about Sandlovitch, Lipsky, and this Munsy? It's Jake who owns your tenements."

"Yeah, on paper. But those guys work as a team. Nail one, you nail them all."

"I may be too skeptical. But you, Jimmy, are suffering from too much optimism. Do you have any idea how old Abe must be by now?"

"Your age?"

Max shook his head. "Older."

"Early eighties?"

"Late."

"That's old," I admitted.

"Jimmy, Abe Kacherginsky is in all probability dead. And

has been for a long time. To speak with him you would need a séance."

Max went into the kitchen to see to the decaf coffee. I was seated in his study finishing my second chopped turkey on rye. I'd already had a roast beef on pumpernickel and a corned beef on onion rye, and I was debating whether I ought to hit him for a chopped chicken on challah or let well enough alone. The ferry snack had not stuck to the ribs.

When Max returned from the kitchen with two tall mugs of decaf and a plate of brownies, I sent him back for more sandwiches. I dipped into another Dr. Brown's Cell-Ray soda. I never kept the soda at home, but always indulged myself when I was at some relative's. For them the beverage was a way of life. Just as it had been for my parents.

So were the books lining Uncle Max's study. There were shelves and shelves of them, a lifetime's worth of reading. I'd learned enough Yiddish to decipher some of the titles, but I already knew what a lot of them were. I 'd been coming to Uncle Max's Abingdon Square home since I was a kid. When he and Sadie had first moved here back in the twenties, Greenwich Village really *was* a village—neat and orderly, and loaded with real bohemians—not the messy tourist attraction it later became. Max used to read out loud to me and Danny in Yiddish. Sholom Aleichem, I. L. Peretz, sometimes Mendele Mocher Sforim, the classic trio, whose collected works took up three shelves. There was a lot of Sholom Asch, too, whose *Three Cities* I'd read in English as a teenager. Poets such as Mani Leib, Abraham Reisen, A. Lutsky, Reuben Iceland, and Yankev Glatstein. Max told stories about them so often, I figured they were part of the family tree. The Singer brothers, I. J. and I. B., had a shelf to themselves. Peretz Herschbein, whose play *Green Fields* I'd seen as a Yiddish movie years ago, took up half a shelf. His son had gone on to become music director at the Ninety-second Street YMHA, and I'd caught some nice concerts there. As a kid I'd been convinced that half the world spoke Yiddish, just like most of the guests who visited our home. It was almost true, too.

Uncle Max returned with my chow, helped himself to a brownie, sipped some coffee, and said, "So Abe told this woman that the police had given him his limp?"

"Shot him while he was making off with his ill-gained loot."

"Abe liked to tell stories. A gangster was one of the things he never was."

"Didn't pay enough?"

"It wasn't his style. What Abe did was hire gangsters."

"That's the way of the world, Max."

"You remember, Jimmy, his specialty was shakedowns: You don't pay, your store has troubles. A broken window first, spoiled produce next. Then if nothing helped, a fire. A few blocks away, Lipsky and his bunch were doing the same thing."

"They have run-ins?"

"Who knows?"

Having polished off the chicken sandwiches, I was now gobbling the coffee and brownies. Before someone could take them away from me. "These brownies are okay, Max."

"The woman in the bakery will be pleased," he said dryly. "It was Jew robbing Jew, of course."

"All in the family."

He shrugged. "The police, they also got their share. So there was really no one to complain to."

"You're sure these were the good old days?"

"Who said they were good? When you are young, everything is good. Anyway, it didn't last."

"Storekeepers ran out of money?"

"Just the opposite. You remember what Olinsky said? They made enough to leave the neighborhood, open bigger stores in better sections. More coffee, Jimmy?"

"That was fine."

"Another brownie?"

"Three are enough, thanks."

"Well, Abe went into another business. In the garment industry, the fur trade, you control trucks, already you have one foot in the door."

"He wasn't a milkman, eh?"

"Wait. From one truck to another wasn't such a big jump. Although in those days the milk wagons were pulled by horses."

"He actually drove one?"

"Who said anything about driving? He became a big shot in the dairy workers' union."

"An honest job?"

"If Abe was involved, it wasn't honest. On the other hand, Jimmy, maybe it was. I mean, by then he was no spring chicken anymore. So maybe he settled down."

"And eight years ago he was already retired."

"That's right. With a pension, health and burial plan; this last one he might already have used."

"Max," I said.

He nodded. "I just thought of it, too."

"Ought to be a detective," I said.

"That is how we can find out what became of him."

"The union."

"Sure, what else?"

CHAPTER 43

I GOT BACK TO THE HOUSES AROUND TEN.

For the last few days, since the police roundup, the rowdies had been toned down, the noise kept to a threatening growl. Now they were in full roar again, as if their layoff had renewed their vigor. Under other circumstances their recovery would have been almost inspirational.

Only a few were out on the street and they were well enough behaved. The ruckus was going on behind closed doors. Party time again.

I paid a visit to Hawks.

"Started quiet enough," he told me, "but it's been picking up steam."

"Anyone bother calling the cops?"

He nodded. "Sure, last time was a pretty good lesson."

"And?"

"Didn't work this time. No law against having a party, not at nine, least ways."

"Sounds like a couple dozen parties."

"Wasn't this bad then. Officer said, they keep it up past eleven, we got cause. Call in again, they'll come around, put a lid on, maybe even carry off some of the worst offenders."

"The worst offenders," I said, "are used to nights in the slammer; they consider it a vacation."

"What do you think we should do?"

229

"Have a chat with our neighbors. That's the neighborly way, isn't it?"

I wanted to kick open the door, but it was open already, doubtless for any stragglers who might arrive.
I entered.
A wave of odors almost swept me back into the hall. I smelled cigarette and marijuana smoke, plenty of booze, sweat, and a touch of perfume from the ladies.
Bodies were piled on couches, on the floor, on beds; they squirmed, chattered, drank, and smoked. Bodies formed standing clusters that shifted and changed shape. Rock thundered. No one even glanced my way. For a guy with a healthy ego, it was mortifying.
Putting two fingers in my mouth, I let loose a shrill whistle.
Heads turned slowly, reluctantly, as if swiveling on rusty hinges.
I made some more sounds. By the time I was done, I had the attention of at least half the crowd, no mean achievement.
With less yammering, the rock was taking center stage. I followed the hammerlike beat to a cassette player, killed the volume.
That did it, all right. The damned music was the biggest narcotic of all. Without it, withdrawal symptoms immediately set in, that is, consciousness began to return. I used the moment to state my case.
"My name's Gordon," I said loudly. "I'm one of your neighbors."
Glazed, puzzled eyes fixed on me as if "neighbor" really meant escaped reptile from the local zoo, and the revelers couldn't quite figure out what I could possibly want among *them*.
"There are working people in this house," I continued, "who've got to get up early tomorrow; there are old people here, infants, not to mention guys like me who want some shut-eye."

230

The glazed eyes still stared at me uncomprehendingly. My words of reason were falling on deaf ears. Stronger measures were called for.

I clapped my hands together. The sound was loud enough to startle even me. "Party's over!" I bawled. "Everyone up and out! Let's move it!"

A tall black man climbed off the couch. "Man, who t'fuck you tellin' to get out?"

"You, pal."

Others began standing up; the fog was lifting. I could see resentment in some faces, anger in others; they were the ones to watch. I edged up to a wall, put my back against it.

"Hey, guys," I said into the sudden quiet. "No one says you can't party, shoot up, or get smashed. You just gotta do it at a reasonable hour."

They weren't listening. Feet shuffled toward me. Hands became fists. The glint of metallic objects caught my eye, too. I wondered if these lads were sober enough to remember they weren't supposed to kill the tenants, just make them miserable.

"Hawks!" I yelled.

Hawks stepped in through the half-opened door, moved to his right. Men poured in after him. Eighteen, all told. The advantage of sheer numbers was with the rowdies. But our boys were cold sober; it made a difference. A couple carried bats. I saw a tire iron, a foot of plumbing pipe, three hammers, and one cane. Benjamin, the cabbie, held a chair leg; Caloney, the tire iron.

Carlos was there, too, leading his mercenary crew. Not counting the ex-super, there were seven of them. They made up in size what they lacked in numbers. I didn't know how they fought and hoped I'd never find out. A roughhouse brawl would sink us all. I'd drummed the message into my neighbors' skulls, and Carlos had laid down the law for our recruits. All they had to do was remember.

"Okay," I hollered into the silence so the folks in the other

231

room wouldn't miss my wisdom. "You've had your fun. If these guys were cops, you'd all be busted. This is your lucky night. File out, and sleep it off."

I pointed to a fat rowdy by the door. "You!" I barked. "Move!"

The guy glanced around as if not sure "you" meant him. I'd tried to pick someone who didn't look like a hero. My victim's eyes scanned the room searching for a rescuer, then, when none materialized, he skedaddled through the doorway. I let my breath out.

"Next!" I yelled, pointing to a runty guy, no taller than five three. "Move!"

He went, too.

I picked two more easy marks, who took their ladies with them.

The black guy who'd first made for me was still standing. He was my test case.

"Okay, friend, your turn."

He glared at me.

Four steps brought me to him. I spoke low, almost into his ear. "Go out under your own steam, or get carried."

He swung. I thought he might; with everyone watching, he didn't have much choice. I blocked his right with my forearms, stepped back. Carlos and one of his boys grabbed him from behind, pinned his arms, and hustled him through the door. I hoped the efficiency of the operation was not lost on the spectators.

The rest of my band fanned out across the room, keeping close to the walls, their pacifiers in plain view.

I raised my voice. "You want the cops, I can call them."

Caloney leaned on a guy by the door; he didn't wait on formalities: he left. Others followed his sterling example. Knives had disappeared. Fists had unclenched to close around half-empty booze bottles and beer cans that were being carried away. Pretty soon we had the place to ourselves except for one skinny black man, and eighteen vigilantes.

"How about you, friend?" I asked.

"I lives here."

"Got a lease?"

"Yes, sir."

Guy had it in a dresser drawer, no less. I studied the document, which seemed genuine enough. His name was Preston, and he was down as paying out eighty-one bucks a month.

"Mr. Preston," I said. "That your tape player?"

"Sure is."

"Looks expensive. Don't want to lose it, eh?"

"Uh-uh."

"No more parties, Mr. Preston."

"Right. I get you. No more parties. Right."

"Have a good night, Mr. Preston."

"You, too."

We left, my crew trailing behind me.

"That," I said, back on the street, "is intimidation."

"Worked real fine," Hawks said.

"Usually does—the first time."

"We move on to the others?" Caloney asked. He seemed eager.

"What time is it?"

"Ten to eleven."

"Change of tactics," I said. "Keep 'em guessing, off balance."

Caloney's eyes lit up. "What do we do?"

"Call the cops."

"Shit."

"Listen, they'll be waiting for us, Ed. Some of the rowdies we chased are sure to have spread the word."

"Big deal. You afraid of them? Lemmie tell you, my friend, we can clean up the entire bunch. Tonight."

"Yeah. And join them in the hoosegow."

"Who's gonna blow the whistle for chrissakes, those flakes?"

"Yeah, those flakes, Ed; they discredit us, they've won another round. Maybe the whole game."

"So what was this," Caloney asked, "a fuckin' one-night stand?"

"Peace, brother," I told him. "We can hit 'em again next time they act up. That's what 'off balance' means."

"Hey, Stu, since when're you such an expert?"

I nodded knowingly. "Got it straight from the private eye."

"Canfield? That kid's still in diapers, for chrissakes."

"I looked him up, Ed; guy's really a pro."

Hawks jumped in to my defense. "Mr. Canfield's doing a fine job."

That was too much for Caloney. He threw up his arms and stormed off.

"Man's a hothead," Hawks said, not for the first time.

I turned to my boys. "We're calling the cops now," I said. "And we don't want them to find us on the street when they get here."

The neighbors trooped off to their homes. Carlos and his crew faded into the night. I returned to my flat and good as my word, called the cops. The guy at the desk recognized my voice, no less.

The building was quiet. I found a Chopin étude lurking in my radio and let it put me to sleep.

Next morning, bright and early—almost, it was ten-thirty—Max called the office. And we were off and running for Brooklyn.

CHAPTER 44

"MAX," KACHERGINSKY SAID, "WHAT HAS HAPPENED TO YOUR HAIR?"
Max touched the top of his head gingerly. "What is left
seems to be in working order."
Kacherginsky shook his head. "And where did those lines
on your forehead come from?"
"Heredity," he said.
"*Nu,* Max," Kacherginsky said, "it takes all kinds of people
to make up a world, fortunate and unfortunate."
The old duffer was right. He obviously had an unfair
amount of hair. It was white, but in glorious profusion,
climbing right down his brow to form a widow's peak. He had
a bristly white mustache like a cossack. And while there were
some lines crisscrossing his face, they were nothing to speak
of. His cheeks had a cherubic, rosy tinge to them. And the
glasses he wore could hardly be called thick.
"Max," he said, "you are how old now?"
"Seventy-five, Abe."
Kacherginsky nodded sadly as though Max had said a
hundred and twenty-five and sinking fast. Or revealed that he
had, in fact, been dead for many years. "I myself," he said,
"am eighty-six, but thank God, who would believe it?"
Max said, "You have become *frum,* Abe?
Frum means pious. In our family everyone was a secularist.
I assumed that the old-timers of the Jewish underworld did
not, as a rule, have a season ticket to the local synagogue.

"At this stage in life," Kacherginsky said, "it doesn't hurt to observe some of the formalities."

Max raised an eyebrow. "You go to shul?"

"On the high holidays."

"Well," Max said in Yiddish, "then anything is possible."

"So I've always believed." Kacherginsky replied in Yiddish, smiling; he seemed to have his own teeth, too. He switched back to English. "It was my motto, you know, when I was in business."

"His business," Max said, "was doing the impossible."

"And his business"—Kacherginsky nodded toward Max—"was seeing I didn't do mine."

"It was a living," Max said. "We both got by."

"Thank God." Kacherginsky raised his eyes skyward.

"Another formality?" Max asked.

"It can't hurt."

Max turned to me. "I don't believe him."

"He never believed me," Kacherginsky said, "no matter what I said. Even if it was the truth."

"You told the truth sometimes?" Max asked.

"I must have. Maybe it slipped out without my knowing it." Kacherginsky winked at me.

The three of us were seated in an enclosed garden, Max and I in deck chairs, Kacherginsky in a chaise longue. Vines climbed up the glass enclosure. Green foliage was everywhere. Plants and flowers were in full bloom. It was summer in midwinter, another modern miracle.

Where we were was the United Trades Retirement Home. And Kacherginsky had already said more than once, "It's not just a house, it is a home." Which I took to be the punch line of some hoary joke about a whorehouse. If I could put him and Olinsky on stage, my fortune would be made.

Kacherginsky was dressed in shorts and a short-sleeved, multicolored shirt with parrots and palm trees on it. The shirt hung loose over the shorts. His stomach, far as I could see, seemed to be firm enough. The guy had a cane, of course, but he'd probably had that all along.

Max had taken off his vest and jacket and loosened his tie. Not having a tie, I'd merely removed my jacket and rolled up my sleeves. A couple of hours in this joint and I'd start worrying about sunburn.

"My nephew here," Max said, "has some questions for you, Abe."

Kacherginsky sighed. "It's been a long time since anyone has asked me questions; I miss it."

"Mr. Kacherginsky—" I began.

"Call me Abe."

"Abe. To what do you attribute your obvious good health and longevity? Bad living?"

"Ha! He's a comedian. Young man, you should come again when it isn't business and I'll tell you some stories."

Max said, "We are here, Abe, about an old friend of yours."

"I have many old friends. Most of them, of course, are in cemeteries now."

"Moisha Gretzberg," Max said.

"Gretz. He changed it."

"We know," Max said.

"He was not a friend of mine."

"This we know, too," Max said.

"His methods I never used. He is still alive?"

"Yeah," I said. "And still up to his old tricks."

"Abe," Max said, "you were living in a building that Gretz bought."

"This is about *that?*"

Max nodded.

Kacherginsky folded his arms. "So maybe you should tell me what has happened that makes you so interested."

"Sure," I said. And told him. He listened attentively through my recitation. Max leaned over once to smell a flower.

Kacherginsky remained silent for a moment after I was

237

done; his eyes had a distant look as if he was peering back into the past, getting a bead on his fellow crook. "I never liked him," he said. "He was no gentleman. He did things, you should pardon me, that only a *putz* would do."

"'Prick,'" Max said.

"Thanks," I said, "I know what a *putz* is."

"You speak Yiddish?" Kacherginsky asked me.

"A little. I'm better at understanding."

"When I was a young man," he said, "I didn't want to hear about Yiddish, although I spoke it like a fish swims in water. I wanted to be a Yankee. Today, I could die for a Yiddish word, but the few *alte kockers* here would rather speak their broken English than two words of *mama-loshen*."

"Abe, you have become a patriot," Max said.

"I have been one for years," he said. "Anyway, about Gretz, he bought my building, that's true. This was maybe nine years ago."

"Eight," Max said.

"*Nu*, eight. You know, I saw him *before* he bought. In the lobby. He was inspecting, seeing what was what. Right there, I went up to him. He was surprised, I can tell you, like I was a ghost. 'Moish,' I say, 'you are looking good.' If God didn't strike me dead on the spot for lying, I knew I would live forever."

"And what about the other times?"

"This was the worst lie, Max. I say to him, 'Moish, I know your game. Not here, Moish! No monkey business! This is my home, these are my people, you understand?'"

"They were your people?" Max asked.

Kacherginsky shrugged. "I knew a few of them, more or less."

"Gretz understood?"

"He had a wooden head, how should he understand? So I gave him a good warning. What I know about the man could fill a book. I told him a few things."

Max said, "Short book, ah?"

238

"Medium." He shrugged. "Who knows how much of it was true? A lot were stories I had picked up. From the old days I had, however, firsthand knowledge."

"How did it go over?" I asked.

"He was not happy."

"He could," Max asked, "be arrested on this? You had proof?"

"What proof? I should go looking for proof? There is the statute of limitations, too, you understand. These were not new things. But a *tummel* about who and what he was, this was the last thing he needed. For him it was bad if people began screaming 'gangster.' It could ruin his buying the building, that was for sure. Maybe also his real estate license it would jeopardize. And for all he knew, I had something up my sleeve that could, after all, interest the police."

"So, Abe, what happened?"

"Then nothing. He gave me this look, you know, and walked away. Listen, next week, I caught the flu. When I was a youngster like your nephew here, nothing could keep me in bed. But now? I was sick and went right to bed. For me, the neighbors provided. Each day or two a different one, so it would not become for anyone a burden. What they brought me was food and the *Forvertz*. My radio and television, I had. On this day, Bradford from upstairs was doing me the favor. He was a learned man, a retired teacher. When I asked the first time for the *Forvertz*, I had to explain exactly what this was. A nice man, but a goy. The thing is, we both had plenty white hair, and a mustache, too, although his was more trimmed. We wore glasses and were even the same height. Also, at this age, what you are to people is an old man. Describe one, you are describing ten others. So this day, I sent him downstairs. And when he returned, there were hooligans waiting for him in front of my door. *My* door. Maybe they rang the bell and there was no answer. I am a sound sleeper. When I met Gretz, I was carrying with me my *Forvertz*. So this they knew. In which apartment I was, was no secret. Bradford, I gave my keys, and he went straight with his package to my door. They thought it was me and they killed him. One, two, just like that. Next week, in the middle of the night, I left with two suitcases through the back way and went to live with my sister, may she rest in peace."

"Abe," Max said, "you have a limp, a cane. Bradford had these, too?"

Kacherginsky smiled. "What Bradford had was a hernia, and he didn't like operations, so he lived with it. After climbing stairs he would walk funny. Max, not for one second do I believe that in front of my door they thought they were killing Hugh Bradford. I am lucky to be alive."

"Abe," Max said, "at your age, anyone is lucky to be alive."

"You're right," Kacherginsky said. "I always was lucky."

CHAPTER 45

"BLOOM," I SAID.

"Spare me, Mr. Shaw."

"It makes sense."

"Only to you."

"And Kacherginsky."

"The man, Mr. Shaw, never came forward."

"Why should he?"

"He a citizen?"

"Sure."

"Then he has some responsibilities."

"To put his neck in the noose?"

Bloom shook his head impatiently. "We're not in some jungle. We have what is called the rule of law."

"Didn't do Bradford much good, did it?"

Bloom sighed. "Gretz was never a suspect in the Bradford killing."

"That was your mistake."

Bloom glanced down at his file. "There were competent men assigned to this case."

"Sure. And they had a hundred just like it on their desks."

"Big town. No end of crime. Still these men did a good job."

"Terrific."

He turned some pages. "The muggers were seen running away."

"Good descriptions?"

"Lots of them."

"So?"

"One's for a black man."

"Anything wrong with that?"

"Everything. All the rest said Caucasian."

"Variety's the spice of life," I pointed out.

"Not this much variety."

Bloom read off a dozen IDs while I sat there. It wasn't an encouraging recital. "Sounds like a gang," I complained when he was done.

"Two men. That's what all our witnesses agreed on. IDs are always chancy, Mr. Shaw, and often at odds. It gets worse when the witnesses don't actually see a crime being committed."

"They were all on the street?"

"All. No one in the house itself saw a thing. Nor was anyone seen running from the house. If the pair had simply walked from the building, no one would have remembered them at all."

"They were hardly remembered anyway."

Bloom laced his fingers, smiled tolerantly. "Why should they be? Two men jogging down a block, no one yelling for help."

"You have a couple of IDs here about a tall and a short guy; you mentioned them before."

"A couple, yes."

"I've got a pair that fits the bill perfectly. One's the new super at Ninety-fourth Street; the other guy's called Bugs; he works for Gretz."

"It's eight years, Mr. Shaw."

"You won't accept Kacherginsky's word for it?"

"Reopen an inactive case because some resident of an old-age home thinks he remembers something? Come now."

"It's a retirement home. And the guy's as sharp as a razor."

"Be reasonable, Mr. Shaw."

I sighed; it was heartfelt. "How are the Sprint reports coming?"

"They are automated, my men aren't. They're still sifting through them, trying to put them together so they make sense."

"Any progress?"

"Some."

"May I see a couple?"

"Of course."

"Mind if I take notes?"

"Help yourself."

"I appreciate this."

"We try to cooperate."

"Uh-huh."

CHAPTER 46

"I'D LIKE TO SEE MR. MUNSY," I SAID.

"You have an appointment?" the receptionist asked.

"No."

"What is it in reference to?"

I gave her the names of my three landlords.

"He knows these people?" she asked.

"Uh-huh."

"And you are?"

"Stuart Gordon."

"Have a seat, please."

King Enterprises had a sprawling office suite in one of the tall, stainless-steel buildings that have grown up all along the Avenue of the Americas. From my twenty-first-floor vantage point I could see their kin through the wide windows. A breathtaking sight if you were a contractor.

I cooled my heels for about ten minutes, but I had confidence the boss would give me a hearing. My confidence wasn't misplaced. A secretary appeared, smiled, and escorted me down a short corridor into a huge, wide-windowed office.

The man behind the desk had a round, ruddy face. He was in his late fifties with thinning black hair, parted on the right. He wore a dark blue suit and tie and a couple of large rings on his fingers. A jeweled tiepin matched his cuff links.

He rose and we shook hands amiably enough across his desk. I sat.

"What can I do for you, Mr. Gordon?" He had a hearty baritone, the type that might make you want to buy a building or two in your spare time.

"It's what I can do for you, Mr. Munsy."

"Yes?" There was a sunny flicker of real interest. As if I'd come to sell him a property at half price.

"I'm here as a representative of a tenants' committee."

The flicker flickered out. "Tenants' complaints aren't taken up here," he said coldly. "We have agents for that."

"It's not your building."

Munsy glared at me. The excellent character references I'd handed his receptionist were obviously forgotten in his irritation. "What exactly *is* this about?"

"Your colleagues, Gretz, Jenkins, and Lipsky."

He nodded slowly. "I know these gentlemen; we are in the same business. I also know hundreds of others. I don't recall any substantial dealings with these three. If you have some problem with them, I suggest you take it up directly."

I fished out Lathem's list from a breast pocket. Stretching over nearly three decades, it detailed the game of hopscotch the three had played with Munsy. Except for King, the acme of stability, company names came and went. But behind them, gloriously entwined with Munsy, were our three sneaky, old-line landlords. I cleared my throat and started reading. I used my best monotone, the one I'd learned as a kid by watching *Dragnet;* it always made the guilty squirm.

Munsy's face began to take on a rosy tint. Halfway through, he broke into my recital.

"What the hell is this?"

"Proof."

"Of *what?*"

"Your long and honorable relationship, Mr. Munsy, with the three aforementioned gentlemen."

His stare was frigid. "I don't know where you got this, or what you want, but I think you had better just leave. Now."

"I've got another list," I told him.

"I don't give a damn what you have—"

"You might call it an elaboration on the first."

"Out!" The guy was half out of his chair.

"It's from the police," I said.

The magic word "police" brought Munsy up short before he could get around his desk and throttle me.

I said, "Sprint reports. Computerized printouts of crimes. It took some digging, you understand. No one company run by your trusted colleagues lasted long enough to acquire much of a record. But once you start correlating all this, it becomes very interesting."

Munsy slowly regained his seat. "What is this, some kind of shakedown?"

I waved the sheet of notes at him. "Common property, *police* reports, hardly the stuff of shakedowns." I sat back. "Of course, no one's put all this together yet; not fully."

"What does it have to do with me?"

"These crimes happened in buildings that you later bought."

"That's your big discovery?"

"They were emptied by one or more of these guys you barely know. Torn down. And up comes your property."

"Any crimes in *my* buildings?"

"That's not quite the point," I said.

"Isn't it? My advice to you, Mr. Gordon, is that you have a talk with these other men, not me."

"Thanks, I already have."

Munsy produced a half smile. "And now it's my turn; is that it?"

"Something like that."

"You crazy, Gordon?" He leaned back in his padded chair. "Where'd you get this information of yours?"

"Harry Canfield."

"*Who?*"

"Private detective. Hired by the tenants on East Ninety-fourth Street."

Munsy's eyes opened wide. "You *are* crazy."

"First to admit it," I agreed.

"Ninety-fourth Street?"

"Jenkins, Gretz, Lipsky. They've all got a piece of the action." I grinned at him. "Can you be far behind?"

"Get to the point, Gordon. You haven't shown me anything yet. You're wasting my time."

"Sure," I said. "Canfield works for me."

"You?"

I nodded. "My committee."

"Ninety-fourth Street again."

"Uh-huh. Guy's in my pocket, so he gave me these to play with, do whatever I think best."

A sneer played across Munsy's face. "And what would that be, Mr. Gordon?" The man, apparently, was still hooked on his shakedown theory.

"Simple," I said. "I want Gretz to call off his goons, pull up stakes, and get lost. And I want you to deliver the message, Mr. Munsy."

"Me?"

I smiled. "Yeah."

"Why should I do that? Is there any earthly reason I should put up with this a second longer?"

"You've got a luxury tower on West Forty-seventh Street," I told him. "Gretz took over the houses that were there before and did his usual fine job for you. He made a slight error, though. Ran into an old friend of his who lived there and decided to have him killed. You know how it is between friends? The boys Gretz sent around nailed the wrong guy, one Hugh Bradford. Abe Kacherginsky, the intended victim, walked away. I've got Kacherginsky, I know who the two thugs were, I think you're tied to it, Munsy, and if Gretz doesn't pay me a visit by tonight, I'm going to blow the whistle on the lot of you."

CHAPTER 47

I WAS ENSCONCED IN MY DILAPIDATED EASY CHAIR, WHICH SEEMED to embrace me with a special fondness this night, as if finally acknowledging a dear friend. I was dressed in a denim shirt and jeans, thick cotton socks, and my New Balance running shoes—although I wasn't planning to skip out unless things got really hairy. The shades were drawn. I was giving half an ear to Korngold's violin concerto. The composer had been a boy wonder back in Europe, the critics comparing him to Mozart. He wound up in Hollywood writing film scores and his reputation hit the skids. Now, he's been dead long enough for his work to make a mild comeback; the comparison to Mozart, though, is only a distant memory. Whenever I hear his music, I still think of some ancient big-budget opus starring Tyrone Power.

I was having trouble concentrating. It wasn't all Korngold's fault, either.

The knock came at eight-thirty.

I flicked off the radio, took a deep breath, and went to the door. No sounds came from outside in the hallway. No helpful peephole let me size up the situation. I put an eye to the crack between door and frame, which was just warped enough to give me a partial view of the hall. The crowd of killers I half expected weren't in evidence. There was only one guy. It was too dark to see much of him. I opened the door.

Manny Gretz stood before me in black raincoat and hat, his hands thrust in his pockets. He marched in without a word as if he owned the joint, which, come to think of it, he did.

"Mr. Pupik," I said.

That earned me a glower, but no small talk. He followed me tight-lipped into the next room. I pointed him to the easy chair. He sat. I hauled in a kitchen chair and made myself comfortable.

Gretz took in my abode with a single glance, a sneer on his face. "Hey, Rockefeeler," he said. "Nice place you got. A real palace."

"Thanks. It has character."

He waved a hand. "You wanna stay here? Stay. You an' the house can rot together."

"Very generous of you, Mr. Pupik."

"Gretz," he growled.

"Anything you say, Mr. Gretz. You ought to know," I said. "I heard it used to be Gretzberg once."

"Who cares what you heard?"

I smiled at him. "You do. Or you wouldn't be here, right?"

"Wise mouth. I don't want you bothering my friends, hear?"

"Munsy said he hardly knew you."

"We had business once."

"Sure. Jenkins, I hear, used to be Sandlovitch." I shook my head reproachfully and squirmed around on my kitchen chair, which I realized now would never take the place of an easy chair. "Lieb Lipsky only switched his name to English, but Jenkins sounds like a convert."

Gretz gave me a long, hard stare. His voice, when he spoke, was a low rumble: "Stick your nose in, someone gonna cut it off. I told you. Only you didn't listen."

"If I listened, what would I know? Not about how you squeezed storekeepers on Delancey Street. Not how you found scabs for bosses. Not how you tried to kill Abe

Kacherginsky and got some other guy instead. You don't talk about that."

"It's a lie."

"Sure."

"Hey, *pisher*, you think I go around killing people?"

"Uh-uh. You have it done by others."

"What others?"

"Bugs."

"What Bugs?"

I gave him a pleasant smile. "One of the two guys who hit Bradford."

Gretz sneered. "Mr. Nobody. How come you ain't a judge, a DA? You so smart, know everything, you should be rich. You rich, Mr. Nobody?"

I grinned. "Other guy's right in this building. Some coincidence, eh?"

Gretz scowled. "*You* they should call Bugs. Your head got air in it."

"This other guy," I said, "is on your payroll; he's the super here. You gotta know *him*, Gretz. Good old Luke, right?"

Up above, through the ceiling, a TV could be heard blabbing away. Even if the picture on the tube showed a slum, it wouldn't be *this* slum, and that would be an improvement for the viewers. Probably, it was something more cheerful, a murder, maybe, one happening to someone else. Other TVs were sounding off in the house, too. No rock. No parties. No screaming and fighting. Maybe in deference to Gretz. Or maybe this was the rowdies' night out. Or maybe they were grabbing some shut-eye before getting back on the job. Even Dracula had to sleep sometimes.

Gretz eyed me sullenly. "You been talkin' to Kacherginsky, ha?"

I remained silent.

"Old *kocker*," Gretz said. "Shooting off his mouth. Who's gonna listen to him, old crazy *kocker*? Ain't nothing left upstairs."

251

"Uh-huh," I said. "Tell me, if I got all this from Kacherginsky, who did *he* get it from? How would he know about Bugs and Luke?"

"You askin' *me*?"

"There were witnesses, Gretz, who saw your boys running away. No one knew who Bugs or Luke were. No one tied you to it." I leaned forward. "The cops didn't ask the right questions, go to the right people. But *I* did."

He squinted at me. "Who are you?"

"Just a guy who doesn't like being pushed around." Cagney would have said as much. And after the scene was shot, and the director yelled "Cut," he'd go back to his own life. Lucky Cagney.

"You talkin' through your hat," Gretz said.

"Then you have nothing to worry about."

A small smile played across his lips. He shrugged a heavy shoulder. "You got more worries than I'll ever see." He made a play of looking around. "Listen, say I gave you ten grand, ha?"

"Say you do."

"What happens?"

"You tell me."

"You go away."

"For ten grand?"

"Yeah."

"I was thinking more along the lines of a hundred."

"I ain't hearing you so good. Even Kacherginsky ain't that simple."

I shrugged. "Manny," I said, "what good's money if you land in the jug?" I gave him a friendly, open-hearted grin. "This is no time to be stingy. Pay with a full hand, Manny, be generous. First the hundred grand—right?—as a goodwill offering. Then we sit down, figure out what comes next. Maybe you want to toss in Bugs and Luke, eh? Kind of a bonus. The hundred grand, of course, is just a down payment. You've got to forget about these houses, though. Write them off, Manny, cut your losses." I made my voice smooth, syrupy, and earnest. "All this is for your own good, Manny; I have your best interests at heart. Play ball with me, you'll come out all right. Fuck around, it's curtains." I sat back and smiled at the big lug.

Gretz gazed at me with considerable interest, as one might at a talking bedbug. It was hard to tell in the weak light but his face seemed a shade redder. "You want to join the dead, ah?"

"Come on, Manny, this isn't forty-five years ago. The threats went out with war bonds and victory gardens. Time to grow up."

Gretz rose slowly, as though he were lifting a great weight. "Idiot," he said.

He lumbered to the door without a backward glance, opened it, and was gone.

I rose, went to the door—peered out into the hall—and closed it.

I returned to the bedroom. Behind the drawn shade, I heard the window rising. Harry crawled in off the fire escape. "Cold out there," he said.

"Pretty warm in here. For a while."

"Kid, you're the Dustin Hoffman of the gumshoe set."

"Maybe. I thought any second the guy was gonna pull a gun and end our chat. Along with me."

"When he didn't kill you at 'curtains,' I knew you had it made."

"That's what they said in his heyday."

"How would *you* know?"

"Heard it in the movies. Guy's a landlord, not a critic."

"That's where you lucked out."

Harry put his gear down on the bed. It consisted of a gun, camera, and tape recorder.

"Get it all?" I asked.

"Sure. Since my paralysis wore off, I handle cameras and tape recorders just like anyone else. Even better."

"Handy with a gun, too, I bet."

"No one stays alive when I start blasting."

"That's what I was afraid of. Know what to do with the tape?"

"You've only told me a dozen times."

"Let's go get a drink somewhere, okay?"

"First sensible thing you've said."

CHAPTER 48

"MORE COFFEE?" I ASKED LUCY.

She nodded and I refilled her cup. Lucy looked her perky, energetic self in a no-nonsense grayish-blue skirt, white, blue-buttoned blouse, and gray wool jacket. The people's shamus. If I needed a good imitation of high society for a job, I'd have to dragoon Daphne, or hire an extra hand. So far high society had given our agency a wide berth.

Midmorning blitzed through my office window. I poured another cup for myself, too.

"Sorry I took so long on the Berk thing," she said. "I had some loose ends to tie up on your other stuff. And Berk was hard to get a handle on. Primrose stonewalled. I called numerous times, Jim, once as a tenant ready to talk turkey. Another time I was a lawyer with money for the man. They said to send him a letter. I cozied up to a secretary in their elevator, told her I knew Berk from bygone days, but hadn't been able to reach him during this trip to the Big Apple. She just shrugged. And he never showed up in the main office as far as I could tell. I tried his home address. The man told you he was married, had grown children. That's news to his neighbors. Your Mr. Berk has lived there for twenty years, and if he has a wife, he's kept her locked in a closet all this time. He'd have to. Hookers used to show up regularly years ago, and no Mrs. Berk who had the run of the place would have put up with it. No one has seen him for the past couple of weeks, neither the families on his floor nor the super. He might be off on vacation. Or on some kind of trip for his boss. Mr. Berk isn't the type of man to talk shop with his neighbors. Most knew he was in real estate, but that's it. The guy has a house in the country, a mile or so outside of Accord, New York. A couple of people knew about the house, but only the mailman could tell me where. Berk takes a month off each summer, fills out a change of address card, and the mailman gets to reroute his letters. He remembered. Berk does go up there for weekends any old time. I called Accord information and was given Berk's number. I asked for the address and was given that, too. I tried to call him at least a dozen times but drew a blank. I could keep looking, Jim, if that's what you want, but frankly I think you're wasting your money."

"God forbid," I said.

"Hey, not bad," Billy Hall said. He was looking around my office, a half grin on his narrow, pale face.

He folded himself into the client's chair, which is distinguished from the conference chairs scattered around the room by an extra layer of padding. Only the best for paying customers. I offered him a drink out of the brandy bottle I kept in a desk drawer to impress the innocent. Having been innocent myself not so long ago, I knew how important that was. The kid actually said yes, at eleven-thirty in the morning. Some kid. I poured myself a third cup of coffee to keep him company, and my nerves began to feel wired. I'd have been better off with the booze.

"How you doing with Bugs?" I asked.

Billy widened his grin, stuck out his narrow chest. "Nothin' to it."

"You've remained discreet?"

"Guy don't know I'm alive."

"Been reporting on my movements?"

"Sure. Like you said. You been hangin' around the house,

256

talkin' to neighbors, goin' for walks, and havin' dinner with people I don't know."

"Dull life, all right. Any problems?"

"Uh-uh. Got him eatin' outa my hand."

"Okay, good job," I said. "I'm pulling you off this guy, Billy. Got something better in mind." I pushed three photos across the desk. "Know the fat guy?"

"Nah, friend of yours?"

"Bugs's boss. You showed a lot of incentive in taking these, Billy, lugging your camera all over town, just waiting for a chance to snap some of the people I've been seeing. Went so far as to climb my fire escape last night."

"That's when I took 'em, huh?"

"Yep. Along with this." I tossed him the tape.

"What's this?"

"Chat I had with this guy. You taped it."

"I been busy." He grinned.

"Exceptionally. Bugs will be tickled pink to get these."

The grin went west, leaving Billy stranded in my client's chair. "I dunno." The kid looked doubtful, fidgeted, took a swallow of brandy. "Bugs got his moods. Don't take much for him to fly off the handle. See, even if it's like somethin' he oughta know, he don't expect it, there could be lotsa trouble."

"What you do, Billy, is explain how much you like working for him. How you're sure he's going to the top and you want to go with him. That comes first, before you pass along the goods; it'll smooth the way. You have a tape recorder?"

"Sure."

"Listen to the thing before you give it to him. You're the guy who recorded it, you should know what's on it."

Billy nodded uncertainly as if hoping I might change my mind, or he might dredge up the courage to say no.

I reached for my wallet, counted out a dozen tens and handed them over. "Hazard pay."

"You said there ain't none."

"There isn't. But you never know, do you? That's why being

257

a double agent pays so much better than being a flunky. Welcome to the fast lane, kid."

Bob Perry sat in the client's chair clad in his trademark flannel shirt and work pants, his lumber jacket on his lap. The three guys holding down the other chairs had been recruited by him.

"What you're being paid to do," I told them, "is make yourselves conspicuous. You're all witnesses to a crime that happened way back. Just gawk at this guy Bugs so he gets the idea he's been IDed and get the hell out of there. That's all. Keep a car nearby for a fast getaway. Bugs is kind of touchy. Bob will steer you to the guy, and he'll be watching, but you'll have to stay alert. Any questions?"

There weren't any.

Bob and his troop filed out, and I went into Harry's office. He was busy typing out a report to one of our clients. From the look on his face, it was not one of our better efforts. I sank into a chair, Harry swiveled to face me, and I briefed him on developments.

"Bob'll be camping on Bugs's doorstep for a while. What we ought to do," I said, "is bug Bugs's phone."

"Poetic," my partner said. "Bugs talks? I thought he just grunted."

"Always a first time."

"Bob's sticking with him?"

"That's the idea."

"Carl Springer's free," Harry said. "He bugs like a pro."

"Nice. He can spell Bob, too."

Harry said he'd call him.

"Right. Then maybe you better drop around to the houses, have Carlos round up the boys, and put some of our tenants on patrol."

Harry smiled. "Action at last. If it's one thing we soldiers of fortune prize, it's combat. Especially if other guys are doing it."

258

"Probably nothing's going to happen."

"Ah, but if it does—"

"Can't hurt. Get a couple of snapshots of Luke if you can. Guy lives on the ground floor of my building and looks like Frankenstein's younger brother. Have some guys with you, he may not appreciate the attention."

"I'll rent a bodyguard."

Back in my office I tried Berk's number in Accord. The fourth time this morning. No dice.

I called Uncle Max, gave him the lowdown, and asked that he take over the office.

I called so long to Harry from the doorway, told him that Max would arrive soon.

"Where you off to?"

"A wild-goose chase," I said cheerfully.

CHAPTER 49

ACCORD, NEW YORK, WAS NO DOUBT A LIVE WIRE IN DAD'S DAY, BUT it bore all the marks of a certified cadaver now. The buildings were mostly boarded up, weathered, and sagging. The gaunt, leafless countryside didn't improve their looks any. On my way through I saw one general store, a bar, and two buildings respectively labeled POLICE and FIRE DEPARTMENT. The cops could spot drunk and disorderly merely by looking out their front windows at the bar, a real advance in crime fighting.

I stepped on the gas and left the hamlet behind. There were a pair of public radio stations at dial's end, both dispensing classic fare, so I let my tape deck lie idle. Everything was canned, of course, except the announcer, but the radio somehow seemed more companionable than a tape. Haydn's Horseman Quartet was appropriately galloping along with me, casting a bit of light on the dour, wintry surroundings.

The fifth gravel roadway off the highway that I explored proved to be right. A mailbox, the size of a birdhouse, said T. BERK on it in bold letters. I continued up the road and came to a clearing. Only one building. And no sign of a car. Not so hot.

The house was a modern two-decker job, in natural, unpainted hues, resting on stilts. There were plenty of windows and they were all dark.

I parked, climbed a row of wooden stairs to the sun deck, and looked down. A small tarpaulin-covered swimming pool was out back, and endless trees. That was it. I turned my attention to the house. The sliding glass doors were locked. Venetian blinds obstructed any view of the interior. I went down the stairs to try the basement. Berk must have been careless, for the door opened when I turned the knob.

The air inside was musty. I glanced around the cellar, saw nothing of interest, and went up a short flight of stairs to the first level. The kitchen sink contained some unwashed dishes. The fridge held at least a weekend's worth of food. The milk container's expiration date was last week. My hunch seemed to have been only half right: I had gotten the where, but loused up on the when. Hardly a stroke of genius.

I went into the bathroom. An open, fully stocked shaving kit was on the sink. Berk, maybe, was planning a return visit. Or had just been forgetful. A mattress on a folding bed was in a bedroom. The bed, replete with sheets, pillows, and blankets, was unmade. Next to it on a chair were a brown pair of pants, yellow shirt, and underwear. Shoes and socks were on the floor. How about that? Berk might have neglected to do the dishes or make his bed, but it was hard to imagine his driving off stark naked. Maybe he had a complete change of wardrobe handy?

I frisked his pockets, found a wallet with a Visa and American Express card, a driver's license, and a social security card all in the name of Thomas Berk. There was also a hundred and eighty-eight bucks. I couldn't see the guy being *that* forgetful.

I went to the closet, half expecting to find Berk hanging there, but only found a jacket and a tweed topcoat. A key ring was in a topcoat pocket, and an address book in an inside jacket pocket. I stood there by the closet slowly flipping pages, as though I'd stumbled across a rare literary find. I turned up the home and office numbers of our three landlords, four firms whose names I didn't recognize, a dozen or so persons living in one or the other of the five boroughs, and half as many out of state. Lipsky's entry was the most interesting. Four listings: home, Primrose, East Broadway, and one on Mercer Street in Soho. From east to west was nice symmetry, but what did it mean? Again the Shaw penchant for hunches reared its head. Maybe this one would manage to outwit the family genes and lead somewhere. About time, too.

I pocketed the book and keys and began looking for signs of violence, a reasonable enough course under the circumstances. I poked around under the bed, revisited the first floor, and gave the basement a second go-round just in case Berk was stuffed into the boiler. He wasn't.

It was getting dark now. I went outside, got the flash from my car, and peered under the house. That was simple enough since the house was on stilts. I found nothing.

I looked around. The forest would make a dandy burial ground. And one just about undetectable, at least for one guy using a flashlight. So much for being Super Dick. For all I knew, Berk had decided for some reason to take a powder, and this was his way of muddying the waters.

Thinking of water reminded me of the pool. I strolled over, got down on one knee, rolled back an edge of tarpaulin, and shone my flash into the water, which in these parts is never drained in winter. Each summer the water is purified. And for all I know, the locals, in winter, go ice skating over it.

The man floating faceup would never do any of these things again. He still wore his white-and-tan-striped pajamas. His mouth and eyes were open as though in surprise at having received a visitor so late in the season. There were no waves in the pool, no motion of any kind. The stains over Berk's chest hadn't even washed away.

I replaced the tarpaulin carefully, got a hanky out of my pocket, and wiped away at where my prints might be.

I rose on legs that had a wobble to them and peered

around. When the cops didn't rush out of the woods with drawn guns, I went back to the house. I spent the next forty-five minutes wiping any place I could possibly have touched. Then I turned out all the lights, closed the door behind me, and drove back to the city.

CHAPTER 50

MERCER STREET WAS HALF EMPTY. THE ADDRESS I WANTED TURNED out to be an ancient loft building squeezed between other lofts. Streetlamps receded toward Canal Street. A few cars drove by. Lone walkers scurried along. The temperature was falling. Factories had once dominated the area, but artists lived here now. There were plenty of businesses, too.

The front door was locked. I tried different keys from Berk's key ring, and presto, it opened. That encouraged me.

The interior hadn't been improved much since its days as a factory. The floor looked like dirt but was probably wood underneath. The walls had doubtless been painted when Coolidge was president, but neglected thereafter.

The elevator, at least, had been spruced up. That is, you needed a key to make it run. I had one, courtesy of Berk's key ring. It ran. Not quite noiselessly—the gears hadn't seen an oilcan in a dog's age—but well enough to get me to the ninth floor. Sending the old thing down again to the ground floor where it belonged and would attract no attention, I took off along the hallway.

Frugal lighting had turned the place into perpetual twilight. Metal sheets covered most of the doors as if break-ins were commonplace here. Made me feel less of an outcast. Do what everyone does.

KASKO IMPORTS was the logo on one door, Z&P PUBLICATIONS

on another. A third merely had a name: FLETCHER. That took care of the ads. The rest of the doors bore no inscriptions at all. I was looking for suite 12, but if the doors had numbers, I couldn't see them. I ended up going from door to door trying out Berk's keys. Definitely not state-of-the-art detection. It took some time but not forever. A door with enough metal on it to stop a bazooka shell obediently clicked open when I inserted and turned the right key.

I stepped into darkness, felt around till I found a light switch, and discovered I was in an office suite about as presentable as Lipsky's East Broadway hangout. The white walls had turned a discouraging gray. There was plenty of exposed plaster. The parts of the wall that were still whole were beginning to flake. A cracked leather sofa was the only furnishing.

I left the door open the merest crack to prevent that closed-in, trapped feeling. I extinguished the light, hauled my flash out, and went into the next room. It held an almost dust-free table, six folding chairs against one wall, and a pair of black metal filing cabinets against another. I hadn't brought my blowtorch along so I put my faith in Berk's keys again. You've got to believe in something, right?

A peek in the last room revealed a sink, a disconnected stove, and an unplugged fridge. That was all except for a metal door with a bar across it. Fire exit. Not bad. Nothing like another escape hatch when you're breaking the law.

I returned to the middle room, clicked on the lights, and got busy trying out Berk's keys on the filing cabinets. My faith had not been misplaced. I got them both open in jig time.

I stood in the weak light admiring my find and began sifting through a wad of files. Some folder headings had a familiar ring to them. They were the same addresses Lathem had dug up and that I had passed on to Bloom for his Sprint check. I and my stringers had visited some of these very places hunting for scandal. Here were the tenants of each house, where they had moved, and how much it had set back the relocaters. Not much as a rule, I saw, but that was hardly news. The properties once emptied had occasionally been kept, but usually sold for development; the name Munsy kept cropping up here.

I already knew all that. What was of greater interest were the other files that made up the bulk of material in the cabinets. They had, as far as I could tell from a cursory perusal, one thing in common. The wicked trio was nowhere in sight. Other firms, other owners, were listed. Rensler, whom Berk had called "the boss" at our first meeting, appeared more than once. These were the well-mannered stooges trotted out to nod, smile, and shake hands. Lacy, I saw, was ubiquitous, either as Lacy or Berk. Pitts was there, too. Along with other guys who might or might not have been them.

Very enlightening.

One bit of personal research still remained to be done. The files were chronologically arranged. I had a vague notion what year I wanted, and as it turned out, I was off by only four. What I had come up with was a tenant's name. I stood gazing at the name on the sheet, far from overjoyed at finding it there. But joy had little to do with this business. For joy, I listened to Mozart.

I closed the file and got down to my real job. I fished a notebook and pen out of a pocket and began taking down names and addresses of firms, owners, and building managers. It meant going from folder to folder, but I had time to spare; the whole night if necessary.

Bloom's Sprint reports had shown plenty of crime, but that, along with tourism and culture, is what the Big Apple is noted for. To trip up our trio a lot more was needed, more than the city had managed to come up with so far. But maybe I could give them a hand.

My theory, which was simplicity itself, seemed to have panned out. What good, I had asked myself, was using a lot of phony names if any cop with a search warrant could find them? No good at all, obviously. The thing to do was bury the stuff somewhere where only you and your trusted coconspirators could get at it. Records were important. You needed them for taxes. Among other things, they would help prove, if anyone asked, that your fly-by-night outfit was really legit. What you wanted least of all was for someone to string all your fronts together, feed them into a computer, and come up with a pattern of major felonies.

What they wanted least of all was what I was aiming at.

My jottings were progressing nicely, and I was humming a bit of Beethoven's Fourth Piano Concerto in celebration, when I heard the noise in the hall.

I stopped humming and listened.

The old, cranky elevator was creeping up its shaft. Visitors. But not necessarily to this floor. There were dozens of offices in the building.

I turned, stretched out an arm, and flicked off the light. Safety first. But not quite safe enough. What I should have done was get the hell out of the office. Only I still had a bit of work left. I stood fast. And the work ethic nearly did me in.

The elevator pulled up with a clatter; its door rattled loudly. Running feet. There was just time enough for me to pull my gun out before the office door burst open.

Silence. No lights snapped on in the outer room. I heard heavy breathing.

I stood there as if nailed to the floor. I could feel the gun barrel become sweaty in my palm. I wasn't likely to win a waiting game. The fire exit was risky. I might not get the door open in time. Or if I did, might find myself bottled up on the staircase. Even so, my feet began inching in that direction. Any change of scene had to be an improvement.

A voice called, "*Pisher*, that you?"

Gretz.

A voice I recognized as Lipsky's said, "It's him, who else it gonna be?"

"What you doin' there?" Gretz called.

"He's a thief," Lipsky said.

"Nothin' to steal," Gretz said. "Table and chairs worth shit. You wastin' your time, *pisher*. Better come out. You want something, we can talk."

I said nothing. But my feet had come to a halt. My feet had a mind of their own.

"Hey, *pisher*, cat got your tongue?"

"He's shy," Lipsky said, "'cause we caught him stealing."

"*Pisher*, you shy?"

What I'd done, of course, was set off an alarm when I'd opened the door. Max would have looked for it. I had talent, but was still a bit green. The alarm wouldn't ring in the building itself or at some agency. These lads wouldn't want strangers here. It would go off directly where the boys could hear it, in their offices or homes. Lipsky lived in Manhattan, so he'd get here first. And probably cover downstairs till help arrived. Gretz in this case. Leaving Sandlovitch. And maybe a truckful of goons. Which explained why the pair was stalling with all this cute talk.

The back door was beginning to assume a magnetic attraction.

"Hey, *pisher*, you want money, we got money. Plenty money. You wanna talk, we'll talk."

I said nothing.

Gretz said, "How'd you find out about here? Someone tell you?"

I positioned them. I couldn't be sure, but their voices seemed to be coming from farther back, near the outer door. It would be open a crack, letting in just enough light to nail me by if I tried to get out that way. Behind the couch would be a nice safe place to wait, and that's where I figured they were. If I was very careful, I might be able to reach the fire door without their hearing.

"*Pisher*," Gretz said. "You settle for fifty grand? Enough to keep you happy? This is between us. Before was about the buildings. No more. We make a deal now, you ain't got no problems."

None at all, except staying alive. I took one step, then another. I had a long way to go. I felt like a cross-country hiker getting set to cover the state. The fire exit would be locked from the outside, but pushing the metal rod should open it on this end. Unless it had been changed from the old days. And locked from the inside, too. By the time I found the right key, I might not need it. But were these guys ready to leave their cover and risk their necks in a shootout? Would they even hear me?

Lipsky said, "You want the money, you gotta say so."

I took another step.

"We got a deal, or don't we?" Gretz asked. He sounded impatient. Of course he couldn't be sure it was me. It could have been *anyone*. But what did it matter? The talk was just filling time.

Another step.

"Be smart," Lipsky was saying. "You can write your own ticket, mister."

A sound reached me. It was very slight, no more than a whisper. It came from the direction in which I was heading.

I stopped moving. Moving was the last thing I wanted to do.

Something that could have been a key turning in a lock clicked softly.

I heard nothing more. Except the pounding of my own heart, which could, I was certain, be heard in the next room, too. My mouth was dry, like a piece of ancient parchment. All of me was covered by perspiration, not just my palms; it was dripping in my eyes and over my upper lip. My stomach began digesting itself. I had waited a bit too long.

I moved again, but backward, quietly retracing my steps. I reached the table and crouched behind it.

"Listen," Gretz said. "You wanna good apartment, I throw it in for nothin'. Extra, see? So there ain't no hard feelings."

I didn't hear noises from the fire door anymore. I tried peering into the darkness. Sweat kept dripping in my eyes. Both exits were sealed off now. I was caught in the middle. They'd have every right to gun me down as a trespasser. It occurred to me that I hadn't changed my will. Daphne would get nothing. On the other hand, what was there to get?

"You sleepin'?" Gretz demanded.

I blinked my eyes trying to clear them. Something dark and bent double slipped from the last room into mine. It moved silently across my line of vision.

Gretz and Lipsky were still talking to me. The dark shape drifted toward the voices in the outer office as a moth might, attracted by a flame. I hid behind the table, all but became part of it. If I was right, there'd be just enough light out there to illuminate our guest. Only he couldn't know that. I wondered who he was and what business he had here.

I blinked, and the shape was gone, vanished through the connecting doorway. A second of silence. Then Gretz spoke; there was astonishment in his voice. "*You* was in there? *You?*"

Lipsky screeched, "*You crazy, Bugs?*"

And that's when the shooting began.

CHAPTER 51

I SAT IN BLOOM'S OFFICE, MY EYES BLOODSHOT, STUBBLE ON MY CHIN. I kept nodding off. I tried another sip of coffee. It didn't help.

Bob Perry sat next to me. He had on a blue-and-red-checkered flannel shirt. His gray work pants were neat but uncreased. His lumber jacket was keeping my trench coat company in Bloom's closet. Bob looked his usual self, like a farmer in town for the fair.

Bloom returned to the office, went around his desk, and sat. He wore a three-piece black suit and muted striped tie. He laced his fingers and said, "Not even in intensive care."

"They looked like goners to me," I told him.

"No vital organs hit," Bloom said.

"There must be a God," I said.

"One that wanted them to stand trial," Perry said.

"Small room like that," I said, "how could they miss each other?"

"Nerves," Perry said.

"They'd have bled to death," Bloom said, "if you two hadn't come along."

"Ambulance service saved them," I said modestly. "Not us."

"We didn't just come along," Perry pointed out. "We were behind Bugs every step of the way."

"Mind running that by me again?" Bloom said.

"Sure," I said. "My partner, Harry Canfield, taped a meeting I had with Gretz, took a few snapshots, too. He gave the tape to this guy we know who does audio editing for the record companies. He fixed it for us so the tape had Gretz telling me that Bugs had killed Bradford. And he was giving me the guy along with a wad of dough so I'd lay off. I made sure Bugs got his hands on the tape and photos. This Bugs is no mental giant. I didn't know what he'd do, but I had hopes it would be interesting. Bob and I tailed him. I'm guessing, but the rest probably went something like this. Gretz and Lipsky called Bugs, arranged a get-together. The Soho office was a nice unobtrusive spot. It's probably where they routinely met. Bugs figured it was a setup. He had keys to the building. He used the fire stairs, crept up on the pair, and started blasting. They blasted back. Bob and I were on the fire stairs about a floor down and still climbing when we heard the shots. We ran up and found the three stretched out on the floor. There's no phone up there, so Bob ran down to find one, and I sort of looked the place over. You know what I found in their files."

Bloom nodded. Through his window, a clock tower said eleven something. The sun's rays across it made the red bricks glow as if they'd been freshly scrubbed. Somehow, unreasonably, this reminded me of hamburgers. I was hungry.

"I know you had your doubts," I told Bloom, "but Bugs and Luke do look right for the Bradford job. Put the screws on 'em, you may get more than you bargained for."

"This isn't the dark ages, Mr. Shaw. They'll have lawyers; it's not that simple."

"What is?" I said. "This kid Billy Hall can tell you things, too."

Bloom nodded again.

"Think I can go back to my own life now?" I asked.

"For the time being."

"You'll keep me informed?"

"If I must."

"I'll always be grateful."

"Go!"

We went.

At home I ate, showered, shaved, called Harry at the office and filled him in on last night's doings. "I figured a convoy of thugs would descend on me," I concluded, "and was all set to vanish down the fire stairs, but they never showed."

"Cops beat them to it?"

"Looks that way."

"Hot stuff," Harry said. "We had a little of our own, too, yesterday. I think Luke tried to set fire to your building."

"Only tried?"

"We stopped him. The patrol was out in full force, tenants, hired hands, everyone. We went from house to house, top to bottom. Caught him in the basement with a nice-sized bonfire. Not mattresses, either. The real McCoy. Paper and wood doused in gasoline. He said he was putting it out. Smelled smoke, ran down to the cellar, and there it was. Believe what you will."

"I'll try and suppress my suspicious nature."

"Very virtuous. Otherwise there wasn't much action. Our citizens' patrol seems to have scared off the heavies. Even the rowdies were keeping a low profile."

"All power to the people, eh?"

"True," Harry said. "But it took the Napoleon of investigators to get them there."

I stood looking up at the tenements. The same sun that had done such a knockout job outside of Bloom's window was lighting up the southeast side of the houses, too. Only here it left something to be desired.

I didn't go directly to my flat and pack. I dropped in on Ned Hawks first.

Again I sat opposite him in the straight-backed armchair

275

with the yellow pillow. The place was as neat as ever, and a lot less noisy.

"Quiet," I said, pointing out the obvious.

"Been this way since the patrols. You had the right idea, Mr. Shaw."

"Going to stay like that, too," I told him.

"Think so?"

"Know so."

Hawks had on faded trousers and a light blue work shirt. He and Bob Perry shopped off the same cut-rate rack, no doubt.

I gave him a rundown of how things stood. It took a while because I went into some detail. I was going to clip the committee for a princely sum, and I wanted them to know they were getting their money's worth.

"What I think's going to happen," I finished up, "is that Gretz will lose these houses. They'll go into city receivership and you people may get a crack at owning them."

Hawks looked surprised. "Never imagined it would end with us getting the buildings."

"It's not quite in the bag," I said. "Let Lewin represent you, she's good at this sort of thing."

He nodded.

I glanced over at the photo on the wall. The grinning threesome: Hawks, his wife, and daughter. They seemed eagerly to be awaiting life's next exciting turn.

"Mr. Hawks," I said. "Berk wasn't exactly a stranger, was he?"

Hawks looked at me.

"Our pal had a different name in those days. He was in charge of emptying the houses. I presume his methods were about the same."

Hawks said nothing.

"The accident that took the lives of your family, it happened in the building, right?"

He shrugged a shoulder, sighed. His voice sounded

276

scratchy when he spoke. "I was working nights. May and Betty were home alone. There was a fire, a bad one. They didn't make it out in time. Police came, said it was an accident. Gas leak in the cellar. No one at fault, no one. . . . Couldn't believe my eyes when that man showed up here. I knew what he'd done. . . ."

"You burned those mattresses, broke windows and locks. You were going to head him off, weren't you? Bring in the police early."

"I was careful, Mr. Shaw, saw that nothing got out of hand."

"Yeah, you were careful. The first to sound the alarm when the mattresses were on fire. I remembered that later. A lady called Norma Windfield was hanging around the houses at the time. She saw someone breaking windows and said it wasn't anyone from Primrose. That got me thinking. It seemed too soon for Berk to start busting locks, breaking windows. He'd only be calling attention to himself while folks were still moving out on their own."

Hawks shrugged.

I said, "When Berk began to ride roughshod over everyone, just as he had twenty years ago, it brought it all back, didn't it?"

"Man's a murderer."

"You followed him, waiting for your chance. Accord was far from home, must have seemed like the ideal place. You shot him, hid his car somewhere, and came back to the city, no one the wiser."

Hawks licked his lips.

"Temporary insanity, Mr. Hawks," I said. "Could happen to anyone. You sane again?"

He remained motionless. Which was obviously what a sane person would do.

"Good," I said. "All this is pure speculation, of course. Even if the cops suspected something—and there's no earthly reason why they should—what could they prove? Berk literally had hundreds of enemies. Thousands probably."

Hawks cleared his throat. "You aren't going to say anything?"

"What's to say? You didn't confess just now, did you?"

He shook his head uncertainly.

"Well, there you are."

The tenements were eventually taken over by the city, where they still remain, tied in red tape. The landlords have yet to go to trial, but they will. Bugs is slated to testify against them. The murder of Tom Berk remains unsolved, as does Norma Windfield's. The tenants' committee came through with a *very* generous bonus, which was only fair considering the bang-up job our agency did. I took Uncle Max, Olinsky, and Kacherginsky to dinner at Dobson's. We had a ball.